©TheExpirement

Credits

The Expirement Series and Darktronics are property of ©
Penelope J Bailey 2016

Thanks to my proof readers Darren and Robin.

Also to the reader for reading.

All characters and events are pure fiction and are not based on real events.

The Expirement Series send your thoughts on twitter @theexpirement

The Expirement Series is Trilogy
The Box (Part 1)
The Day Was Thursday (Part 2)
Revenge is Bitter Sweet (Part 3)

Let me know what you think you can contact me on twitter: @TheExpirement or #theExpirementSeries

Ian
Thanks for listening & your advice.
Enjoy
P J Bailey
12-Mar-19

1 –Expirement Series

©TheExpirement

Prologue

The box arrived promptly at 8.00. The sirens were sounding in my lab as I walked carefully up to the box.
It had been carefully wrapped in brown paper and stuck with glue; the address was handwritten so I was careful not to rip any evidence, as I didn't know if this was for real or a test. My heart and gut were telling me this was for real; I didn't want it to be, not today. Not today of all days.
I took a deep breath and pressed the yellow switch on the console in front of me. Finally the sirens have stopped and my office filled up with a team collecting the data.
I could see my boss pacing behind the group of scientists; he was worried I was worried.
I carefully took apart the box piece by piece, studying everything as much as I could.
I looked over to my office and I saw the angst on their faces, the lab, my lab was under attack.
Then I saw the reason for this box... a clock stopped at 8.
I held it up to my boss who was stood silently watching.
He nodded.
We were under attack, full attack..

©TheExpirement

Chapter One

Today was the day I am going mad, I am pacing up and down in my office.
It's hot in here; the air con has just gone off for testing. Humph, I need coffee and doughnuts. I grab my baseball jacket as I leave my office and walk slowly down the corridor, it is cooler. As I reach the double doors my mobile phone starts to ring.
"Morning sweetheart"
I chat to my gorgeous girlfriend as I continue walking to the coffee lounge.
My name is James Kieran Folster and I am a scientist in the leading security firm Darktronics. These are my memoirs about my life and the craziness that decided to enter in to it.
At the time I was in my twenties and like now I had short black hair, unlike now I kept myself clean shaven when I could. I have blue eyes, 5ft 10, occasionally exercising, and I liked going in to work comfortable wearing something that I could do my long hours in. I enjoyed wearing my suits and getting all done up, but mainly I wore just general work trousers with my favourite t-shirts and shirts and jumpers. I think that's me in a nutshell.
Now let me take you back to the day that things started to change. The coffee lounge is one of the few places you can relax in this place, but sadly I have a very busy day ahead and once I have my coffee black with two sugars and my jam doughnut, I head back through the lounge and the double doors, the long quiet corridor is a breather before I am back in my lab.
Now my office come lab is basically what you would see in any other office. But this time it has a secure lab area which is sterile and allows me to do my testing.
"What do I test?" I here you ask

©TheExpirement

Well that all depends. As I mentioned earlier Darktronics are a leading security firm. They secure anything from well your front door to bombs. Therefore, we test new stuff to help with that, the downside to the job (apart from the paperwork) is what we receive from the outside.

Anything can arrive and its part of my job to keep Darktronics trading safely. Mind you safety can cost you your life. Never under estimate your enemies and what they like to send you for fun. Talking of which the lab sirens are now ringing in my ears and my robot Dennis is carrying today's test.

Wish me luck.

The box that Dennis is carrying in to my lab has already been searched for visible signs of anything deadly, so it is a relief to know that maybe, just maybe it's not a bomb. But one can never be complacent; sadly in my five years of working here I have buried friends and seen colleagues lives changed forever.

By now I have changed in to my lab suit, in the safety area between my office and lab. I thank Dennis and reach down to pick the box up. Don't worry I am not going mad talking to a robot, the camera on the side of Dennis shows there is indeed a real person at the other end of the camera feed. This is Dennis himself Dennis McDonald an old army officer who was indeed over the moon when I named the robot after him.

Anyways I do my thing and my office computers are going mad as I tap the data on the lab console. It will take me about two hours, in which time I must have decided was this box a test or for real. If it's for real you hit the yellow switch on the console and all your friends arrive, if it's a test then you hit the red switch. Either way you might not see lunch. I take a deep breath as I take the last item out of the box and today it's a carrot...hmm interesting, I've already tested a grape, melon and peas today but not tested a carrot before. I look

©TheExpirement

for signs of tampering and then start to take a sample to see if there are any poisons.

I decide overall due to all the different objects this was a test, too many pieces of fruit and veg today maybe this is the management's way of saying too many doughnuts. I hit the red switch and I go decontaminate myself. After my shower which is to the left of my lab area I read the report on my computer. In big blue letters it says "Test Completed"
Phew.
Then my office phone rings.
I look at my watch its only 10.30am
A typical morning.

©TheExpirement

Chapter Two

There were no more typical mornings that week. But before I go on about the rest of my week I will go back to that afternoon. I was ordered from the phone call to go and visit my boss after lunch. I had assumed (wrongly) that it was about the test box. After putting down the phone, I cycled to lunch. Lunch was in town, where I met my girlfriend Fiona in the local café. The café was your typical gossip central for the town, it was more relaxed during the day with your waiters wearing jeans and tops with Grace and Tom Café logo on them, if you ever arrived here at night the café would be a posh diner with the very same waiters wearing black tie.

I remember walking in, it didn't seem as busy. Fiona was looking relaxed in her skin tight jeans, brown boots and a white blouse with her leather jacket on the back of her chair

"Hello" she said

"Hey sweetheart" I replied kissing her on the lips

She had already got us a table and had ordered me fish and chips (my favourite) and because I usually finished late it saved us cooking a full meal in the evening.

I remember looking at her with excitement. She had that sparkle about her.

"Darling…" she started

"Hmmm" I replied

"I am going to apply for a job at Darktronics"

It took me a second to take in what she had said

"Really" I replied that was about as good as a response as I could muster.

Working at Darktronics was a good idea but it had its downsides too. I worried too much. Fiona was my dearest girlfriend who wasn't currently working and I knew she was bored. To be fair I couldn't say no to this, which was until she described the job.

©TheExpirement

"What will you be doing?" I then asked as she looked sternly at my "REALLY" response.
"Fire testing"
I nearly choked on my chips, but I don't think she noticed...well not much
"Look I know you're mad, but please James I'm bored. I can't be someone's PA and I'll be dammed if I become a call centre agent." Not that any of these jobs are bad, but this wasn't my Fiona. I had to agree.
I calmed down and took her hand
"Darling, I love you and I worry about you. I'm pleased, go for it. You'll be fine"
"Thank you….I start on Monday" she said calmly
I tried not to respond. The waiter came over to the table and asked if we needed anything.
"A bottle of your finest champagne to take away please" I replied
This had successfully shocked Fiona.
"You're not mad that I didn't tell you?"
"No, because I'm pleased you have found something that you'll enjoy. Keep you out of mischief" I said happily even though my mind was going ten to the dozen with extreme worry. "And the champagne?"
"Well you'll just have to be good and wait. I'll see you at home my sweetheart"
And with that I leaned over the table and kissed Fiona.
I then walked out of the café and cycled back to work.
I walked back in through the automatic doors to the office, the reception which was fairly typical. Big glass windows, bright white walls. The reception desk was wooden and looked more to me like a hotel reception than it did an office. But everything else was pretty much run of the mill. There were armed security guards and they checked every inch of you every time you entered and left the

©TheExpirement

building. This made you feel safe as well as a little nervous. Behind the reception were not your typical receptionists. They were trained to do well anything to be honest, but I won't go in to that now. The reception was busy today, the press were all sat in a corner interviewing idiot of the year Paul Jones a right idiot who was pretending to be the best scientist. He was the boss's nephew, not that the boss liked him by any stretch of the imagination but because the boss had lost his sister to a nasty car accident he had promised to look after her son. Shame. Great shame. Anyway I started walking through ensuring that the armed security guards would indeed see my pass. You were almost x-rayed every time. But I breathed a sigh of relief when I crossed the Darktronics rug, the logo which was a blue three headed spear. I was clear. Clear of all the front of house nonsense that keeps the Darktronics public face. As I walk through two automatic sliding doors which have the words Staff only embossed on them, you are reminded why you should never take your eye of the ball. The wall of remembrance, bears the name of all those who have died in service. Most days I do take time to look at the framed photos of my best friends who have sadly died on these very premises. As you reach the end of the corridor before another set of sliding doors, the last part is dedicated to the worst disaster this company has ever seen. However, what stops me from looking at this today is the time. Sure enough there it was time to go and quickly change in to my posh suit and see the boss.

First rule of seeing the boss, where a suit and tie. He doesn't actually mind if you turn up in anything, but I was specifically asked to dress smart. My mind wondered from the wall to what did the boss want…hmm maybe it was something to do with Fiona's choice of employment. I headed up the stairs; you have a choice at the end of the remembrance wall through the doors to go in the lifts or the stairs. As I am only up one flight of stairs and my office door is right

©TheExpirement

next to them I always take the stairs. Unless of course I am carrying anything and considering the coffee lounge is on my office level of course I take the stairs all the time (wink)

I quickly shower and change. I am five minutes away from seeing the boss. My mind does focus on what Fiona said to me at lunch. Maybe this is them asking if I'm okay with it. Of course I'm okay; I am just a natural born worrier.

I walk out of my office and instead of the stairs I take the lift. No way can I do five flights of stairs in five minutes. I hit the level button and I try and relax. But as I reach the floor I spot an envelope with James written on it. Stuck to the lift door, I wonder if that's for me. But I decide that avoiding it is always the best policy. I walk out of the lift and turn left; there is the bosses' door. You can really miss it, but I have known the odd new comer to go in to the janitor's cupboard next to it before now. Through the bosses door you are greeted by his PA who is leaving next week. Can't say we are going to miss him, but to be fair he has been loyal for the last two years I'll give him that. He waves me in and there is the boss, he too is as ever smartly dressed.

"Ah James please take a seat" he says quietly firmly

Darktronics' boss is Ralph David Mearlow.

He is wearing his dark grey suit, a crisp white shirt and claret red tie and polished black shoes. When I first met him I remember feeling slightly intimidated as his beard and short hair gave him a rough and angry sort of look, but I did meet him when I was 15 with my father many years ago. I now stand slightly taller than him and the years show on his face, but even with his rough angry look the kindness and care he has for this place shows through his blue grey eyes and respect he shows and as for his office is well minimalist. Not a lot in it. A bookcase holds his books and files and a wall is full of all his certificates, photos and memories and his desk has well his phone and a note pad and some pens. There are some photos up of his wife Felicity mainly with work and the same with their three children.

That's it. I know it's hard to imagine, unless of course you are minimalist yourself. But here am I sat in a specially brought in chair.

"What can I do for you sir?" I ask

"Well how long have you been working here?" he says whilst looking out of the window

"Five years today sir" I reply

"And how long have you and Fiona been together?"

"Five years sir" I say proudly, quietly rejoicing in my head that I have remembered such a date.

"I see she is starting in our fire testing department on Monday" he says turning to finally sitting down and looking at me.

"Yes sir, I am sure she will enjoy it" I say trying not to show my worry

"Hmm, well I didn't bring you here to talk about that, but I just thought we should see where you were"

I nodded. I wasn't sure I understood his following but it was always polite to nod. "Well as you seem to be the leading tester, having completed all your tests to the highest order, I am giving you the chance for promotion"

"Thank you" I responded, I was very impressed.

"You understand that this won't be easy"

"Yes sir"

At this point I stood up and his office door opened.

In walked Philip Dowing who was the senior field tester. Now he was the opposite of Ralph, loyal but I would say a wannabe Ralph. He was quite a thin gentleman with a pin stripped suit, his freshly cut brown hair oozed a bit of smoothness that I just didn't trust. Plus his blue shirt today didn't hide a new tattoo which was peeking just above the collar. I focused back to what I had just been told.

"Ralph" he said shaking the bosses hand
"James, Philip is here to witness this statement"
I nodded
I was now terrified
Then the boss spoke as he too was now standing
"James Kieran Folster, as of today you are now under full observation for the next three months. You will undertake a series of tests that will allow Darktronics to look in to every aspect of your work and life both in and outside of this building. Do you understand James?"
"Yes sir" I simply replied
"On completion of all these tests you will be scored by Philip as to whether you are suitable for the role as a field tester. At the end of the three months you will be summoned here to my desk to be read the results. In exactly three months of today I will expect to see you hear at 9am. Don't be late most of all James this will be the toughest test of your life. So good luck and see you in three months. "
"Thank you sir and thank you Philip" I replied smiling.
They both nodded and I turned to leave the room. "Ah James, your set of instructions..." Philip started to say
"Envelope in the lift?" I asked
Philip smiled Ralphs PA had been too eager this morning to get his jobs done.
As I walked back towards the lift I could feel myself shaking. I had indeed just changed my life forever.
I carefully unstuck the envelope from the lift door; that man did like his sticky tape. I was lucky not to rip the envelope as I took it off the lift door. When I reached my floor I nearly fell over the broken down signs in front of the lift. I smiled; it was the bosses' way of ensuring the instructions would always get to the right person. As I

©TheExpirement

turned to my office door, the janitor Rock Simons had just cleaned my office

"Hey Rock, you can clear the signs I have my instructions"

"Cool man, I shall double check with the big man, see if he's finished for today"

I smiled; Rock was very much a cool dude. He had made many a dull evening interesting when he recalled his stories of his travels about the world and I really must ask him to tell me the one about how he became a janitor. I remember it to be one of the most interesting but I can't fully recall the details. Anyway, it was nice to see an old friend, he must have known something was up as I entered my office and there was a fresh cup of black coffee and two iced doughnuts with a note saying

"Sorry man, only had iced, but hey if you accepted the job congrats and good luck; Laters Rock"

I smiled as I dunked the first iced doughnut in to my coffee. That calmed me down no end; I then picked up my phone and dialled out.

The phone connected and there were ten rings before they answered

"Jack speaking"

"Hey Jack speaking its James"

"Yo, this must be serious"

"Don't tell me wrong time of day again"

"Yeah, but don't worry, what's up?"

"Field agent testing"

"Your kidding"

"Nope"

"When did you get your instructions"

"Today"

"Shit man that is serious" Jack paused and said

"You opened them yet"

"No, I only just got in to my office"
"Sure no worries, don't ring anyone else, open them"
"Sure?" I asked
"Yeah. Good luck, I'll call you tomorrow, see you soon bud"
And with that I put the phone down.
I took the envelope which I had laid down on my desk and I opened it.
Inside it had a set of instructions. Now the envelope was a pocket C3 and was fully packed with instructions.
The a4 paper had been folded and came in two sets, separated by paperclips one green and one blue. Come to think of it I don't think the colour of the paperclips mattered, but for some reason I always remembered them.
Anyway I opened the first set this was the set with the green paperclip. I saw that there were ten pages. Judging by the thickness it looked that the second set had a lot more in it.
I took a deep breath and read page one.

"Dear James, your first instruction is to well go home. I know this may sound strange but the job you have agreed to go for will over the next three months take a lot out of you. This job is a test of not just how well you perform at testing but at how you as person can react to shall we say interesting situations. Now for the next week I will not expect to see you anywhere near this building. Fiona will be asked not to start her job for another week to allow you to both have some quality time. Go and enjoy the time off and be in your office usual time a week on Monday. Regards Ralph
PS Don't take these instructions home as I want you to relax.
There it was the first set of instructions and well I had a sneak peek at the other instructions which told me to do certain things at certain times on the Monday I was to be back. I smiled as I

©TheExpirement

"Where have you boys been" Samantha asked

"I showed him round my allotment" Patrick replied

She laughed, well as it's a nice warm evening lets cook sausages round the fire and we did as we were told. Patrick now looked extremely relaxed, but I was worried was this something we should worry about, the following day the answer was yes

I remember being awoken by the birds in the trees it was really early and then I heard a car draw up. I thought it might be a local milk service or something but then I heard a scream. Fiona startled awake as I was now out of the bed and opening the door. I told her to stay there

"Patrick, Samantha" I shouted

"Down here quick" Patrick replied

Patrick was comforting Samantha. A box was on the floor containing a very gruesome picture. David Kerr tied up and covered in blood.

It was time to worry.

©TheExpirement

Chapter Four

My initial reaction was to ring the cops, like any normal family would. But no not us, Fiona said that there must be more too it, maybe this was part of my test. I closed my eyes and tried to picture the instructions in my mind. And to be fair it didn't take long to visualise the paragraph 4.1 of page 9. Which stated and I quote "You will be tested how you deal with personal issues, your family will never be put at risk but a conflict of interest will arise. Be alert and never assume."
That was one of the rules, I racked my brain and tried to reason why they would pick on someone who was supposedly dead and not say my girlfriend Fiona who would be working there soon.
Patrick was calming down Samantha, she was worried and to be fair it was like seeing a ghost. I decided to get out my work mobile and ring the office.
After a short phone call I was reassured that the testing hadn't begun and that any threat made against my family was indeed sadly real and was to get the details to them as soon as I could possibly do so.
They were going to investigate. To be honest this company had it all. There wasn't just the Fire testing and the Science testing departments oh know Darktronics was a rabbit warren of many different things. Let me take this opportunity to tell you exactly what Darktronics is and how it came to be.
Darktronics was a firm that was founded back in April 99. David Mearlow took over a set of three businesses, just like other big businesses this was built from the ground. David Mearlow was as you guessed it the boss's dad. He apparently was a giant over in America and had made his fortune. Whilst the legality and history of how he made his fortune is built on rumours one thing we do

know for sure it was just before he died in 1980 that he had bought all the little companies that now make up Darktronics.

In 1970 he had bought out the Fire testing company – Missions. These were a little unknown firm based in Devon, but they were very good at researching new ways of Fire prevention and alerting people to fires which gave them status in the local fire departments across Britain. The company was bought out as the researchers couldn't then keep up with demand after their newest fire prevention kit saved the lives of a local boarding school. Since then Darktronics have built the Missions prevention kit which is now standard across many schools worldwide. The fire testing department now looks at moving this forward and even making your humble fire extinguisher that much better.

Next on Mr Mearlow's shopping list was the Science lab, which my dad ran. My dad had run this ever since he was old enough to run a business. However, with no thanks to some rogue colleagues my dad's reputation in the science world was dwindling until David Mearlow arrived. To be fair whilst everyone knew what David was up to, he did get my dad's reputation up before buying out the firm which allowed my dad to retire. That did hit dad for a while until he realised he could fulfil his travelling dreams when his first retirement cheque came in. Now my dad's company was named after the family name. Folster, this was the proudest moment when dad had built the science business. His clients which are now very much still with Darktronics were people like your millionaires who had houses and businesses to keep safe. The boxes that I now test began when my dad had a European client; he had received a box of objects which at the time meant nothing. In a way like my carrots and various vegetables, anyways they were soft toys, but each toy was laced with a poison. It was a sign from his enemies that they would poison his children if he did not comply. Hence the reason for anything can be in a box. My dad helped build the company

©TheExpirement

within Darktronics our family name is honoured by a science scholarship.

A few years later in 1978 David bought in the Forensics which was originally in each team. He then took on a local Security Firm who employed former soldiers. That's why we have armed guards at the front door. Highly trained and not to be messed with. That's when he built the crime and forensic units who now keep us safe and sound.

By the time these three elements of Darktronics were settling in everyone could see that David was getting sick. No-one knew if it was cancer or just that he picked up every bug going. Two years later he was gone but had left specific instructions for his oldest son Ralph (my boss) to continue with his plan.

Next for Ralph was to build the site we now work in. That was a little complicated because the site that was the most suitable was full of little shops.

Whilst apparently his dad was going to wait until their leases ran out and ensure they couldn't afford to re-lease. Ralph realised that the people working in Darktronics were more than likely to need these services. So he asked the coffee shop to come under the brand, they now do indeed supply my lovely coffee and doughnuts. He then went next door from the coffee shop and into the hairdresser and they were very much delighted as they had wanted to expand. So just left of reception is the hair salon. Newsagents also came aboard, however security checks found they couldn't be trusted, so Ralph ensured that a new team from the chain were running shop. Then finally the medical centre which provides both medical and dentistry services. Ever since the darkest day in Darktronics the medical practice has provided counselling.

Ralph was seen as ruthless when he was project managing the build. The locals who were against the big build were very quickly dealt with even though some had influence on the planning boards.

But in truth he wasn't really like that, it was his minions. Whilst yes he was about to open the doors to the world's biggest science company he cared about the people who were in it. A trait many said he didn't get from his father.

All the companies that were taken over with really only the odd exception like my dad, the staff were all employed in to Darktronics. Many didn't even have to sign new contracts they were kept on their own terms until their contracts ran out and then they were given new ones which were better or the same.

When I was looking for a job there it did seem too good to be true. Having met Ralph, just as I turned 15, when my dad had to go for a business meeting there.

Now as I had said a little earlier Darktronics has more to it than just what I deal with. After a year of running, Darktronics expanded its doors. It delved in to the travel industry, crime and nuclear. Something you wouldn't automatically assume would happen when really it was just a science company. Our clients grew, we had business people, we had you the public who would buy our alarms, and thanks to Felicities love of animals we had veterinary clients in many of the areas who needed help to prevent poaching. Also the crime part became really an extension of the local police, they were just grateful that we had a crime lab that they could use.

Back to where we are with the Kerr's. Patrick was now pacing around the lounge; Samantha had taken a sleeping pill and gone to bed. It had hit her hard. Fiona was sat quietly in the kitchen. No-one really knew what to do.

I was waiting for the team from Darktronics to turn up. So in reality this is crime and forensics units. They turned up in their black vans with someone who I really wasn't expecting.

©TheExpirement

Chapter Five

All I could see was this lanky lad in a black suit and tie, his long jet black hair was cut to a short back and sides, I was impressed, then I noticed the trainers on his feet, I smiled.
"Jack?" I said as I opened the door.
"Hey bud" he said
waving his men to go round the house. I was told later that this was standard procedure in case anyone was watching or had left anything behind.
"So when did you join crime?" I said as I took him in to the lounge
"Oh I got asked to run them last month. Problem was couldn't tell you, cus there were some shall we say sensitive investigations going on"
That now all made sense to me, some of my fellow colleagues were suddenly sacked without warning and without chance to appeal. Who knows what they had been up to, all I knew was I needed to keep squeaky clean.
I introduced the family, Samantha was still in bed, but Jack understood.
"Patrick, you best show him the letter"
He nodded and went to find it.
I explained to Jack and Fiona about the letter. Jack was worried that this was something against the family. He grew even more concerned when I said
"David Kerr died in a car accident."
Jack was immediately on the phone
"Hey can you get me a warrant..."
He was asking for the right to dig up David's body. Something that made us all cringe. But it needed to be done.
We needed to make sure David was dead.

©TheExpirement

A few hours later, Samantha came down from her sleep. She looked refreshed, but you could see that she had been crying.

"Hey Samantha" I said

"Is your team here?" she asked softly

"Yeah, I'm going to take you to my mate Jack, he needs to ask you a few questions"

She nodded as I took her in to the kitchen. Patrick was looking upset. He hugged Samantha as they passed each other in the doorway to the kitchen.

"So what can I do for you Jack"

"I need to know everything about David." He said simply

She gave a full account of their history, but what was interesting was the latest story about him.

I sat down at the dining table and listened.

"I remember it was like yesterday, it wasn't long before the car crash."

She took a deep breath.

"I had a phone call from him, saying that he needed my help. I had at the point assumed it was something to do with moving house. He had just brought a brand new four bedroom house. I was so happy for him as he was finally settling down." She smiled

"I met him at the local pub the Bay Horse. We went inside and had drinks, he had a whisky and I had a white wine. After our first drink he said that someone was blackmailing him"

She paused this was getting really difficult for her now.

"I asked who, but he showed me this name. The problem was it was just some random letters. I guessed it was a street name. But I couldn't fathom out why he needed my help, after the second drink he said that I would know the name. He was told that I would know and I couldn't work it out."

Her mind was reliving this, I could tell by her face that she was playing this out. After a sip of tea she continued.

"I was quite good at puzzles at that point and I tried matching the letters up with patient names, cryptic puzzles, you name it the lot."
"And did you find a name?" Jack asked
"Well yes, but not until after the car crash, it was only a week later when the car crash happened"
This was really hurting now; I could see tears forming in her eyes. I reached to the box of tissues on the side.
She took one out a carefully dabbed her eyes.
"We got the phone call on Monday afternoon. Patrick was doing some house calls and the hospital needed someone to come to do the identification. So I agreed, I called Patrick and said for him to continue his rounds. As I was near the hospital anyway it made sense.
I remember him lying there looking at peace and I remember them asking me if I wanted his personal items. All I remember was nodding and being given a clear plastic bag."
She turned to look out of the kitchen window. She dabbed her eyes even more now.
"In the bag was his phone and so before I met Patrick I decided to look and see if there was some more information about who was blackmailing him. It turned out that the random letters were only part of a message and there was an anagram. I did the anagram on a napkin and it spelt out my husband's name. Of course I was shocked there was no way he could be blackmailing him. I explained everything to Patrick and later the police. They sadly said that this was another one of those cases."
"Ah the cases where they try and frame a family member" Jack suddenly said
Samantha nodded.
I stood up from the table and looked at Jack. Samantha smiled and said "I hope they haven't"

©TheExpirement

Of course she was referring to David's body. That was tomorrow's nightmare. Jack seemed content for now. He and his team made camp in the meadows and kept watch that night.
Out of respect for the family Jack decided it was better if we didn't go with him to David's grave. Whilst Fiona and I decided to go for a walk and try and get some air, Patrick and Samantha decided to go through some letters that David had sent them just in case there were any clues.
Jack called me just before lunch
"We are doing tests James"
"What sort of tests?" I asked I tried not to sound too panicked.
He explained that whilst there was a body they had to see who it was. There was nothing to say that the body was definitely David. The meadow Fiona and I were walking in was muddy but there was a sense of quietness and feeling relaxed before going back to tension and stress. We stood there for a while just holding hands as we looked at the views. It was a precious moment, one that I wouldn't forget.
As we walked back we could see that Jack was back and hopefully we would know more about what was going on.
Samantha was crying as Jack explained to them what they needed to do. It had hit Samantha hard, the thought that David maybe alive and in trouble made us all feel worried and tied in knots not knowing what to do.
Jack pulled me aside after he had finished things explaining to Samantha and Patrick.
"It's going to be a while for the tests to come through. I am worried about leaving these two on their own"
I nodded, of course Fiona and I were due to start work soon and this wasn't going to be a straight forward investigation. I asked Jack to stay
"Patrick trusts you and Samantha trusts Patrick"

"Yeah thanks James, I don't want this family to worry too much."
"That's why you are best placed Jack, don't think about this one too much" I said
He looked concerned
"Okay, I will stay as the tests should be complete and if they get any more letters or parcels at least we may get a lead"
I breathed a sigh of relief, I couldn't leave Patrick ad Samantha worrying too much about it. I just needed to let Fiona know. As we walked back in to the house I saw her talking to her dad
"Dad, don't worry I won't be testing straight away"
Yikes that conversation the one where she tells dad about the new job. I know she had been stressing about telling him as he was a worrier like me.
"But I don't want you getting hurt" he said sternly
"Dad look I understand, I won't do the testing for at least several months and it means we have all the care we need."
I smiled as I then saw them hug. I knew this was going to be tough. I just didn't realise at that point just how tough.

©TheExpirement

Chapter Six

It was now Monday morning, we had arrived home late Sunday. Not really recommended when you have two nervous individuals, sorry I mean extremely nervous.
Seriously I thought Fiona was ill when she spent an hour longer than normal in the bathroom.
But to be fair as I sorted out some breakfast she came down the stairs looking absolutely stunning. Yes I know I am biased but I think every man will have one of them moments.
Anyways this isn't telling you my story. Now where was I ah yes I remember. It was nice out, but we were both really tired. I was worried about my first day and Fiona had to come in as a newbie. Whilst the security aspect had been all sorted she had to register at reception. I kissed her goodbye at the front door; she was expected one hour earlier than me due to all the paperwork.
I then carried on having my breakfast which was just toast that's all I could manage. How Fiona managed to eat toast and cereal and then I found out later a croissant I am not sure. Maybe she was comfort eating.
I arrived in the office on time and quite pleased with myself. The cycle ride in was quite pleasant and for once I wasn't too stressed about the school kids walking on the cycle paths and being generally annoying.
Fiona had decided it was best to drive in, as point one the car park was nearer to the fire testing department and point two was that today wasn't a full day to day and if mum needed her then she could just get in the car and drive. Sensible, organised.
For me it was going to be a strange day. I worried too much about reading the instructions.
But I remember that they were interesting and that had been one of my first jobs. Read both packs of instructions.

However, now going back earlier in the story I talked about the paperclips and how they didn't matter. I remembered they were blue and green. But that day the shade of blue had changed, I rang the bosses PA and they advised that I was correct the instructions had been changed.
Check, if that was a test I didn't realise, but at least I hoped I had passed it.
I put the instructions down and sipped a coffee, then the desk phone rang it was Jack.
"Hey how it's going" he asked he sounded relaxed
"Yeah well I just read the instructions, so waiting for the craziness to begin, but can't really be too focused"
"I understand, yeah I had some of the tests come back, the good news is we really do believe this is David..." Jack paused he never paused unless he was giving bad news.
"What's the bad news?"
"The picture is a fake, so someone and honestly we don't know who yet is targeting Fiona's family"
I sighed, I was relieved that the picture was a fake. Jack must have pulled some serious favours to get that result back quick.
But he was right, someone was targeting Fiona's family my family.
Three weeks later and there were no leads still on the case.
Fiona though was getting used to her job and was loving it. She had been mainly understanding the products, doing a bit of procurement and research. But now it was time for the testing training. Whilst I knew most of it was simulated and perfectly safe this was the part that gave me the most dread.
Let me take this moment to tell you about some more of Darktronics history.
Through the doors in reception there is a wall dedicated to each member of staff who has died, even those who retired or left.

But at the end of the wall there is a whole section dedicated to its darkest day in history.

©TheExpirement

Chapter Seven

This day happened two years after its opening in 99. My late father Jonathan wrote this in his memoirs. I will relate to this as if it was yesterday.
It was the summer of 2001 I am currently watching the news and the birds are singing in the trees. I have one final act to do in helping Darktronics establish its science lab and that is to visit Darktronics today and hand over some paperwork and ensure that some legacy items are put up in the new lab.
I turned the television off and took my time walking to Darktronics. I decided to go the scenic route and enjoy this gorgeous weather. Half an hour later I reach the reception area, they give me a visitor's pass and the head of the science lab comes out and greets me. We are old friends and I smile as I am relieved to see that the lab is in such great hands. Geoffrey Rogers is his name and I had trained him up just like my own son.
It was an hour or so later when we were sat in the lab doing some research. We heard a massive boom and the evacuation of site notice came over the speakers. Like we had been fully trained we left by our nearest exits, however what greeted us wasn't the gorgeous day but bellowing smoke and people running, running for their lives. Both Geoffrey and I were fully trained in first aid and I remember running to the point of contact, he was stood there shaking like a leaf. He was devastated, nothing like this had happened before and nothing could have prepared anyone for the horrors that we saw that day. I calmed the guy down and then realised why he was shaking, his whole arm was covered in some sort of acid I believe or some chemical. He was in shock and going downhill fast. I called over for some help, Geoffrey appeared and then ran to get some kit, luckily the new first aid kit that had arrived hadn't been sent out to the departments yet, so it was all there,

everything we needed. We treated this poor man and left him with a colleague who was a bit more with it. As I got my bearings others had set up a first aid area and had a routine going of patients. Geoffrey and I helped where we could, at times writing on people to say what their status was and if they were dead we got their identities, so we knew the families could try and get some closure. Time that day seemed to pass slowly, but it hadn't. Things were suddenly calming down as ambulances took away the injured and private ambulances took away the dead. The site was eerily quiet and I took a deep breath to see what else needed to be done. That was when I was approached by the senior fireman. He came to me and asked me to go in to the building. "My guys need your help in their identifying something for us" he said

"Okay is it safe for me to go in"

He nodded, but did ask me to wear protective gear as there were some fumes and smoke still lingering. I agreed and went with him, after getting in to my gear I went in, I saw Geoffrey helping out some patients who were waiting for the ambulances to return. I was amazed that we hadn't been hurt and that we could help.

As I walked in, the place was dark; the firemen were still cooling down parts of computers and lab equipment. Then as I walked closer to a bank of desks three firemen parted. They revealed a computer. I then read what was on the screen; somehow this thing was still working.

My stomach churned as I read the code, it was his style and as I worked out most of what the code did, I nearly fainted. Geoffrey had been responsible for killing what turned out to be 100 people. He had done it by setting up various triggers in the lab and the triggers were connected to poisons and flammable gases you name it he had done it. He had aimed to kill more, but he said at his trial that it was fitting. They had given him 100 days to turn the science lab around, but he had failed and that he would be sacked. This meant no golden handshake. But when asked about why the fire testing department and not the science department, he turned and said "Because they are not the best in the world, my team are" So why was I James so worried? Well sadly Geoffrey had followers and no-one ever got to the bottom of the pile. Everyone was re-checked hell even tripled checked, but no-one was ever sure if he had un-finished business. Plus fire testing brought its own risks with it. Various people have had burns or a few accidents; I guess like my job you could never be fully away from danger. However, it was time to let my girl do what she did best. As long as she arrived safe and sound home each night that's all that mattered. My days were full of more and more testing and the weeks rumbled on. There were even less leads than before on the case and my tests were getting harder. The week of fitness was coming up and been in my spare time I had been working out more. Haha yes sadly no more iced doughnuts or coffee in the morning. Fiona had me on yoghurt and well cardboard. But I have to say every time I look in the mirror hell I look good. One day I was doing some reports in my office when my mate Jack turned up un-announced. "Hey bud" he said as he strode in to my office with no knocking

"Jack, what are you doing here?" I asked standing up from my desk and giving him a firm handshake

"Hey sit back down, I have news" he replied and I did, he perched on my desk.

He took out some folded pieces of paper from his jacket. "It's not great news, turns out David was indeed being blackmailed and turns out the person was working with Patrick at the time"

"no way, seriously?"

"Why a doctor you ask, well I asked the same question myself James, I really did"

"Was it patient related"

"I think so, I think what happened was the patient was someone close to this doctor and Patrick had stepped in to say that he couldn't be treated"

"Oh so they went after his brother?"

"Yeah but I think they got Patrick confused with David"

I took a moment, they were really after Patrick?

Jack had indeed read my mind. He knew what I was thinking, I sighed

"Don't worry, I have Patrick under guard. They shouldn't be able to get through"

"Can't you arrest them or something?" I asked hoping for a straight yes or no

He took his time

"We don't know where the hell he is"

He showed me the picture, I didn't recognise the guy. His name was Martin Kowl. Sorry Doctor Martin Kowl.

Jack then departed, he asked me not to do any investigations and I decided it was best for everyone not too. Little did I know I was about to have some problems to deal with of my own.

Chapter Eight

It was a week after Jacks visit that I started receiving strange post at work.
It wasn't the normal post and in the second set of instructions, the one with the blue paperclip, I found a pictorial piece of paper which clearly stated what should be expected for the promotion tests.
The post didn't fit any of the briefs, I was worried.
I was even more worried when Fiona rang from home advising that we had a parcel at the post office to collect. We hadn't ordered anything and we weren't expecting any parcels. My mind was now racing to make sure that my next move didn't cause us to make a mistake.
I decided it was best to go and talk to Philip, he was out on a job but after his colleague rang him, I was picked up by a Darktronics lab van. Philip had sent it over, he was worried. As we drove, the driver was silent; however, I could hear my heart beating fast. Philip rang me and asked how long we would be. The driver suddenly stopped the van.
"What the hell?" I shouted
He jumped out of the front seat and opened my door.
I kicked him in the chest keeping the phone open with Philip so he could hear everything. Then noticing he had a gun in his jacket pocket. As I kicked him again before he got u, the gun had fallen on to the ground beside him. It made me feel sick but the adrenaline was telling me to drive. I ripped his pass off his neck and decided to take the gun.
I jumped into driving seat and started driving fast. Philip gave me instructions.
It was indeed time to be worried. It seemed like hours before I finally got to where Philip was. He was relieved to see me, but as soon as I stopped the van and saw real Darktronics staff I just broke

down there was nothing to stop me. I needed air, I had for the first time in my life killed a man.

As I walked around the field drinks tent, I suddenly realised I recognised the name on the guys pass. It was Martin. The Martin that Jack was trying to find, that's all I remember for the rest of the day. I fainted and woke up the next day in hospital with Fiona sat asleep in the chair.

I was relieved that I was alive.

After I had woken up fully and the nurses had done their checks. Jack walked in

"Good morning" he said

"Yeah" we shook hands

Fiona hugged Jack and said she was going off to find coffee and some breakfast.

"What the hell happened?" I asked Jack as soon as Fiona walked out of the room

"Turns out that there is more to this Martin Kowl"

"Oh okay"

I pondered the thought, I didn't know then what I knew now, but something was on my mind that day.

"Turns out, he's dead" Jack said without showing too much emotion

"Well I did pretty much hit him hard"

"No not that guy, your so called driver was impersonating him"

"Do you think..." I started to say

"Yes James, I think someone is playing you, all of us and no I don't know how ugly this is going to get"

Fiona then walked in with welcome coffee and some food, she had popped out to the local café and got us a bacon roll. I was starving. Jack laughed as I practically only took two bites to eat the roll. He did offer his, but I refused, I was trying to be good. But Fiona then made me really smile, she took out a paper bag and there was an iced doughnut. I spent the next week in hospital, Darktronics wanted to ensure that I was physically and mentally ready for work.

©TheExpirement

Chapter Nine

The next couple of months were going to be some of the hardest of my life.
Fiona was busy working on her fire testing course one evening studying away, when I received a call from Philip.
"James, we need you to come to Darktronics please. Code 9825"
I phoned reception, I will just before finishing that conversation tell you about the receptionists. A little earlier I advised that they could do well about anything. It's true, as you come in to reception you are greeted with five young ladies or five young men depending which day it is.
No mixing of men and ladies on any day.
Each are trained to exacting standards
From left to right we have receptionist one who are highly trained in martial arts and first aid, this is usually Sally and Mike.
Receptionists two and three belong to the TA and are highly qualified Army soldiers who have seen action in various countries. These are usually Frank, Debbie, Kerry and Andrew. As for number four, well no-one really knows what they do for sure, but they are your direct line to the Home Office and anyone beyond that.
Usually George and Marie, finally that leads me to number five who in essence is highly trained in all things well IT. They run the high powered security systems in the front of receptions and in some of the secure areas around Darktronics. Daniel and Felicity are usually in the number five spots. However, as I have mentioned the word usually throughout my description. All of them are able to do each other's job, all have served and all are highly trained. So as I was saying they can do just about well anything.
Back to the conversation, and the code I have received the code from Philip
"Darktronics reception how can I help" Sally answers

©TheExpirement

"I have a code for science lab" I say clearly
"Yes, please enter your code now" she replies
I put in the number in to the phone
Sally then confirms it and I breathe a small sigh of relief. This is for real and I am now expected at Darktronics. I decided to drive that evening, whilst I did sometimes do night cycling, I didn't know how long I was going to be and we were due rain.
I arrived at reception
"Good evening Mr Folster" Sally advised
you were always greeted by the person who confirmed your code; it was another layer of security.
"Good evening to you" I replied and re-entered the code.
I then went as normal across the Darktronics rug and up to my lab. Philip greeted me
"We have a package waiting for you" he said as I walked in to my office. A team were already in place.
I could expect this at any time and any place; this was a test of working in different conditions.
I placed my bag down and walked in to my air lock doors and changed in to my lab suit. Dennis delivered the package, it made me smile seeing Dennis, there was a post it on the front of him saying "Good luck"
Whilst everyone wasn't supposed to know what you were doing, everyone knew. It was like a family, which back then we didn't realise was going to be fully tested.
I thanked Dennis and place the package on the counter. It was a padded envelope; I did some swabs and started feeding data in to the lab's computer.
An announcement then came over my labs speaker
"You may proceed" Philip advised
I replied by simply nodding

41 –Expirement Series

as I began to carefully open the envelope, my stomach did a few churns. From the corner of my eye, I noticed that the video camera in the top left of my lab moved.
It never moves.
It shouldn't move.
It can't move
I have tried it.
I then made a code signal via the labs computer to the team.
Philip then left my office and went out.
Act naturally I thought and so I decided to continue opening the envelope.
I peered inside and there was a bag of white powdery substance and a clear plastic box with drawing pins closely packed inside.
Then I pulled out a set of wires and to finish a box of matches.
My aim was to analyse each individual item and then not just decide if this was a test or real but which item or items were the most dangerous.
After about thirty minutes Philip returned to my office.
No news was bad news, he couldn't tell me anything because he didn't want me reacting. We now know that someone was watching me and had hacked in to the video camera system. This was someone who was on the inside or had been on the inside.
My stomach was still churning as I analysed and entered data.
Several hours later, I was finally in the air lock doors changing back in to my t-shirt and jeans. As I entered my office I picked up my soft hooded top, it was welcome. I was cold. Philip then asked me to follow him.
We walked up the stairs to his office; it wasn't too far from Ralphs and we you could hear some serious shouting going on.
Philip made me a cup of tea as I sat down on one of his many computer chairs.
He then explained

"You are right, the camera did move"
I took a sip from the tea
"I assume someone's hacked" I asked
"Yes, I think that is security in Ralphs office"
It made sense, any sort of breach and he would be livid. He prided himself on the fact that the systems were the world leaders. Any sort of breach in this place could lead to loss of jobs and even lives. We sat in silent drinking our tea when Ralph walked in to Philips office.
"Good evening" we all pretty much said at the same time.
Ralph pulled up a chair and asked us both to sit close
"You've probably heard that I have had a breach in security"
"Yes sir" I replied
"Right, well the good news is it was one of our testers"
"Oh one of our well paid teenage hackers" Philip said
Ralph nodded
"You were right on it tonight James, I am just glad it was noticed tonight, we have the press coming in tomorrow" Ralph said, you could hear the sense of relief in his voice.
"Telling off security was needed as they had assured me that no-one should be able to get through with our latest upgrades"
He was angry, he was livid. This had indeed upset the apple cart. I suspected there were some important things going on tomorrow and well this was all that he needed.
"Now, I want you two to be my eyes and ears tomorrow please" he said sternly.
We both nodded, I sipped the last bit of tea out of the takeaway cup and threw it in to the bin. Philip couldn't help but smile. As the bin was the other side of the office.
"Good shot…" Ralph began to say
We all laughed, it was nice to break some of the tension

"Now tomorrow we have a new set of companies coming in to see if they want to become part of Darktronics, this could lead us in to space"

Ralph then stood up from his chair"

If you see anything in any of your areas out of place, you do whatever is needed to remove them"

The air between us turned serious and tense.

"Do you understand what I am asking you to do" Ralph said

"Yes sir" Philip and I replied in unison

I took a look at my watch, tomorrow was now today.

©TheExpirement

Chapter Ten

I thought about sleeping in my office, I had a sleeping bag stored away for such matters but Philip and Ralph wouldn't stand for it and sent me home. It was a welcome relief to climb in to bed and see Fiona sound asleep. She stirred slightly as I made myself comfortable. It was about three when I had gotten in to bed. They had asked me to be in a 10 so that I could get some sleep and food. Thankfully my body had decided to give me a goodnights/morning sleep; I wasn't too surprised to find myself alone in bed some hours later, shame as I could have done with a morning cuddle.
Anyway I climbed out of bed and went in to the shower. Fiona then came in to the bathroom
"Morning sweetheart" she said
I opened the shower door and saw that she was standing there looking gorgeous as ever. She then climbed in to the shower with me.
A few moments later it was time for me to leave; I was surprised though to see that Fiona was still here.
"You got the day off?" I asked grabbing an apple from the fruit bowl on the kitchen side
"Yes I need to run a few errands"
I smiled and gave her a big cuddle and kiss, how I loved her so much. Which every time I kissed or cuddled her reminded me of how I must indeed marry her one day.
I drove in to the office as it was raining, I had my posh suit and tie on, as I wanted to make a good impression.
However what greeted me at Darktronics wasn't what I was expecting.
I was greeted by Philip as I parked my car. There was an ambulance parked near the science labs

©TheExpirement

"Come quickly its Ralph" he said I got out of my car. I quickly locked it leaving all my stuff behind

"What happened" I said as we broke in to a run, so much for wearing the suit

"He has been stabbed"

I was in shock

Of course Ralph would have loads of enemies or rivals who wouldn't want him around. But to actually try and kill him… hmm the list was a lot shorter.

We made it to the back fire exit when we saw the paramedics bringing him out on a stretcher he was alive.

He spotted us and moved his hand as if to wave.

Philip somehow saw that as a signal and we ran up the flights of stairs.

As we entered Ralphs office the forensics staff gave us gloves and covers for our shoes just in case we touched anything. I wasn't sure why we're here, but I followed Philips lead. He knew what he was doing.

He touched a key port and then asked me to put in the code from last night. I did so and cabinet door then unlocked. It didn't open, then Philip got a key out from his pocket and opened it. I then had to enter the code again. Somehow I just remembered it; I was starting to feel worried when I saw what was in the cabinet.

"Really" I said

"I understand James, this is all new to you. But Ralph has every faith in you. Trust me and trust him". All I could do was nod, I was worried.

I picked up the gun and Philip put it in his holster. We then got out some bullet proof vests. I wasn't going to be carrying a gun as I wasn't yet trained. But it still un-nerved me.

I also grabbed a black diary; this had everyone's name in it that could be a possible suspect.

I was now investigating the recently attempted murder of my boss Ralph Mearlow.

As for the companies who were being shown around today, yep that's right that job fell to his nephew Paul. Whilst he was useless he did have the gift of selling, he could sell you anything if you gave him half the chance.

At least he would keep the press out of the way too. We needed that and we met him in Philips office.

"Paul what can we do for you" Philip said

"I just want to make sure you find who has done this"

"Yes we will" I said

"I thank you both for getting here and doing what he asked. When I found him he gave me this" Paul said and he handed Philip and piece of paper. It was covered in Ralph's blood.

"Good luck today" I said as Paul left the office

"And you" he replied and with that he was gone.

©TheExpirement

Chapter Eleven

Philip opened up the piece of paper
"Jenkins" he read aloud
"That rings a bell" I said quickly moving to his computer
"Sorry do you mind"
"No not at all" He motioned me to continue
I logged on to his computer, we were meant to do that only in an emergency and this was one of those times.
"I remember a Jenkins from the fire of 2008" I said as I entered our online history database.
It contained every single event in Darktronics history and there was even today's stabbing of Ralph already entered.
I typed in Jenkins in the search function, it was worrying, and something was nagging me at the back of my mind. I wasn't quite sure what it was and then I remembered as the results appeared
"What is it" Philip asked he was stood there with his arms crossed
"You won't find a Jenkins in the diary" I said
"why?"
"Because it was Jenkins who died in the fire"
"Explain" he said
"The fire was started in the crime lab, there was a fault in one of the electric points or so they thought at the time. Jenkins was the crime lab PA and thought he could put the fire out but sadly the smoke got to him first." I saw Philips reaction
"Revenge?" he asked
"Not revenge, he had a younger brother at the time who was helping in security and they didn't know how Jenkins had managed to get through the doors as they shouldn't have opened"
Philip now looked really stern and almost upset.
"Last night hack"
I nodded and typed it in to the database

"Jenkins brother Sean is the one who put in the planned upgrades."
The page haunted us for a few moments.
"Time to find Sean and time to get our crime unit" Philip said.
And with that we walked out of his office.

Normally I would have rung Jack as he was leading criminal investigations. But he was still busy working on the Martin Kowl case and to be fair this was now finding a fellow colleague not someone who was an impersonator.
We walked calmly through the corridors; everyone was whispering and talking about the attempted murder.
On the way Philip rang the hospital
"He isn't dead and he's out of danger" he then said to me" after having a short conversation with someone.
I smiled, I was glad they hadn't managed to kill Ralph.
We then found ourselves in the reception, sadly some of the press recognised us and came running over
"You must be proud that Darktronics are going in to space" one journalist shouted
"Yes we are, now Paul has the full brief and we have some very important meetings to attend too"
Philip said calmly.
The press knew they were being fobbed off but they ate it up and rushed to see where Paul was. It was part of our training to deal with the press; you didn't need anything leaking out the way you didn't intend.
Out of the front doors, we turned down a side alley which took us directly to the crime lab where a young lady named Leona greeted us.
"Glad to see you two" she said and showed us in
"I am glad to see you" Philip said giving her a kiss on the cheek. I got a handshake. Philip wasn't married and some weren't sure of

©TheExpirement

whom he was interested in, there was a book being run in the corridors of our science area. Leona was an outside favourite. Anyway, I smiled and we carried on to her office.
"Don't make yourselves too comfortable" she said as we tried to find somewhere to sit.
There was paperwork everywhere, on what looked like seating, but you couldn't be sure.
"Why not" I asked
"Well I need you to answer a few questions" she said in a tone that made you wonder if we were now suspects.
But before she continued Philip advised her
"I believe this is evidence, and we have inkling that Sean might be your guy"
She took us in to another room and closed the doors.
"Sound proof" she said to me directly, she had read my mind.
"Why Sean?" she asked
"Well he was the brother of Jenkins, the one who was killed in the fire with the faulty security doors. He failed last night with some security upgrades and let's just say Ralph blew his top" I said
Her face dropped, she understood, she knew what we had said to her
"Okay fine, you two go with my assistant Greg and look at some video for me"
Leona was now going to go find Sean.
We followed Greg who had been directly outside the door waiting.
"Right, here you go lads, here's the remote and well see if you recognise anyone on this, I'll be next door if you spot anything so give us a shout like"
And he left us watching the video of someone stabbing Ralph.
I had seen blood before, but it was like watching a horror movie.
But then we caught a glimpse of a face, he had tried to cover it up, but a reflection from a lift door gave us all we needed. There he was

©TheExpirement

Sean was standing in front of the lift with blood all on his clothes. We shouted for Greg.

Chapter Twelve

It felt a little bit surreal; here I wanted to know what had happened this morning.
Greg then interrupted my thoughts
"Okay guys what do we have here"
"We recognise that as Sean"
"Okay I will ring her ladyship"
We all smiled, to be fair she was the boss and it made sense, she was good.
Leona was amazed at how quickly we had found some evidence for her
But then Greg said
"Right we must go to were Leona is, she wants you to see something"
My stomach started to churn, part of me just knew that we were indeed being driven to identify Sean.
Greg took us out of yet another entrance; it was a rabbit warren of confusing corridors.
Thankfully though we were outside before you knew it and there was a police car waiting for us.
Greg jumped in the front, Philip and I got in the back
"What's your feeling on this" Philip said quietly
"I think we are going to identify Sean"
His face turned slightly worried
But then all he said was
"Interesting"
I then wondered
Was this a test, a test of my ability to cope with the unexpected, to cope with death of colleagues.
I was even more worried now.

©TheExpirement

Question was should I ask.
Before we knew it we turned in to a long main road
it was massive, the houses were extremely posh, and most had
secure gates at the front of them. Others were well kept and from
what I could see had amazing front gardens.
You could tell they had money down this road. The road itself was
lined with trees and there was well no dirt, the road seemed newly
laid and was kept up together.
The young blond police officer turned in to a drive.
I sat there for a second just before he had turned off the car engine
and I took in the view.
A detached three-storey house, black front door with police tape
over it, I am guessing at this point that Jenkins had a big pay-out
and this was where the money was gone.
Philip, who had gotten out before me, was looking pale as he
knocked on the car window
I then got out of the car. I followed Philip in to the house, we were
given some shoe socks by the officer on the door and some gloves.
"Don't try and touch anything" Leona suddenly said as she
appeared from a side room
"Sure" I said
I was guessing my gut feeling had been right considering that Philip
was looking rather pale.
I took a deep breath as we walked nearer the room. It was full of
forensics doing their thing

Then I saw it, the body.
Sean Jenkins was very much dead on the floor of his own house.
"Is that him James?" Asked Leona
"Yeah, its Sean"
"Okay that gives us our second confirmation, let's get this body out"
Philip was chatting to one of the forensic photographers

I only heard his last couple of words
"Get Jack"
And with that he turned to me and asked me to follow him out.
Things hadn't gone to plan.
As we walked back through the hallway that led us straight to the front door
I could smell something interesting, I had smelt it before. I couldn't put my finger on it but I knew I had smelt it before and not that long ago either.
"James, let's go we need to meet Jack"
Philip called me over from the waiting police car.
I wanted to know where the smell had come from as we were driven out of the drive
I asked Philip
"Did you smell something in the hallway"
"Which smell?" he asked
"The one that wasn't quite strawberry or liquorice"
He shook his head
"If you don't mind me saying sir" said the young blond police officer
"Go ahead" Philip advised him
"I did and I smelt it in Mr Mearlow's office this morning"
That's where I had smelt it before, it was a clue a massive clue in my mind and we needed to remember it.
We drove to Darktronics where Jack was standing outside the car park.
Philip hadn't said anything else to me on the way, he was worried and I could tell.
Philip instructed the young policeman to pull over. As the officer stopped the car, we both got out.
"Jack" said Philip
"Good to see you Phil"

©TheExpirement

"Maybe different terms next time" Philip replied shaking Jacks hand.
Jack acknowledged my presence and then we started walking
"Where are we going?" I asked
"Don't worry James, you'll see" Jack said
He was wearing black jeans and a red plain t-shirt; this was unusual normally Jack would wear a posh suit and a crisp white shirt. I was concerned; we were walking to a part of Darktronics that I didn't know existed.
It was a small set of rooms that was connected to the crime building, or so I thought. That was the first set, we then went down stairs and we were underground.
The first door on the left was secured by a code lock. Jack opened it and then turned to Philip
"Right then, we are now secure we can now start talking"
"Someone want to tell me what the hell is going on"

Philip turned to me, but Jack stopped him from saying anything, so I continued
"I HAVE NO IDEA WHERE THE HELL I AM, AND WHAT THE HELL HAS GONE ON THIS MORNING"
I shouted, I don't normally shout, but I was beginning to feel annoyed.
"Okay James, don't worry we are about to tell you"
Jack said calmly, to be fair it was nice to see him, he was a good friend and someone I could trust.
Philip smiled and had gone to get us all a hot chocolate and some chocolate biscuits. This place was suddenly heaven
"Right let's sit" Philip said as I smiled at the tray of goodies he brought over. He appeared from a kitchen at the lower end of the room
"What is this place I asked" taking a seat

The room was like a school classroom in some way, the walls were covered in blue notice boards, and there were pin marks where stuff had obviously been placed. But the seats were soft instead and there were old desks as tables. . Filing cabinets filled some space near the kitchen
"This is a sound proof evidence room" Jack said
"Its where we do the really sneaky beaky stuff" Philip advised
We drank our welcomed hot chocolate and then Jack went to one of the filing cabinets and pulled out a briefcase.
"Let's get down to business" he said

©TheExpirement

Chapter Thirteen

There was nothing I could have foreseen about this meeting. My gut feeling about Sean had been right, but right now it was now telling me nothing. I wasn't sure if this was real or a test.
Hungry for answers I had to sit patiently for Jack to put up his bits of paper and photos.
My stomach churned slightly when I saw the pictures of Fiona's mum and dad and the box they had received.
"Right over to you Phil" said Jack
Philip stood up; he straightened his jacket and took a deep breath.
"About four months ago, Ralph and I made plans for you James to be moved in to our promotion programme. To ensure this I was tasked in setting up some exercises for you, many of which you are going to get over the next month or so as agreed."
He paused.
I nodded, I was worried with what he said next
"However, on the day of your meeting with Ralph and I, we received this letter here"
He pointed to a scrappy piece of paper which I couldn't read it from where I was sitting, but before I could move closer Philip read it aloud.
"Dear Ralph, time for revenge, hope your guinea pig is ready for some exciting tests. Watching you always R."
"Who the hell is R" I asked
"That's what we have been trying to find out" Jack suddenly said.
He was now sat down looking through a pile of papers
"Okay, what happened next?" I said looking at Philip hoping for some straight answers
"Today was meant to be the first time you saw a threat on our boss, Ralph's so called stabbing was indeed a fake."
Relief filled me like I had never felt it before, I was sure it was real

"But Sean is dead" I then suddenly said without realising it.
"Yeah. Someone this R is, trying to play us we believe. That strawberry liquorice smell…" he paused
He could see I suddenly was in deep thought and I was.
That smell, I suddenly could picture back in my mind the office where Ralph had been so called stabbed. It was strong by the exit door and by the secret cabinet that Philip had picked the gun from. Then my mind took me back to the morning of the box arriving at Samantha and Patrick's, there was that smell again.
"What is it James?" I could hear Jack saying to me, he was about to say it again when suddenly I was back in the room
"That smell I have smelt here in Ralphs office, at Sean's and at Samantha's and Patricks" I said
Jack was now writing those place names on a small white board he found at the back of the room.
"Is that the scent of our R?"
"Could be" Philip said
and with that we took a moment. This was something big we had found ourselves in and to be honest we didn't know what was going to happen next.
Jack continued, whilst Philip went to out to get more supplies. I wasn't sure where the hell he had gone, because he didn't go out the same door as we had come in.
Anyway it gave me and Jack time
"Is this a test?" I asked him
"No, sadly not my friend" he said he turned to me with a look that was serious but concerned.
"Do we really know what we are dealing with?" I asked
"Nope, but thankfully Phil here is back with supplies and we can explain some more"

He was seriously quick I thought, but then again there was more to this than they were letting on, I was just a piece in the puzzle but I just didn't know which piece.
"So what do we know?" asked Philip
"Well, we have the letter from our anonymous R"
"Have we run that against any past employees who did our head in?" I asked
"Yes and there is one hell of a list all with names with R"
Jack showed me the list he had been talking about, sorry I mean lists. There was one list that contained employees that had the name starting with R and that's forename and surname, the other list was nicknames beginning with R, but that was shorter and the final list was people who had sadly passed away. This could be revenge and this could be deadly.
"Okay, sorry I asked" I said after reading through the lists. There wasn't anyone really standing out.
"Sean died about two hours after we found Ralph" Philip said as he opened some of the carrier bags that contained our supplies.
"Crisps anyone" he said passing out a big multipack, I was getting hungry, and it had been a busy day. This worrying was making me eat, no dieting this weekend.
"So we know someone was watching him when he entered his house?" I asked as I tucked in to my bacon flavoured crisps
"No" Jack said firmly
"Okay so he was killed at home then" Philip said
"Yeah, that's what Leona found out" Jack advised, he then showed us some pictures from the scene.
"They are pretty gruesome I'm afraid"
"He's a good photographer" I said looking at the detail that had been captured.
"Why thank you" said Jack suddenly
"You were the photographer?" I asked

©TheExpirement

"Yeah man" he said he could see I was ready to blow again
"Okay, before I go mad, I assume this was a plan?" I asked sternly
Philip then stood up from his chair and decided to tell all
"Okay Sean was hired to play stab Ralph which he did, but we then saw he was asked to get in to a car outside Darktronics. I was worried when he didn't turn up at his agreed safe point."
"Which was?" asked Jack
"The Grange Hotel room 650"
"Anyone been there yet?"
"Leona is going there now" Phil said
"Excellent we should get some more answers" Jack said whilst he opened a bottle of pop
"Okay what the hell do we do?"
"You boys can now help me analyse this evidence" said a voice behind us
"Leona" Philip said with a smile.
Jack winked at me.
I laughed.
Then we saw the boxes and bags of evidence.
Hence the supplies I thought. We spent the rest of the day looking at the evidence. To be fair it was paperwork and computer tech, Leona had advised us that her police were too busy to get this done. I wasn't sure, turns out the chief was in town to check on the Darktronics Police and there were more high profile crimes as this was currently under the Testing protocol, in plain speak that's fake crime.
Which made sense considering this was all meant to be part of a test for me.
This then made me wonder if of course this was an attack on me.
Jack wanted us to stay here overnight, Philip and Jack argued over this I stood and waited
"Look you can't expect us to get anywhere tonight" Philip said

©TheExpirement

"No I don't, but this is sure the safest place we can be" Jack said trying not to get angry

Jack didn't do angry he did terror, he was my best friend but never cross him on a bad day.

They carried on for a little while longer constantly going over the same. I decided it was time for me to stop waiting

"LOOK" I shouted

they both turned to me, I think hoping to see something that made them stop worth it?

"This could be a threat on me, which means my girl Fiona could be in trouble. Now if you don't mind you too, I would like to get this evidence clear so that instead of sleeping in some cold room I can go home and sleep in my own bed"

They both looked at each other resigned to the fact that I was right. Jack called his minions as asked them to ensure that people were safe, so that was Fiona for me, Leona for Philip and as for Jack, well no-one was sure if he had someone or not.

I was even more relieved when we agreed that bedtime was to be two in the morning. We had been sifting through CCTV footage and doing various sketches of people we recognised, constantly crossing them off the lists if we found they had an alibi. Two in the morning arrived and Philip turned off the computers and ushered me out Jack followed me.

There was a door from the kitchen and there were three beds all covered in sleeping bags and blankets, then on top was a toothbrush, paste, shaving kit and a flannel, part of the supplies that Philip had gotten us; he acknowledged my thanks when I sat down on the bed. I was relieved that they had thought of everything. A small bathroom was off to the left of the kitchen we took it in turns and before you knew it I was in dream land. Sleep was at a premium that evening as both Philip and Jack snored; a bit of surround sound would be the best way to describe it.

©TheExpirement

However, luckily for me I had my mp3 player with me and the ear phones dulled the sound just enough for me to sleep again. I woke up a couple of hours later to the noise. So I was glad of the next two hours sleep.

Jack then woke me up with breakfast, which wasn't bad, black coffee and croissants which were extremely nice.

We got back to looking at the footage, Philip was yet to wake, it was about an hour in that we started to worry

"I think we should wake him" I said to Jack, realising that it was late.

"Yeah I think he just needs his beauty sleep"

Then we heard his phone ring, no answer

"On the other hand" Jack said worriedly as he jumped up from the seat, we then hurried to the bedroom

Phil stirred as we walked in

"Hey buddy, time to rise and shine" Jack said loudly

"What time is it?" he asked looking very groggy

"Err 8ish" Jack again said it loudly, I could see what he was doing, he wasn't convinced Phil was shall we say with it.

"Sugar, I never sleep that long" as he sat up in bed,

"You okay?" I asked I wasn't convinced as he looked pale

"err a little dizzy" he managed to say and with that he went down like a sack of spuds.

Jack pulled out his phone and called for help

Leona and a paramedic arrived, the paramedic worked on him for what seemed like ages

"Any ideas?" asked Leona as she paced up and down the room

"No, we were all locked in here last night" Jack said, I hadn't realised that we had been, but I understood why.

"He allergic to anything?" asked the paramedic who had stepped out of the bedroom to the kitchen where we now stood

"Yeah liquorice" Leona advised trying not to blush

©TheExpirement

"That's why he was pale near Sean's house" I said
we found that one of the croissants smelt of liquorice and the others seemed fine.
Now we were confused
Was this an attack on Darktronics?
Was this an attack on Jack or even myself?
Was this an attack on Philip?
That no-one was sure enough, Leona jumped in the ambulance with Philip.
Jack put his hand on my shoulder and said
"Come on, time to leave and get Fiona"
And with that we went outside and drove to my house.

©TheExpirement

Chapter Fourteen

Fiona was already outside our house with two small suitcases. As we stopped Jack turned to me and said, "Right then, seems like my message got through, time for you two to live in our safe house"
"No way, Jack, come on" I sternly said
"Look it's not that bad, I'll be there and so will Ralph" I sighed it gave me some comfort that Fiona and I wouldn't be alone in the safe house.
I decided there was no real fight in me for this one and Jack then advised that we would still be going to work, it would allow him to monitor us and what goes in and out.
It made sense, I was just angry that we had to leave the comforts of our own home.
I took a deep breath and got out of the car, Fiona smiled at me it was a strained smile. There wasn't anything I could say to her, she was worried and I didn't have the answers.
She kissed me on the cheek as I held her hand; I smiled as I then noticed that she was wearing her lucky green bracelet. I had given it to her on our second date. She smiled back as she could see I was remembering how I got the bracelet for her.
I had decided to impress her by taking her to a fancy restaurant. I was completely bowled over by her by our second formal date. Coffee at the local café didn't count. So that day I was returning from work. My boss, the mad professor said I could go and do library study, but he did not want to see me again and he never checked up on me. So as it was raining I decided to take the bus, but I left a little late, luckily I was able to flag it down and it stopped for me. As the bus reached town, I suddenly realised that I didn't have my phone on me, even though I was supposed to call Fiona to tell her where to meet and time. Yikes, I was worried. I laugh now,

but that day I was panicking, the old lady next to me must have been watching me as she turned to me
"Everything okay, my dear?"
"Yeah thanks, second date" was all I could muster
She smiled and turned back to watching the traffic out of the window.
As I got off the bus at the next stop, the rain was continuing to pour down, so I ran to the next phone box, which was a rare find, luckily for me it was working and I remembered Fiona's number off by heart.
As I exited the phone box, the rain hammered down soaking me right through. So I sought shelter by a market stall where this guy was selling bracelets. He sold me this green one for half price. I met Fiona at 6 that evening and she was impressed by my gift to her
"Thank you, that's lovely"
I told her the story of how lucky I was that day, from that day forward that was her lucky charm.
Now today as we moved to the safe house luck needed to be on our side. Jack hurried us a long a bit as we put the suitcases in to the boot.
We were driven to the safe house. None of us talked; I just held Fiona's hand tightly and hoped that everything would be okay. When we arrived, Jack had taken us down many streets and back roads, so we weren't sure where we were. But as we turned in there were big black electronic gates which seemed to auto open as the car got near them, but later on we were given key fobs which would open them. I was slightly terrified of losing it.
The combination number which should you ever need it was changed daily so you would have to ask security every morning.

I was quite impressed by the big house, it was like a mansion, Fiona was still extremely quiet but I understood as nothing would be like home.

We walked in through the front door which was a solid oak light brown door. There was a gold coloured lion door knocker and no letter box. Security greeted us there; we wiped our feet on the door mat as we stepped in. A long posh hallway greeted us, it wasn't carpeted, but there were small tables against the wall of which some had vases of flowers on them others had drinks and other bits and pieces.

When we reached the end room, which was the security hub with loads of people in suits all working at computers, all wearing radios I saw a map of the estate was up on the wall. That was when I realised how big this place was.

I felt safer when Jack showed us to our part of the estate, a more accurate description than a big house.

"So guys you will have your own area, a flat if you like" he said as we walked back down the hallway up the stairs to a front door.

It was white, with a black number 53 on it and a normal looking lock.

He grabbed a set of keys out of his jeans pocket and opened the door.

We were greeted by a fresh scent; you walked straight in to the lounge which had a flat screen television on the wall, a leather corner couch and a coffee table which was also the fish tank too. Neat I thought as I saw the goldfish swimming around in it. I wasn't sure how we fed the fish but then Jack turned my attentions away "Bedrooms are en-suite and the kitchen is over there" Jack said as he pointed to a door over in the left hand corner. The hard wood flooring was also covered by some rugs, Fiona who still hadn't said anything decided to go and look in the bedrooms. Jack looked concerned

"It will take her time" I said, hoping that time wouldn't be the long sort.

I walked in to the kitchen and saw all the modern fitting and fixtures, and a big oak dining table which could fit twelve round at least.

"So what are the rules" I asked Jack

"Go to work as normal, be you, but don't let anyone know you live here, if you think you are being followed go to your home"

"But what about mum and dad" said a voice behind us

"They can visit no problem, you just need to plan it in. Or visit them with our protection" Jack said as he looked at his watch

Fiona came and stood next to me, holding me tight.

"Right time for me to go do, I will check in with you guys later, oh and the fridge is full of food or you can ring security for takeaway and the full rules are in your safe"

He then closed the door behind us.

I turned to Fiona

"What's the bedroom like?" I asked gently

"Nice, let's make some tea" she replied quietly

that was our first night in the safe house.

I didn't sleep much that night, not just because of where we were, but because I hadn't yet found the safe that Jack had advised contained the full rules of our stay.

I didn't want to wake Fiona but she was worn out and I was happy to see that she had managed to go straight to sleep.

I quietly got out of the big king size wooden bed, they really like their oak in here I thought.

I walked through the bedroom and went in to our en-suite bathroom.

I closed the door behind me, so that any noise I made wouldn't wake Fiona.

©TheExpirement

I smiled; I had to think like Jack, where would he have placed the safe.
I checked the bathroom cabinet, I then checked behind the toilet and this had taken a fair few minutes.
Then the door opened, I nearly jumped out of my skin
"Sorry" she whispered
"Did I wake you?" I asked turning to the sleepy Fiona
"No, I couldn't work it out either, until I had a thought" she said yawning
"I don't think it's in here" I said about to walk out
"Don't go, it's here, do you remember when you told me about you and Jack on holiday?"
"Oh the missing box set of his favourite dvds?"
She smiled, it made us both laugh we said it together
"Shower"
And with that we climbed in to the shower and found that the dial had more numbers than it should have. Well little markings, only seen if you were looking for them
"Hmm now we have to think of a number"
I said hoping that it would be something straight forward
"When did you go on that holiday?"
"1005399"
That indeed was the number a panel then opened towards us
There was the safe, I was impressed it made me feel a bit, dare I say it, safer.
I reached in and found an envelope which Fiona opened it contained all the rules
Then the other was a hand written note
"Well remembered man, it makes me laugh too" I read out loud
A photo was also enclosed in the note and it was a picture of me and Jack outside the villa we had gone too. Good times.
I hugged Fiona

©TheExpirement

"Right sleep time, we have work tomorrow and we can read the rules then" I said kissing the top of her head

Sadly the morning came to soon and we had a wakeup call from Jack

"Morning, how was your sleep?"

"Good, do we drive?" I asked tiredly

"Nope, Ralph wants to see you so we shall drop Fiona at work and then go to his home"

I then sat up in bed as I hung up; I wondered what the day would have in store.

Fiona stirred

"Breakfast first?" I asked

"Coffee please" she said and with that our morning began.

After breakfast we jumped in to the back of Jack's car. I took in the luxury seating and wondered if Jack actually owned a car or whether he just used the company cars. I smiled to myself and sat back and relaxed, Fiona was staring out of the window watching the posh big houses go by. I wondered if today was going to be normal but then I remembered we were going to see Ralph. This was going to be interesting.

As we approached Darktronics, Fiona grabbed my hand tightly

"Stay safe" she whispered and she kissed me on the cheek

she then got out of the car and I was glad to see that the receptionist Sally was there to great her. Safety was now our priority.

"Don't worry, I've got every angle covered" Jack said as he was now turned round in the driver's seat looking at me.

"Yeah but I don't know Jack. This is tough"

"Right now all we can do is work out the evidence and it's time to go see Ralph, so come on jump in the front and let's well go"

And with that I did as I was told

©TheExpirement

My heart though was aching for Fiona; I could see she was watching us from reception.
Jack then drove us to Ralph's home
"Hello Jack" said a soft voice over the security system
"Hey Sabrina, can you let us in please, Ralph is expecting us both"
"Okay" and with that Sabrina buzzed us in
"Whose Sabrina?"
"Oh that's a cousin from his wife's side of the family"
Jack advised as we then drove up a very long drive.
The house was more modest than what I was expecting
"I thought it would be a bigger place" I said as we exited the car
"Nah, don't forget this is the work house" Jack advised laughing
"Yes I have one in France and another in America" Ralph suddenly said making us both jump
"I apologise Mr Mearlow" I said
"No need to apologise, now come along we have work to do"
Jack and I then followed Ralph to a side door it was well all a bit surreal
"Jack has been filling me in with what's been going on"
"I have despite doctors' orders" Jack said
Closing the door behind us
We were now stood in a little room it was fresh, the windows were old fashioned
"I thought you were okay sir" I said taking in to account what Jack had just advised
"Yes, well I still needed to be checked over and sadly my boy the old blood pressure is up and so I must take it easy"
I nodded
"Now tell me James, who do you think is behind all this?"
"To be honest sir I don't know, I have looked all through the names and there isn't one that stands out. "
Then as we went silent a thought came in to my head

I broke the silence, I had to say it
"Of course there is one thing that is common"
"What's that James?" Ralph asked
"Someone must have known about Sean and the test"
"Agreed" Ralph said standing in his suit he know had his arms crossed I have his attention
"And that we would find him"
"True" Jack said
"Are we looking in the wrong place?" I asked tentatively knowing that Jack would then say it
"Your kidding James, you don't think anyone on the inside could have pulled this off?"
Yep was it someone on the inside
"They also knew about me going to see Philip that day when I got attacked"
"Wait here" Ralph suddenly said
He called Jack over and then they disappeared through the next door which was opposite the door we had entered through. Had I just messed things up? I paced around the room it wasn't very big I felt like a caged animal
Then Jack peered round the door "You can come in now"

©TheExpirement

Chapter Fifteen

"Now what you are about to see you must never and I mean never tell to anyone" Jack advised
"Okay Jack" I said not realising what I was about to see
"Oh my days" I then said as we entered a room full of televisions
Ralph was talking to a technician who was fixing one of the screens. As it came back to life the technician quickly went out of the room and Ralph turned to me and said
"Now I understand where you were coming from James, someone on the inside and it would make sense"
"But" I then added
"Now what you are seeing is every inch of every corner of every room of Darktronics"
"Even the bathroom?" I said pointing to the top left of the screens
"Yeah, I tend only to check that when someone is rumoured to be doing something they shouldn't"
"Only Jack and myself know about this" Ralph said
"Okay, so what you are saying is that somewhere here we might be able to spot or would have spotted the person doing this"
Both Ralph and Jack nodded
"Okay fine, so it's not someone in the ruddy office"
I then said I had to concede
"Don't completely forget about that idea" Jack said
Ralph then continued
"Just because we haven't spotted them yet, doesn't mean we won't"
We sat down on some cinema like seating, it was much comfortable than the seats in Darktronics.
Jack was going back over some evidence that they had found on Philip when he got poisoned.
"I recognise that guy" Ralph suddenly said looking at a photo

©TheExpirement

"Is that Lyons?" I asked
"Yeah, you heard about that story?" Ralph asked
"Dad told me all about it, it was the next biggest thing since the disaster"
"True talk of the town"
Jack then showed Ralph some other old photos
When something caught my eye
"What the hell?" I suddenly spurted out
"What's up James?" Asked Jack
"Top right hand screen" I said pointing
I walked up to the screens to get a closer view
"We can rewind if that helps?" Asked Ralph who had now stood up
Jack grabbed one of the many remotes
"Here you go" handing me a silver remote control
I rewound for the last ten minutes
"You see that?" I then asked them
"I think you maybe on to something" Jack mumbled as he started looking for his phone
"Over on the side" I then said
"Thanks"
"I didn't see it..." Said Ralph concerned
"It's a loop, someone has fiddled with your camera in my lab"
Ralph's face turned to a very stern look.
Jack was chatting to some people on the phone there wasn't much we could here, but I had some tea made for Ralph.
We were now in his lounge
"Thanks" Ralph said to Sabrina as she handed us the tea
"Your welcome, I am now off to college, I'll be home tomorrow"
I could see that Ralph would normally argue with her by the tone in her voice and his look.,
But he had bigger fish to fry today and he was worried for the integrity of his business let alone anything else.

©TheExpirement

"She has a not so nice boyfriend" Ralph then said to me after looking a bit better after sipping some tea
"No need to explain sir"
I said
He smiled at me
"Any news Jack" he then said
Jack was now off the phone and was waiting to hear back
"I have my guys checking your lab James, only Rock Simons has been in there today"
"Bring him in" I suddenly said
Both Ralph and Jack looked at me,
"Sorry, if you agree, he's good at remembering things like if anyone is out of character"
"Good point…Do as the boss says" Ralph said to Jack with a hint of humour
Jack saluted and did as he was told with of course a big grin on his face.
This wasn't of course a time for laughing but it was a welcome distraction. Rock was driven from Darktronics to the front of the house
"Hey man" he said as I was the one asked to greet him at the door
"hey, good to see you" I said
"Sure thing man, I have been writing everything down that happened today and yesterday"
"That's good"
We stepped back inside and Jack and Ralph were sat ready at a dining table, one of many that were dotted round the house
"How can I help Mr Mearlow" Rock said taking a seat at the end of the table
"Well you can start by saying where you were at 6am this morning" Ralph asked in a very serious tone
"Sure thing Sir"

©TheExpirement

Rock took a moment getting out some pieces of paper

"At 6am I was cleaning the office next to Mr Folster's, then I went for coffee and doughnuts and saw my wife at the lounge. We talked for an hour and then your nephew Mr Jones came over and asked me to go and tidy your office sir"

Ralph nodded

"I went straight to your office and saw this gent who went by the name of Martin Kowl, I never seen him before in my life"

Jack interrupted him

"You say Martin Kowl"

"Yes sir"

"Can you describe him"

"No need to" Rock replied

"Sorry" Jack said very sternly

"Why he's on that photo sir" and Rock pointed to a photo they had on the dining table

"You're sure that's him"

"Yes sir, hey man let me show you this"

Rock pulled out his mobile phone and got up a picture

"This is a photo I decided to take of him whilst I was cleaning"

"It matches" I said taking the photo and phone and comparing them side by side

"You notice anything else" Ralph asked

"Hmm let me see, I could smell this funny strawberry and liquorice about, in your office. That was after he was gone mind"

"How long was he there for?"

"Well I was in there for about two hours doing a deep clean I was nearly done by the time he left"

"Are you sure he didn't see you take the photo"

"Oh he couldn't have cus he asked me if I had a phone and he asked me to put it on your desk, so I did as I was told. I was going to call security right after I had finished but your nephew arrived"

"I see"
"How did you take the photo" Jack asked
"I have a remote control on it sir, so I placed the phone carefully down so that the camera could get a good picture of him"
"Cool" Jack replied simply
"Well done Rock" Said Paul behind us
"Thanks Mr Jones" Rock replied to Paul
"Thankfully not only did he get a photo but he got a recording"
Paul slid his phone to his uncle who promptly gave it to Jack
"It's definitely Jensen"
"Damn it" Ralph said
"I went to school with him, I can't believe he thought it could come back for revenge"
"So who the hell is he going after?" I asked
Everyone turned to look at me
"Darktronics" Jack replied
"Paul, we need to find this bastard and quickly"
Ralph said standing from the table
"Uncle, I do what I can"
"You can work with me" Jack stepped in before anyone could say anything
"I have a plan" I said I was now thinking on my feet we had to set a little trap for the little bugger
"What plan?" Jack asked
"Look, this guy isn't stupid, he's already managed to fool us all"
"continue" Ralph said quite sternly but I could tell he was intrigued
"Let's all pretend everything is normal and we figure a way to well trap him"
"Okay and how the hell do we do that?" Paul said he wasn't one for thinking on his feet"
"That I don't know,, but if we work from the safe house, go to work as normal and see what he has in store"

"Dangerous, far too dangerous" Jack advised
"True, I don't know what the hell to do" Ralph said
"I agree with Mr Folster man" Rock said
"Thanks Rock, but for this to somehow work I need all of us to work together"
"Okay, fine let's try and catch this man" Ralph said
"I'll work on security" Jack said
"I'll get everyone in the cleaning section a phone that you can monitor" Rock advised
Ralph turned to me and said
"We need to trust everyone and yet no-one"
"I understand boss"
"STAFF" he shouted and three armed guards appeared literally from nowhere
"Close this room down now"
We were all now standing round the table in shock
"Yes sir" one of the guards said and disappeared again
Ralph then got a bleep on his phone.
"Right gents come in close" he then said to us all
we gathered to the side of the dining table
"Right as of today, we only trust each other no-one else. You report to me every day with news with no exceptions"
"Yes sir" We all said in unison
that was now a brief or should I say our mission. I was worried as hell as this could cost us our lives but to stop this Jensen Lyons we had to work together.
As we started to leave, Ralph stopped me
"You can't tell Fiona"
"I understand sir"
He then hugged me tight
"Stay safe" he whispered in my ear

©TheExpirement

I then walked down the steps of the front of the house and in to the car

Jack, Rock and I then quietly drove back to Darktronics.

Chapter Sixteen

I was tasked that day to do some normal tests; I mean normal by just dealing with the post that day.
Jack had managed to convince security that this was part of my training.
Of course my training, I was supposed to be going for this darn promotion.
I sat in my office looking at my tasks for that day and cried
yes I know it's not a manly thing to do, but I wasn't afraid of it.
I was panicking and if I hadn't gone for this darn promotion then all of this wouldn't have started.
It was the first time I had questioned myself, was this my fault in some way.
I got myself together and went in to my wash area and cooled my face down and starred at myself in the mirror.
"Come on James, we can do this"
Then the alarm started to sound in my office it was in some way a welcoming sound
"Right time for business" I said to myself
I then entered the air lock between my office and lab and got in to my protective suit
"Good afternoon Dennis" I said quite confidently
"Good afternoon James" He then said back in a robotic voice
Of course I wasn't expecting that, my gut started to churn
"A voice box Dennis?" I asked
"Yes sir, I was going to tell you before this package arrived."
"Okay, that's good, now I have someone to talk to" I said whilst smiling
"So what Dennis do you have for me today?"
"A plastic bag sir"

©TheExpirement

And with that I picked up the bag from Dennis's robotic arm and emptied the contents
Out came dice and other what looked like game pieces.
Was this a message I thought
I put the game pieces together and then panicked
"DENNIS GET ME JACK"
I shouted
"Don't worry I'm here" Jack appeared in my office and was talking over the tannoy system in to my lab
"Was this you?" I asked
"Yes I'm sorry" Jack replied looking quite sincere
"Don't let me near you" I said I was angry I thought Jensen had figured us out already, the pieces were representing each of us in the room earlier.
"Calm down its part of my plan" Jack said
"Fine, I will be there in a min" I growled I was still pissed off with him
"You better have brought me coffee and doughnuts" I growled as I entered back in to my office
Once I had calmed down and had handed me a very nice doughnut and large coffee, he took me through the plan
"Look Ralph only really trusts you and me"
"Yeah so, what's with the game pieces"
"Just keep them close, I want you to keep an eye on all of us"
"Who do you trust" I asked
"No-one"
I understood his answer; it was true we couldn't trust anyone.
"This is a game James, the pieces represent us"
"Yeah I get that"
"The board is Darktronics, just keep an eye on all of us"
And with that he left.
I was worried even more

©TheExpirement

I then ran after him
"JACK"
"Hey" he said stopping just before going through the doors
"Dennis has a voice box, can you check"
"Sure, see you later"
I walked back slowly to my office
I then wondered what the dice had been for
"Roll of luck" I mumbled to myself
Every move we made was going to be watched and the consequences would be played right in front of my eyes.
The next day Jack confirmed that the modifications to Dennis were indeed real and that it wasn't Jensen playing me.
Ralph was now back in his office and had made it known to everyone that due to Philip not being well enough he was in charge of everyone on the promotion programme.
That was regardless of what section they were in, so for me I would get direct emails or letters from him telling me what tests I needed to complete.
Plus it allowed me to directly update him. I was pleased to see Fiona at coffee break but she looked apprehensive
"Hey Hun" I said sitting down in one of their less comfortable seats
"I've been asked to go and study"
She said
"What do you mean?" I asked
"They want me to go and study for a degree at uni"
"Wow, that's magic"
"Yeah, but it's not local"
"Oh, where?"
"Newcastle"
"You want me to see if they can move it?" I asked
She nodded
"Okay, I'll see what I can do"

And with that I went and visited Ralph
"Sadly they are full here" he said
He moved closer to me, he could tell she was my rock
"I understand, the six months is away and then she will be back" He said quietly
"Okay, thanks" I replied
I was disappointed
"Don't worry we will look after her" he then said
"I'll try not to sir"
"And James"
"Yes sir?"
"Fiona and you are like my own children to me"
As I left his office, I felt warmed by his statement, somehow he understood, but the reality was I was losing my rock for six months and that was a long time in my book. I then went and saw Fiona over in the Fire Testing Department.
Jean her boss came out to the reception to greet me.
"Hello James" she said
"Hi, I'm here to speak with Fiona"
"Yes, I had a phone call from Ralph"
"Ah, I assume Fiona has been told"
"Yes, I have my research education team discussing the way forward now"
"I shall take my leave, please let her know I visited"
"Mr Folster, no need to leave let me explain what's going on"
We went in to a side office, I was impressed by Jean, most people saw her as a hard boss, someone who really put a stop to anything that wasn't work. But I saw her as a confident woman who was in her late 40s and that had control over her department.
We sat and she took a moment gathering her thoughts then she explained

"Newcastle are welcoming new students to boost their research fire department. As you can imagine students from Darktronics are a nothing short of gold James, pure gold. That's the other reason as to why we can't move Fiona to another University. But I understand that a move completely is out of the question. Luckily for all of us Fiona will be on a course, where she can do her studying both here and there. The time she has to spend in Newcastle will be very brief, just enough to give them sponsorship and to get us the money we need to branch out"

"Thank you" was all I could muster to that

"Ralph said you were his top man, Fiona is mine, so don't worry I won't let anything happen to her"

I nodded; we shook hands and went back to my office.

Chapter Seventeen

It was a week before Fiona had to start living up in Newcastle; we had a few special times together that week. I loved her to bits and I was going to miss her terribly. I had been just worried about her on her own up there but I worried if the plan my plan was going to work here. I didn't want this to be the end.
On the Friday before she was due to travel up on the Saturday afternoon, we were at the safe house packing a few last items. I had bought her a present, I walked in to the bedroom and said
"Darling I got you something"
She turned to me and smiled
"When can I open it?" She asked trying to keep her brave face on, it was difficult for her and really for everyone. I had even noticed Jack's mood had worsened as the week had gone on.
"You can open this part now and that part when you are on the train"
It was deemed safer that she travelled by train, that way she would blend in and bit better and so could her bodyguards.
She carefully unwrapped the first part of her present
"Wow that's lovely, thank you" she said rushing over to give me a long kiss
It was a necklace with a heart inscribed with our names, I helped her put it on
"I have this too" she pointed out the lucky green bracelet. They didn't match, but we didn't care that day.
Then out of the blue there was a knock on the door
"I wonder who that could be?" I asked as I went back out of the bedroom towards the door
I spied through the lookout and there was her boss Jean was stood there looking very classy.
I called out to Fiona as I opened the door

©TheExpirement

"Jean" I said
"Hello James, I'm sorry to intrude"
"No please come in"
Fiona came out of the bedroom she greeted her boss
"I just wanted to let you know I am coming with you" Jean said with a smile
"But I thought you couldn't" Fiona started to say
"I know dear, but I realise that we need to look after you, I don't think Ralph or James for that matter will every forgive me if something happens to you" She fiddled with a gold ring on her left hand I wondered if she had been in this situation before
She had a kind soft voice, this wasn't the Jean you see at work this was the Jean that only friends and family get to see.
"Well that's great news…care for some tea" I said
"Yes, I wouldn't mind, I don't want to stay for long as I know this time is precious" she said sitting down putting her handbag to one side.
Fiona and Jean discussed their travelling plans and had decided what they should do on Sunday. As on Saturday they were being shown round the university and research labs.
I was pleased that Fiona was no longer to be on her own, I poured the tea
"I also have some other news" Jean said as I handed round the tea and of course dunkable biscuits.
I sat down trying to ignore the frown from Fiona when she saw how many biscuits I had in my hand
"Well you won't be staying in student digs up there my dear"
"Oh, where will we be staying?" Fiona asked
"I have rented a house for us both to live in, if that's okay, I didn't want to make a fuss but I realised we needed somewhere that felt well like home"

I smiled, Jean really did care and I was pleased that Fiona was being looked after.

After Jean had said her goodbyes we spent the evening doing some finishing touches to the packing and then I got the mini lecture about the biscuits.

"I saw you had four Mr" Fiona said as I sat on the couch going through the travel documents

"Four what my dear?" I asked fully knowing that this was about the biscuits

"Look, you have to look after yourself now; you are going to be okay aren't you?" Fiona then said right in my ear and she bent over the couch

"Yes of course" I said giving her a kiss

"I've told Jack to let you do some exercise in their gym"

"They have a gym?"

"Yes dear"

Seriously I had no idea, but then it made sense all the security detail needed to keep themselves fit. I thanked Fiona and then we had dinner together, all too soon morning arrived Jack knocked on the door

"Morning, taxi for Fiona" he said he was trying to be his normal self

"Morning" I said sleepily I didn't get a lot of sleep that night I was worried, even though with Jean being there it had relaxed me, but not enough.

Fiona went and got her bags

"I understand man" Jack said to me

I smiled, I was grateful, the pair of us were as bad as each other, and those were nervous times ahead for us both.

I ensured that Fiona had her second present in her hand bag and I locked our door behind us. I wasn't looking forward to coming home after this, but Jack winked at me and I wondered what he had planned.

©TheExpirement

I sat in the back with Fiona holding her hand all the way to the station, we met Jean who was carrying four takeaway cups of coffee
"These are for you two boys" Jean said
"Thanks" we both replied
"I'll get the bags" Fiona said picking up Jeans suitcase
The train was here already and all too soon the pair of them had found their seats on the train
"I love you" I mouthed to Fiona
I could see tears forming in her eyes, I wanted this all to stop right now.
I then saw Jean give her a tissue and a rather nice looking chocolate bar, which Fiona then waved at me.
I laughed as Fiona then blew me a kiss and the train pulled away.
"Come on bud, we have man things to do" Jack said who also looked as if he was going to burst in to tears. We both cared for Fiona deeply, we were like brothers and there was nothing that could break that bond.
I finished the coffee just as we walked out of the station and found the car
"So what is your plan" I asked Jack
"Oh I don't know, I was just making it up"
"Seriously?"
"Of course not, come on we have things to do"
My mind was never far from thinking about Fiona and I relaxed more when she phoned me a few hours later.
"We made it to the house fine" she said
"Is it nice?" I asked
"Yeah and thank you for my present"
"Good, just take care of yourself"
I gotten her a journal and a pen, it doesn't sound like much, but I knew she would want to write about her adventure and this was probably going to be one.

87 –Expirement Series

"I will, we are just going to the University, this place is like home James, you will see if you can visit, I miss you already"
"I miss you too"
We said our goodbyes and I continued practicing my drives; we were at a golf range. It was a good day now.
Jack was also much relived as Jean had given him a call too. So between us we now relaxed, we enjoyed our golf lessons and then went and got ourselves some beer and takeaway.

Chapter Eighteen

Of course Fiona and I talked every evening, but Jean bless her had done her best to keep her busy. During the day they work working hard at University and the evenings Jean well had lots of plans.
"Theatre tonight, a dinner tomorrow, I don't think I can keep up" Fiona said laughing
"You don't have to go" I replied
"I know, but I want to go, it's fun, plus if I didn't go I wouldn't be able to write any adventures down in my journal"
"Good, I love and miss you"
That was our typical conversation, I wasn't too worried as I was also getting regular updates from Ralph during the day
However, Fiona would always ask about my day too, but I had to keep things simple and not tell her about what I was really doing.
"Theory tomorrow" I would say or "Packages from the fire department" Of course this was true, but I wasn't just doing that stuff.
Ralph had advised I would still continue to be tested for promotion; this allowed us to be flexible with our investigations.
It was day three that Fiona had been away and I was doing my fire training, I was greeted by Rock
"Hey man" he said
"What can I do for you?" I asked
"Well the guys from fire said to give you this" He handed me a new style fire extinguisher, and a brown envelope. I thanked him
"Good luck man" he said as he closed the office door behind him
I put the fire extinguisher in the lab and as I put it on my work station I then noticed some writing on the brown envelope, it was in Rock's handwriting.
I opened whilst still in my lab as this was my most secure room.

©TheExpirement

"Hey man, I found these whilst clearing out the science stock cupboard" he wrote on a plain piece of a4

The science stock cupboard was where we could collect all our consumables for testing, such as testing kits, swabs you name it, it was in there. Now to keep an eye on what we were using our passes all contained a bar code. To enter the stock cupboard we would show our passes at the door and then on each drawer we had to scan our bar code to release the drawer. This would give us a clue as to who was inside the room.

I then emptied the envelope and saw pictures of Jack and his team in Sean's home. These seemed to be recent as the picture contains last week date, but there was something wrong with the photo. I held it up to the light and I could see that it wasn't professionally printed.

Was this a fake?

The other photos contained the other rooms of Sean's house, and then there was a question on the last photo

"Did he look in here?" with a red arrow pointing to a wardrobe.

I didn't recognise the hand writing and decided to ring for Rock. I walked back in to my office and picked up the phone I had some important calls to make "Can you put me through to the security office please?" I asked Mike

"Sure James, please hold" I knew Mike as he was the rugby team captain, I didn't play but he knew everyone and he and I had gone up against each other in a cycling competition, I had beat him by three seconds. It was all for a good cause mind.

"Security office" said Helena Corrington

"Helena, its James Folster, I need some barcode information"

"Certainly, please can I have your reference number"

Our reference number was from the case, Ralph had set one up on the system so we could log all investigation work under a

©TheExpirement

pseudonym, I gave the reference number "Thank you, what date is it for please"
"The last three weeks, stock cupboard" I said
I waited, you had to wait, there was not getting away from it, if you left the call then you were deemed to be a security risk, every so often they would change this logic. I never understood it myself, but it kept us on our toes.
"Downloaded sir, you should have an email"
I clicked on my computer and there was an email from Helena
"Thanks, reference number 9843"
That was the logic, she confirmed the number and we hung up I then rang Rock
"Hey, could you bring me coffee and a blt sandwich please"
"Certainly man"
Of course I didn't want that, but it was our phrase to say please come alone, don't rush and be in the lab not the office. Keeping up with the security in this place was hard and sadly I have lost some friends and colleagues who didn't keep an eye on the ball. I remember when I first started I was working with Hansen, it was late and we were both tired. "Home time soon" he said I remember he was starting to mellow "Yeap, just one more package and Kevin Brown is visiting with it" I said
"Ah Kevin"
Whilst one should never speak ill of the dead Kevin pretended he was more than he really was, quite cocky.
I remember he walked in with the package and that was fine, but after the testing he saw an envelope similar to the one I had found in the lift.
"Don't open that" shouted Hansen
He opened it and inhaled something, to this day I wasn't sure what it was.
All I remember he had decided to open it and said

©TheExpirement

"Don't worry it's for me"
He died a week later. Kevin wasn't a friend of mine, but it was a reminder to us all that we had to keep ourselves safe, our fate was in our hands.
The sirens were now sounding in my lab; Rock was stood in my lab
"Hey man"
He said as I walked in.
We chatted about when he found the photos and which drawer; this would help me narrow down the data I was going to analyse. I also did the test on the fire extinguisher Rock could then take it back and he always wanted to see what I did. It wasn't anything exciting but I was pleased that Rock was able to help and that he had backed our overall plan.
I wished him well and then sat and went to work on the data that Helena had sent me.
I wasn't going to Ralph or Jack until I could be really sure what had happened. I felt tomorrow was going to be a more interesting day.
I decided to stay in my office all night; I didn't tell Fiona when she rang quickly before she went to the theatre.
I was pleased to hear her voice, the data was starting to make my head spin, it wasn't making sense straight away and then I saw a pattern.
Someone a person called A Wilkes had accessed the drawer in question on a weekly basis
I decided to look up this A Wilkes on the staff database.
My heart sunk when I couldn't find A Wilkes on the Science staff database.
I wondered if I could access the other parts, I found that I had access to a few. I then found A Wilkes who worked in the crime lab; I now had a case for Ralph and Jack to look at.
Off I went to visit Ralph, but Rock stopped me before I could get to the lift

©TheExpirement

"Hey man he's gone home, he said to go there if you need to talk"
I smiled; he seemed to know everything I wondered if he knew what I had been doing already.
I got in the Darktronics taxi and was driven to the home of Mr Mearlow, again even though I had been here before was taken aback by the lack of money being shown off in the house.
I smiled to myself and thanked the driver, who I seemed familiar
But before I could check again they were gone and Ralph greeted me he seemed stressed
"Everything alright sir?" I asked
"No Sabrina has gone missing from college"
"Maybe I should go"
"No, you can help"
He took me to the side of the house to the garage. As he opened up the front of the garage I saw where his money had gone, there was a black Bentley all shiny and new.
He smiled; he could tell I was impressed.
"Get in, let's go and find her"
I jumped in the front, I didn't realise Ralph could drive as he was always driven around by people
I was wearing my jeans and my favourite hooded top so I think his plan was that I could go round campus and fit in.
Too darn right gut, we arrived at the college campus and I was politely asked to look for her. I couldn't refuse as I wanted him to listen to me later.
I was looking for a needle in a haystack there were loads of young girls all ready for their big nights out.
I then found her lecture room where she was last seen, no-one was in there, but then I saw two shadows behind a door which had frosted glass.
I then heard her say
"I had best go, I'll see you soon professor"

Hmm sleeping with the professor, never a good idea and not when you have the all-powerful Ralph Mearlow looking for you.

She turned red when she saw me

"Your uncle is waiting for you outside"

"You going to tell him" she asked I could tell she was gutted that she had been found out, she was getting more redder by the second

"Look I am not going to tell him if you end it"

"I can't"

"Okay, so move classes and have a proper relationship" I stated

We walked out of the lecture hall and back to where Ralph had parked

"WHERE THE HELL HAVE YOU BEEN" he shouted

Even I was taken aback

"Sorry my phone died" She showed it to him and fair enough it wouldn't turn on

"Okay, so do you want to live at home?" he asked

"Yes Uncle, I do, but"

"Okay, well do whatever he said and don't you dare go missing again"

All she could do was nod, she realised he knew, her uncle always somehow knew.

We drove back in silence

Do whatever he said I thought to myself...a bug must be a bug I couldn't look for it now as we were going back to his place

"Sabrina, dinner then bed please" Ralph stated as she quietly went up through the front of the house

"The bug James is in your hood"

"Ah, I did wonder, did you know already sir?" I asked fully well knowing that the answer was a yes.

I shook the hood out and out dropped the bug as I handed it back to him he said

"Sort of, I just needed it confirmed"
I smiled
"So what can I do for you?" he asked looking a bit more relaxed
"We need to be secure sir" I said and with that we went to the room with the television screens.
I was tired but I tried not to yawn, I logged in to a work networked computer. Handy I thought as Ralph brought me some coffee
"You shouldn't be doing all-nighters" he stated
"I know sir, but it's lonely in the safe house"
"Ah yes the safe house, I was supposed to be joining you there, but Jack had forgotten about this room you see and I knew that it would be an asset."
"Yes sir, so I was given these photos"
I grabbed my bag and showed him the photos, he was thinking
"I then found out from Rock where he found them and when"
"You downloaded the data?" he asked he was looking quite thoughtful I could tell he was placing the pieces together just as I did
"Yes sir, and here is my results"
"A Wilkes, don't know that name"
"No, but I found this photo of him"
Then it struck me, he was the driver tonight and he was the young policeman
"I think sir we have found a possible connection" I suddenly blurted out
I shared my thoughts, we rang Jack who was at the safe house
"We will pick him up now"
Jack went and picked A Wilkes up from his home, just north of Darktronics, we had tracked the Darktronics taxi.
Back in the Bentley Ralph drove us to Darktronics so that we could meet Mr A Wilkes.
He was sitting on a chair in the evidence room of the crime lab.

©TheExpirement

"Who are you?" Ralph asked
"Alan Wilkes, sir and I had to give you clues"
"Why?"
"Philip sir, I am working for Philip, you can phone him now"
Everyone waited as we tried to contact Philip, because if this man wasn't telling the truth then Jensen had managed to deal another blow to Darktronics.

Chapter Nineteen

Jack was less than impressed by Alan's story; of course we had yet to confirm it. But Ralph knowing Philip had a hunch that this could all be true.

My only worry was that if this was easy for one of our guys to do this, how easy was it for Jensen Lyons to get someone like this in on it all.

Ralph could tell my gut was churning and asked me out of the room

"What's your gut saying son" he said in his gruff tone

"Oh this is true, my only worry is if Philip managed it can Jensen do it to?"

We starred in to the room; Jack was pacing up and down behind Alan waiting to hear back from Philip. Then his phone rang, we went back in to the room

"Hey do you know Alan Wilkes" Jack asked

We couldn't hear what was being said on the other end of the phone but Jack's facial expressions hardly changed.

"Thanks see you tomorrow" Jack said and then he hung up

"Well?" Asked Ralph

"Yeah, he's Philip's mole so to speak"

"Told yer" Alan said

"Who the hell told you to speak" Jack said to him angrily

"Why are you so angry I am one of you guys" Alan said. "Philip told you to tell us all the details, we didn't know if we could trust you?" Jack shouted at him. Alan stood there I could tell he realised he had messed up.

Indeed Alan had forgotten the password and the pass codes, they were then found within his possessions, the problem with Alan was well he liked a few drinks, whilst he was reliable when he wasn't drinking, his hangovers were more blackouts and he wouldn't remember the night let alone the day he just had. Turned out the day Philip had hired him was the same day he was celebrating his kids 18th, and Alan being Alan well had his few too many.

Ralph motioned to me

"Jack, James and I will leave now, you get him to the cells and I'll talk to you tomorrow"

"Sure goodnight you two" Jack said

I waved

"He's being charged"

"Yeah being drunk on duty"

Fair enough

"Look stay at mine tonight" Ralph said as we walked back out to the Bentley

"Are you sure, I don't want to intrude"

As we got in the car he turned to me and said

"You're not, like you I find it hard to sleep when she's not there and having an extra pair of eyes in the house is going to help with little Miss"

"Thanks" I replied agreeing with what he had just said

His wife Felicity is a research fellow hence why Darktronics has a massive research budget. She spends a lot of her time travelling the world getting funding and passing on her knowledge to new schools and departments.

"One day Darktronics will be worldwide, we will have an office in every country" I remember Ralph Mearlow saying in his speech at last years end of year dinner. The dinner was a time for the whole of Darktronics to reflect on what went on during the year. I remember thinking in that car that evening that this year's dinner might just might not happen or be a good one.

We arrived at Ralph's home and I was impressed by the fact that Sabrina was still in residence and she made a point of apologising to both me and her uncle.

©TheExpirement

I was sure then that whilst she meant it, her relationship with the professor wouldn't be over or that she would change classes.

I entered the spare bedroom which was already made up for me; Ralph had ordered his men to get my work suit from my office whilst we were talking to Mr Wilkes. I wasn't surprised by his confidence in me Ralph worked on his gut feeling, if his gut wasn't right then the situation he was in wasn't right. Nine times out of ten he got it spot on, it reminded me that night he was like my father. As I sat on the bed reflecting on the days event, I heard a tap on the door

"Come in" I said

"Sorry, didn't think you would be asleep, I just wondered if you would care for a night cap" Ralph whispered

His staff had now gone to bed, it was his time now to be himself and for once I was now looking at a Ralph in no suit, just well-worn t-shirt and joggers.

"No suit" I said quietly, we didn't want to disturb anyone, we were in his library it was amazing the amount of books that lined the old bookcases

"Ha ha yes I am human after all" he said pouring out some single malt whisky into crystal cut glass tumblers. I smiled it was good to see him in his own domain.

I surveyed the books, most of them were classics, but there were a few books that I didn't expect, but then again this was a family library.

"You can borrow any of them" he said holding out the glasses

"Sadly I don't get much time to read" I took a glass

"Cheers" we both said

"You should read more often, I learnt a lot as a kid reading" he said

"Yeah mother would let me read when I had done my homework" I replied

We laughed. I then stood next to him we were both leaning on the drinks table

"It's going to get worse you know" Ralph stated

"Yeah, I know, I just don't know how worse" I replied as I took a sip of my whisky

"True, but let's just enjoy this moment James, we made it through today and tomorrow I have ensured we meet as a group, so breakfast is at 7"

I nodded I was impressed by his organisation

"James, don't be afraid of what may or may not happen"

"I'll try not to be sir" I said

"I'm here for you"

I nodded. All I could do was nod.

"Right is that the time" he said looking at his watch

Neither of us were going to do sentimental at this point in time, we finished our drinks and went to bed.

I slept well that night even though I wondered just how bad this was going to get.

I awoke realising I had forgotten to set my alarm. I walked out of my room in to the lounge where breakfast was being served; Ralph had decided that it wasn't worth the effort of putting out the dining table for just the two of us to eat. I really wasn't a morning person that day, which to be fair he recognised and quietly went about serving me coffee "Thanks" I said taking it black with two sugars I sat taking stock of the past few days and wondering what might be round the corner for us. "When do the other arrive?" I asked "Soon, but hey don't worry have your breakfast."

I was surprised when a young maid walked in and served me with a full breakfast, of bacon, sausages, poached eggs, toast and hash browns. I started eating it and I did feel like I was rushing it as Mr Mearlow noticed

"Take your time James" he smiled as he said it

©TheExpirement

"Sorry, I'm just hungry" I said apologising again

I was then about half way through my breakfast when in walked Paul and Jack

"Morning all" Jack said

"Uncle" Paul said

"Ah James, our sleuth" he said to me

I acknowledged them both but unable to speak due to stuffing my face with toast.

Jack smiled; I could see he was impressed by the fact that I was having breakfast here.

Once finished we all gathered in the smaller room next door, Ralph had wanted us to be closer together.

As we walked in Jack stopped me

"How the hell did you get breakfast"

"Dunno, guess it was cus I stayed the night" I replied leaving him gobsmacked at the fact that not only had I been served breakfast but I had stayed over.

Rock and Paul were in deep conversation as we entered the room

Ralph followed us in and made sure that the guards were outside

"As we know we were lucky that this Alan Wilkes was one of us" he then said

"Yes background checks show us that he was an apprentice of Philips" Jack then advised us all

"Question is though we must be more vigilant as it may be possible for Jensen Lyons to do the same" Ralph then told us, he wasn't in a mood to be messed with

"I say we carry on as we are, but Jack and James you go to Sean's house and see what Alan Wilkes was trying to tell us"

"What about the footage of the cleaning crew?" asked Rock who seemed concerned

"Paul you can go through that can't you?" Asked Ralph looking at his nephew somewhat nervously

I wondered what he was thinking
"Yeah sure Uncle no problem"
"I will do some background checks as I have to do some staff reports" All of us agreed, we sorted out a few other issues, then Ralph made a sign to Jack who then promptly texted someone. Seconds later I felt a vibrate from my phone as I reached for it
"Ah the Mrs" I said as I noticed Paul to be watching me really carefully. Luckily for me there really was a text from Fiona which I then ensured Paul could see when he walked passed me.
I stayed in the room texting Fiona, the other text which was indeed Jack was telling me to stay so that we could go down to the television room as I like to call it.
However, before we did I asked Ralph a question
"I understand this may not be my place, but do you trust Paul?"
Jack turned to Ralph and wondered the same
He motioned us to sit on the sofa's as we did we could tell the situation was personal.
"I do, but his mind is elsewhere, Paul comes in to a trust fund on his next birthday which is a week away"
"Oh okay" I said
"The problem is his father wanted him to spend it on their family business, my sister his mother wanted him to spend it on his career here."
"I'm guessing no-one won out?"
He shook his head
"No, and I think he may have a girlfriend who is suggesting other, well her ideas for him"
Ralph sighed I could tell it was troubling him
"Right, look let's get back to our situation"
We followed Ralph down stairs and in to the television room
Jack then showed me a recording which was of Jensen in my lab
"He's looking for something" I stated

102 –Expirement Series

"Yeah, you know what?" Ralph asked
"No idea, I don't have any hidden things in there, well only my speech for when I ask Fiona to marry me"
It was true I had decided some while back not to store anything in the room at work. Whilst it was so easy to hide things from Fiona I didn't want her to find the speech, I had it all set out, I just needed a ton of courage. I wasn't sure what Jensen was looking for, or did he put something there I suddenly wondered.
"Unless he put something there instead"
Jack turned to Ralph who had just said that, I was worried "Like a bug you mean?" I asked
He nodded
"Bloody hell"
Jack turned away as his phone was buzzing it was on a pile of documents "Jack speaking" he put it on speakerphone when we realised it was Sally from reception
"Hey Jack, we have a package here which you are not going to like"
"What is it?" He asked
"It's a box, signed by Jensen, we now know how he managed to get through security"
She said
"Don't tell me a mask of some sort"
"Yeah, is that James?" she asked
"Yeah sorry"
"That's okay, err you best sit down, this is a face of Derek Malone from accounting"
I gulped, he was the guy who had helped me and Fiona get a mortgage and had been recommended
"Is it real?" Jack asked
Ralph was pacing up and down
"We think so; Derek didn't report for work this last couple of weeks"

©TheExpirement

Jack thanked Sally for her call and told her to ring back when she had definite confirmation
"So he wants us to know how he did it" I stated
We all stood and wondered what was next in store for us.

Chapter Twenty

The day it started was in fact just like dare I say it a normal ordinary day. The plan so far had worked, we had kept things normal at Darktronics. It's kind of how you deal with some children, if they play up you react they play up some more, should you not react they realise it's not working so they try something else. We had so far successfully succeeded in stopping this Jensen Lyons from acting up again or so we had thought. There is always the danger that when someone goes quiet they are doing even more damage than before and this was certainly the case with Jensen. Jack had recently told us that Derek was killed by Jensen, this was a nasty reminder of what this man was prepared to do, and our investigation in to Sean's house was a dead end. I did wonder if it was a red herring and I started to wonder who exactly was managing this dangerous game.
But most importantly Jean had managed to get both her and Fiona back down here for a few weeks.
I had cycled from the safe house to Darktronics that day as it was nice and sunny, plus Fiona bless her noticed I had put on a few extra pounds and needed some exercise. The fight between Jack and Fiona was funny to watch, it was like brother and sister sort of fight. But my girl finally won out and that was all that mattered, I was allowed to cycle. It was freedom for me for a little bit, the bodyguards did their level best in keeping their distance, but I knew they were there and to be honest I would have been worried if Jack hadn't done his job.
Darktronics that day was busy, Paul was showing around some new recruits from the local University, they were due to start next year when they had all gained their degrees, but these twelve individuals had shown something else a little extra, they were guaranteed a job regardless of degree.

I smiled over and he acknowledged me as we crossed paths near reception, I checked to see if I had any messages
"Let me just see for you now sir" said Kerry receptionist three, I was waiting for a message from Ralph, Fiona had invited him to dinner
"There are two sir" Kerry then advised me handing me two pieces of Darktronics logoed paper
The messages had been via telephone and carefully typed up
"Thank you" I said and then started to read them as I went through the corridor and headed to my office. The first one was indeed from Ralph stating that yes he would be there for dinner and that whilst he wasn't allergic to anything he wasn't a fan of seafood. I laughed, it was good to see he had stated this, Fiona had tried to think of a menu the other night and yep you have guessed it, it contained seafood. I got out my phone and texted her the news straight away, she was pleased as punch that he had agreed to come, but gutted that she had to do a new main. I then gave her a quick call
"Hey I've had a thought" I said
"Go on" she said sounding like she was in a humph over the main
"Look, your mother has some rather nice recipes…" I began to say but then Fiona interrupted me
"Oh the cookbook, that's a massive help thanks sweetie"
"Not them, inside in the back of the book you'll find hand written ones"
"You serious" she said startled
"Yeah, you know we had that casserole the last time we were there?"
"Yeah sure, it was delicious"
"Well I noticed the notes then, you ask her"
Fiona laughed. We said our goodbyes as we were both now heading for our days' work.

©TheExpirement

The second message was more of a cryptic one; it was stating that in my office there was a secret compartment under my lab console. Inside the compartment I would find something of interest. The message then said it was from Jack.
I wasn't convinced. But as I reached my office I decided to check. And check I did.
I changed in to my protective suit as I stood in the air lock and took a deep breath. For some reason though my gut was not giving me anything on this one, I was wondering if I had fallen in to some sort of trap.
I went in to my lab and found that there was indeed a panel that moved, now this takes me back to the first day I got my office with a lab...
"Here you go James" said Hansen (my old professor)
"Wow thank you sir" was all I could reply
I was impressed, I done a lot of hard work and some really boring stuff in my way up to this job
"Now, you enjoy it and you deserved it" Hansen replied leaving me to look round my new office and lab.
I remember looking at the console for the first time, it was bright white and silver with the computers looking so brand new. I had checked every single panel that day and none not one was loose or could have been opened.
But now as I bent down and pressed in a panel, it was loose.
"Don't be a trap please" I whispered
Then Dennis my robot appeared with a sticker on this robotic arm
"Jack did this from Dennis"
I breathed a sigh of relief; I had a mate behind that screen and someone who was looking and checking up on me.
As I opened the panel there was another plastic bag, the same as the one he had put the game pieces in before.

©TheExpirement

I stood up and emptied the bag on the console work top and wondered if this was more pieces to the game. There were two new pieces one which represented Jensen and the other was Philip. A hand written note which I instantly recognised as Jacks handwriting was stuck to the inside of the bag. I carefully removed it and read it.

"Dear James, Sorry had to be discreet as not sure who's watching. I don't trust either of these two, when you have Ralph over for dinner we three will talk. Take care Jack" I was worried Philip had been a side kick to Ralph for some time and I believe he trusted him. I wondered what had made Jack suspicious of him. Was it the whole Alan Wilkes thing, I had my own suspicions. The next day Fiona was up early preparing some bits and pieces for the dinner with Ralph that evening. I was impressed by the trouble she was going to, then I noticed four plates being taken out of the cupboard "I thought there would only be three of us?" I asked

"Ah I invited Jean" I smiled, of course it made sense, she was like a mother figure to Fiona and Ralph was a father figure to me. I cuddled Fiona and grabbed my lunch which I was grateful for that day. I went in to my office which had now been searched for bugs and waited for my next assignment. Jack knocked on the door around 10 and we walked in to my lab area "Why don't you trust Philip?" I asked I was always straight to the point, I didn't really like this sneaking around, we weren't telling any of this to Ralph and I thought that was a slight mistake

"Look I don't understand what we missed at Sean's" he begun to say

He walked around the lab

"Look Jack have we looked in to Philip's background?"

"No, I can't, if I do it will raise an alarm with Ralph"

"That's it, we have to disable that" I suddenly said like a light bulb had really being switched on

"But how the hell do we do that" Jack asked

I was relieved that actually this wasn't a stupid idea but there must be something in Philips background that would make us see red. Or so we thought.

Jack then put his skills in to hacking, I am sure this wasn't something he learnt here in Darktronics, but I was easily impressed by his ease which he got in to Ralph's computer

"Look if we now do a search we can clear it"

I had tabs on Ralph's schedule he was due to be in the coffee lounge and I made a point of checking. I was pleased to see him and Jean talking away about something or other.

I then took my own seat whilst grabbing a coffee and read the local paper I texted Jack to say when Ralph was on his way, by which time of course Jack had already done the check and indeed cleared any trace of doing so.

Nothing.

Absolutely nothing showed up. No connection to Jensen no connection to any organisation against Darktronics and even no connection to Derek Malone. We paced around my office when I suddenly had another thought "Who is always best placed to manipulate?" I asked

"Girlfriends" we then said together

Leona's background check didn't need any hacking, but it came up trumps with some connections.

Turned out she was the one who had done a criminal check on Jensen. To our own background check Jack told me what he had found

"Look James, Jensen was in prison when he was just 16, for drugging his father"

"What drug"

"Um…here you go"

©TheExpirement

It was spelt out in science speak which clearly Jack didn't do, but to you and me it was Doxacurium Chloride, the crime lab were doing Derek Malone's post mortem when they found his faceless body at his home showed up this drug.

"She covered it up"

"The crime lab had ways of getting in to the stock cupboard"

With that I ran out of my lab and then office and went to the stock cupboard

I wasn't really surprised but there lying empty was the drug which had paralysed his dad and Derek. We use it for paralysing objects before they blow up.

I then walked back to my office

Ralph was now sitting in there looking more concerned than ever Jack calmly went through the evidence once I had explained where I had bolted to. Ralph was impressed that we had done this investigation work.

Leona was now on the most wanted list for Darktronics alongside Jensen Lyons.

He was worried though that if Philip was being manipulated by Leona that things might turn nastier than they would of done.

He was sadly all too right. Ralph didn't want to let Paul or Rock know as they were if you like blissfully unaware and that made them look for other clues and we couldn't afford to miss any of those. Ralph decided to keep on track for today as he was more than aware that Fiona would be devastated if we cancelled. "You must meet your new team" he suddenly said and with that a few people filed in to my office Ralph introduced each one.

Darren Michaels who was fresh out of University, he had a strong hand grip and loved playing the guitar.

Finn Marston whom I recognised from accountants " Pleased to be working with you sir" he was shy but I was impressed by his ability with numbers

Then I turned to meet Lucy Lewis, she was the sister of Daniel Lewis who was the Darktronics Rugby fundraiser. "I am pleased to meet you" I said she was from the science area and could really play the violin.

"That's your team"

Ralph stated

"Well welcome" I said I wasn't expecting a team, but I was later advised that they were there to take some of the stress off and I could plan anything I wanted for them.

Excellent.

That afternoon so I could get back to Fiona I decided to send them to the library but not before giving them a lecture ; "Now, in here as you know we get all sorts of packages" They nodded, they knew what I did, they had been well briefed.

But they weren't expecting my next move

"When I first started here, I was given the chance to either experiment or research, as many of you have sadly seen many have chosen to experiment before understanding what you are dealing with"

I had printed off a book list "I would like you to go out and read these books today and tonight, then from the local store they will give you this dictionary of all Darktronics terms. Only by doing the research will you understand these terms. Now I bid you good day as I have to be somewhere"

They were stunned. But they soon were on their way to the library I heard them in the corridor "He's the best, he has seen loads of stuff and I understand my brother and him saw someone die here, I don't want to see that" Lucy told one of the others, they voiced their appreciation of her knowledge.

I was impressed, now it was time for dinner.

©TheExpirement

Chapter Twenty One

I arrived home looking forward to the dinner that evening, Fiona was mixing something in the kitchen, she was pleased to see me. "Hey, you want to make yourself useful?" I laughed, of course I would make myself useful I started to peel potatoes as Fiona was still mixing something "What are you making?" I asked
She simply smiled, she then turned the bowl and put the mixture in to a tin, it was obviously a cake of some sort I thought and she wanted to keep it a surprise, her smile was my cue to stop asking questions. Before I knew it there was a tap at the door Jean was first to arrive, thankfully we were ready, Fiona took a deep breath and greeted her boss
"Jean" they kissed on the cheek they were now great friends
Jean then greeted me in the same way, she then handed me a bottle of red wine which I was grateful for as we had forgotten the wine.
"Thanks, can I get you a drink" I asked as I put the red wine in the kitchen,
"Do you have brandy and a drop of lemonade" she asked as she took a seat on our sofa. I was making her drink when the door was knocked again. I handed Jean her drink and opened the door
"Ralph" I said shaking his hand
"Good evening James" he said smiling
He too had a bottle of wine and I got him a whisky as he greeted Fiona and Jean. I felt that even though things were undoubtedly going to get worse before they got better it was nice to see that tonight we could just well be us.
I joined them in the lounge as they were talking about life in Newcastle
"I don't think I have ever done so much" Fiona muted

©TheExpirement

"But how is the University?" Asked Ralph he was a fan of all things University. He prided himself on the fact that he had a degree and that his family were all educated to the highest level.
"It's delightful" said Fiona
"Yes the research rooms, well let's put this way our money Ralph has been well spent" Jean advised
Fiona made her excuse and tapped me on the shoulder as he passed me
I took my leave and we made for the kitchen
"Time to get serving"
Before we knew it we were sat round the table enjoying beef casserole, roasted potatoes and of course the wine, talking about films, Hollywood, the stars that Jean had met in her early years, it was fascinating. Even Ralph and some pretty interesting stories to tell. I cleared up our plates and was grateful for the fact that we had a dishwasher. Then after a while Fiona served pudding.
It was lemon drizzle cake and custard.
The smile on Ralphs face was well like a kid in a sweet shop
"Looking forward to it boss?" I asked
He looked up at me after taking a spoonful
"It's delicious, you are..." he started to say but then Jean finished his sentence
"A very lucky man"
I smiled; Fiona was positively beaming by this time.
I was a very lucky man.
But things were just about to change.
I had finished my pudding and I noticed our glasses were now empty
"Anyone for a drink" I asked
Everyone nodded, Fiona thought Jean had driven over
"Don't worry dear Ralph and I will be sharing a taxi"

They had actually been driven over by our dear friend Jack, who bless him was a bit miffed that he hadn't been invited to this dinner. But I didn't have time to explain to him why today, but I knew I could make it up to him by saving some cake. As I grabbed the white wine out of the fridge I noticed already a plastic tub with his name written on it. Fiona had already put him aside.
As I took the wine in I stopped still.
Someone was standing in our lounge pointing a gun at Ralph's head
"Don't do anything stupid" the man said
He was stood all in black with a balaclava over his face, I thought I recognised the eyes but I couldn't be sure
"What do you want" I asked, somehow putting the wine down without spilling a drop
Fiona and Jean were huddled together on the sofa
"I want four million in the bank by tomorrow afternoon"
"I don't have four million"
"Ralph here does"
He was silent, why wasn't he saying anything.
"Okay, why?"
"Because that's what he owes my son"
"I don't know you" Ralph then suddenly said
"Yes you do"
The man took off his balaclava and a burned face was revealed. I noticed Jean shield Fiona from the horror, but then she calmly stood up.
"No he doesn't know you but I do"
"What?" I asked
"Don't do anything stupid Rory" she then said
"Jean..." he said
"Yes Rory, now give me the gun"
"I can't"
"Why not Rory, you trust me"

©TheExpirement

"Yes, I do, but this man he threatened to kill me if I don't do as I told"

"Just who asked you?" Jean asked

"Jensen Lyons...oh man he said that he wanted you to all know that he was coming for you"

He then took the gun and pointed at his own head

Seconds later the gun went off, there was nothing we could do

Fiona screamed.

Security then arrived in our flat and everything began moving as if we were in slow motion. We were all moved to another area of the house, Fiona was seen by a doctor who gave her something to calm her down. Nothing had prepared us for tonight, it was just supposed to be dinner.

I turned to Jack

"How the hell did he get in?"

"He has a twin brother who works here and well they swapped"

"Bloody hell Jack he could have killed all of us"

"I know, I'm sorry"

Jean was sat down talking to an officer giving all the details about this man, I stood there and listened as I was intrigued by her story

"Rory was a former student of mine at the all boys' school I taught at. He and his twin brother were burned when a student set fire to their dorm. Of course they never returned to the school, but I was taken aback by the fact they both had identical burns. Strange very strange"

"Who did the fire"

"I remember him as a quiet lad, his name was strange as he wasn't English, no that's right"

She took a moment to pause

The officer pushed for more, but before he could get his question out she then said

"Ruben Oliver, he was foreign and he was asked to leave but I remember he managed to find evidence that proved that the twins had burnt each other and had paid him to make it look like an accident."
The officer took more notes and asked more questions.
"Could this Ruben Oliver be involved still?" I wondered, as right now I needed air and lots of it.
I surveyed the area as I took some fresh air in the back garden; Ralph was resting on a garden bench
"How are you feeling?" I asked
"Better thanks" he said he looked quite pale and yet calm
"I can't believe this is happening.." he began to say when a nervous yet fully loaded Jack appeared behind us
"Right well, sorry to disturb, turns out that this guy Rory was paid three nights ago by Jensen"
"How did we not see this happening Jack" asked Ralph who was now stood up adjusting his shirt and tie
"Sir, his brother is talking, sadly it was all done in cash and well under our radar and the brother only found out tonight"
"Seriously"
"Yeah he woke up in his garage, realised what was happening drove straight over here and well he was too late"
"Crap, damn it this Jensen has really got the better of us now. We need to find this little bastard and soon"
Ralph stormed back in to the house, he was now on a mission
Jack look like the whole world had collapsed around him, " Don't worry we'll get him" I said
He forced a smile. It was plain to see, Jensen was hitting all the right notes, playing each of us in turn.
Just right now the dice were being shaken and we didn't know whose turn it was next.

©TheExpirement

I stepped inside the house, going in to our new flat and checking in with Fiona. Jean came out of the bedroom
"How she doing" I whispered
"She's asleep, I checked to make sure she is okay"
"Are you okay?"
"Yes my dear, and I'm fine. I have seen death before sadly but you youngsters I am guessing not so much" Fiona and I were meant to have spent a few days together before she had to return to her studying and would have eventually go back to Newcastle. Problem was Jensen, it was deemed too dangerous for her to live her and I decide to make the heart wrenching decision to ensure that she had to be in Newcastle. My heart ached so much that I cannot bear to tell you that evening when we discussed, many tears were cried that night. She was having nightmares practically every evening and there was little I could do. However, there was a problem Jean. Jean because she knew a lot about Rory well a lot more than we did, there was an inkling that she might draw attention to her and Fiona. But of course we couldn't leave her to go alone. Even though she was adamant that she would be fine. Jack though decided to sway her by letting her know a little more about Jean. "Jean isn't just a scientist or a former teacher" he advised
"I understand she might be more, but I can look after myself you know" Fiona stated standing there with her arms folded.
"You know she is a former spy too"
"WHAT?" she couldn't help but shout out, it was amazing to all of us.
"Yes, look she has an alternative identity and it's time maybe you both went and studied at another University where Darktronics have helped"
"Are you placing me in witness protection Jack?" Fiona asked, she had calmed slightly but to be fair it was a fine line between calm and angry.

©TheExpirement

"I am"

"But can I contact my parents and James?"

"Yes, we will work something out, you just need some training"

"I understand"

"I agree too" I said hoping they had forgotten the fact I was too standing in the room and that I was her other half.

Fiona turned to me and smiled

"Sorry, I needed to make this decision and be happy with it"

"I know, loves you" was all I could say. I wasn't totally happy she didn't really have to make this decision alone, but deep down I had too much to lose to argue and most of all I understood.

I took a step back and let Jack and Fiona decide what was to happen next, I had my own investigation to do and it was time to go and see Rock.

I met Rock at the local café, as I didn't want anyone to see us at Darktronics; I had also called my new team member Finn. Finn I knew was Derek's right hand bud when he first started in accounting. We ordered our drinks and we settled in

"So how we can help you man?" Rock asked

"I need you to see if you can find these people on the cameras" I asked him, I had photos of Rory, Jensen, Alan and also I had noticed in Jacks papers earlier a picture of Ruben

"Okay I can see what I can do"

"I need your full discretion not a word to anyone else in the group"

Finn joined us a couple of minutes later just as I had planned.

"I need you to do some digging in to Derek's background"

"Okay where do you wasn't me to look?"

"School, where did he go, where did he study who was his classmates"

"I have to ask, why?"

I understood his question; he wasn't part of the team that was investigating this attack on Darktronics.

©TheExpirement

"I will tell you when you have done your investigation, I need you to be objective" He looked at me, he could tell there was more to it than I was letting on and he then he simply said "Okay, but I'm out if I feel threatened"
"Sure"
We shook hands on it and finished our drinks.

©TheExpirement

Chapter Twenty Two

I sat patiently at the railway station; this should have been a day out with Fiona. However, since the incident she needed to be away from here as it was getting all too much for her. I remember Jean and Fiona taking their new identities with some fun, Fiona was even trying to get a whole new wardrobe off Jack, but he wouldn't budge. Sadly though she had to leave her lucky green bracelet and new necklace behind just in case someone could trace her, I was glad to hang on to it as it brought me some comfort. Hayley and Anna were due to start at Manchester, Jean who was now Hayley had pulled some strings and they were glad to start somewhere afresh. Plus I being a Manchester United fan was hoping for a few souvenirs to be brought home when things calmed down. Anyway the day arrived that they needed to leave, sadly I wasn't allowed to say goodbye the way we had done before. But thankfully due to Finn's research I was heading to a town just three stops away. So I got to the railway station way before my train. Jack was even there as he had a security meeting; he wanted to see if Jensen had been in town lately. It was of course pre planned so that we could keep an eye on our girls, I don't remember seeing Ralph there, but Jack advised me the next day that he was. He must have been worried too. I sat reading the free paper and looked at my watch, Hayley had taken an earlier train so I only just saw her go, as for Anna my dear Fiona I smiled as she took the train it was dead on ten and mine was a few seconds later, it pulled in just as hers pulled away. I could see she wasn't happy but I felt deep down that she was safe from all this madness. I took my seat after staying near the door so I could see Fiona's train for as long as I could. I then carried on reading the sports news and I noticed a familiar face in the next compartment along.
Finn

©TheExpirement

I couldn't blame him really, as it was his lead I was following, maybe something in his gut was telling him that there was more to it.
I had done my research on Finn, him and Derek had been good friends ever since they started working to with each other. In some ways they had been like myself and Jack and I, but I did notice that Finn had gone to the same school as Derek just three years younger. So I had wondered if he had followed in his mentors' footsteps or whether it had been planned all along.
I closed my eyes for a bit, it had been a long night; no-one had slept even though Jack had moved us to a new flat and made it feel as homely as he could. I didn't make any move towards Finn before we got to the town. I wondered how long he would follow me for or if he was following me at all. We reached our destination about half an hour later, I took out the address of the lead and I smiled. I stepped off the train and I didn't notice Finn get off, I wondered what he was up too. However my mind was then focused on getting to my meeting on time, I didn't want to be late. I took the quickest way I could find out of the station, which turned out to be the lift. I was taken in by the busyness of the place, I really hadn't realised that so many people used this station. I showed my ticket to the guard as I reached the exit barriers, he smiled and I entered the outside. It wasn't particularly good weather, but the car park which was just right outside contained several taxis' one of which had my name on it. I was pleased as the clouds were threating rain. I showed the driver some identity and he in his black and green top opened the door as I sat inside I wondered who this man really was, but a quick check on my phone showed he was a legitimate taxi driver. I believe this Jensen had put the creeps in us all. As we exited the car park, it wasn't long before I had reached our destination, I thanked him and was about to give him money as I stepped outside, he waved his hand and drove off. I then knew this was part of the meeting. I took a deep breath and walked across

the road, a dog scurried past me as I went in through a small black gate which creaked as I opened it. I saw the curtain move I knew I was at the right house. I rang the doorbell and it wasn't long before an old gentleman I would say in his eighties "Ah Hello James" he said he was wearing a jumper with a crest on it I thought I had seen it before and it wasn't long before I realised where I followed him in, before even having chance to say hello back, he was walking without a stick but I noticed many by the door side, I wondered if they were for walking or for protection. I closed the door behind me "Do come this way, I have tea prepared"
I took off my coat and hung it up on the clothes pegs that were just inside the hallway on the left. I was taken aback really how modern the place looked but the lounge was more shall we say homely. As I entered the lounge, there was another person sitting on the sofa.
"Hello Finn" I said
"Ah, you found me" he simply replied, he was wearing the jumper he always wears to work a school crested round neck jumper, that's where I had seen it before.
"Your Granddad?" I asked quietly
"Yes, I can hear perfectly well you know, and I am his grandfather."
"Sorry, I didn't mean to offend"
"No offense taken, I simply wanted to tell you myself. Now I shall go and get the tea before we let you know more details"
As he did I had a question to ask Finn, but he must have been reading my mind
"There is a station just down from here, I knew that my taxi driver would delay matters if needed."
"Well done indeed" I said I was proud of Finn, he had guts. We needed them.
Finns grandfather brought in the tea; Finn jumped up from his comfy looking chair and helped his grandfather with the cups.

©TheExpirement

Whilst he was a very spritely man and doing extremely well for his age, trembling hands were sadly letting the side down.
Finn quickly took control of the matter and handed me my mug of tea, it was in a proper mug, and no bone china around here I thought. His grandfather must have been reading my mind a family trait I wondered?
"You look thirsty, so I gave you a proper mug"
"Thanks, yes all I had was a coffee first thing"
"Never had a coffee in my life"
He said sitting down in his high backed chair
I was sat on the sofa; it was comfy but clearly not the best seat in the house. But I wasn't complaining, I was looking round the lounge, the log fire which wasn't lit was the focus of the room. It made it feel warm; pictures of the family were framed and sat proudly on the stone mantelpiece. Then I saw for the first time pictures of what I could only assume was Finns Grandmother and mother, they were peas in a pod. I hadn't been able yet to read up on Finns personal life, but as I finished half of my tea I asked the question "So tell me which one of you has the information" Both of them smiled
"Well both of us do really" said Finn "Do go on Finn, your grandfather can then have his time" I saw him move to speak but he appreciated my acknowledgement. "I was as you know at school with Derek, he was my school maths mentor, there were three years difference, I being younger got assigned to him when I got straight A's in my first year."
"Did he recruit you?"
"No, I was asked by another man in our office to join, as he was in my year. But that wasn't the reason I brought you to my grandfathers"
Finn seemed to go tense; this I thought was going to be a sensitive moment. "Derek and my sister Hannah were also best friends; they

were in the same year. Sadly my sister died a couple of years back in a car accident. She had been out drinking with her school friends as part of a reunion. Derek was there, but so was someone else."
I was about to speak as he paused, but I could see this was hurting so I let him say it in his own way, "Jensen Lyons" he said
He stood looking a photo on the mantelpiece, he stood there for a while taking a moment. His grandfather took over the story "Yes, we were never sure but Derek always told us that someone had spiked her drink. She wasn't driving that night but she didn't want to get drunk as she had an interview with Darktronics the next morning"
So Jensen was interfering even back then I thought, "So who caused the accident if Hannah wasn't driving?" I asked whilst I was trying to get all what had happened in to perspective.
"The taxi driver was also killed, but his autopsy showed he was at his countries legal limit, Derek found out that some of the drinks that Hannah had were meant for the taxi driver. Had she not felt drunk she would have walked home." Finn then said he had regained his composure and turned to me
"I see, so you think Jensen thought Derek was going to spill the truth and so therefore killed him?"
Finn nodded and then his grandfather then showed me a school photo
"This is the year of Hannah, in the back row you can see none other than Jensen"
I could his distinct evil look about him
"But why now, you aren't looking for compensation for Hannah's death so why would he be worried?" I asked
we were all concerned
"I believe he is getting revenge, Derek mentored Finn and advised him of all the details, whilst we never wanted anything we gained a

lot of money from the taxi business. Yes Jensen owned the business, we didn't find out until Finn showed me this photo"
His grandfather reached out another photo, this was a copy of one that Jack had taken as part of surveillance
I wondered how he had acquired it but now I was taking in this information
"See this is the same taxi logo as the one that killed Hannah"
The photo showed Jensen using a taxi, but then I noticed he was carrying papers and you could read the top of it which says the administration of Mr Jensen Lyons taxi business
I gulped it was a lot to take in
"May I ask where the money went to?"
"We set up a scholarship for violinists as Hannah had been a very outstanding one" Finn said
"Good lord, so Jensen is making this personal"
His grandfather then advised something more outstanding
"Look as you know we were all part of the St Michaels school, I was part of the rugby tour back in the day, but as I was a fundraiser, they send me each time they do their fundraiser tour a photo. I thought you would like to see some other colleagues, it may be of some use"
It was there was Daniel Lewis, Lucy Lewis, Finn, Damien who worked in fire testing and then I saw a face from the past. Kevin, the guy who was so cocky, he was standing next to Jensen
"They were best friends, I remember being on that tour and wondering if they were going to do anything but go out on the town" Finn's grandfather suddenly said
I wondered if he too got murdered by Jensen.
But my mind was now racing and I had to contact Jack to tell him all what I knew, so I took my leave by thanking Finn and his Grandfather for their evidence, I took copies of the photos which

his Grandfather already had prepared "Take care James, don't underestimate this man, I feel he's not one that ever gives up"
I closed the door on my way out and went for a walk to the closer station. Then I received a text from an unknown number saying "I am walking near the theatre of dreams, may they all come true"
I smiled it was Fiona they had made it their safe and were fully settled in. How I missed her.
Whilst I felt more relaxed now that Fiona had made it to her safe haven, I did feel I was heading in to something that involved danger and I wasn't sure I wanted to enter it. I walked pretty much without noticing my surroundings deep in my own little world. I was suddenly brought out of it by the ringing of my phone
"Hey" I said
"James, can you get to Ralphs place?" Jack asked
"Sure, I am just catching a train"
I hung up, I wasn't going to ask what this was about, but I knew from the tone of Jack this was fairly serious.
It didn't take me long to get back to Ralph's house, I was greeted at the gate by Jack, "Good afternoon" he said looking at his watch "I told you I was catching a train" I said, I didn't like his tone, it was almost he was telling me off for something "No sorry, it's not you" he said in a more relaxed tone then I noticed he wasn't looking at me, I thanked him, for his apology and as we went in through the gates, I turned and saw a blue car pull away, something was telling me that was someone watching.
"So tell me Jack what are we here for?"
As we walked in through the maze of corridors, I wasn't getting much out of him. But he mumbled something as we walked through to the room with the cameras within Darktronics. Ralph was sat there looking quite solemn. Then I realised that something bad had happened whilst I was busy this morning. "What happened?" I asked, I was being quite stern, but on purpose, I

didn't want to be like this, but seriously something had happened I needed to know.

©TheExpirement

Chapter Twenty Three

"Sabrina has been kidnapped" Ralph said very quietly. I nearly had to ask what he said again, but then I saw a picture up on the middle television screen. There she was tied and gagged to a chair
"Do we think this is Jensen" I asked, expecting there to be a yes
"No, it's the lecturer she was having an affair with" Jack said
I wasn't sure how this one had gone down whilst I had been following up the leads this morning
Ralph looked like he was on the verge of breaking down as he was sat in his suit still looking smart, arms folded not knowing what to do or where to look.
My heart sank as I was given a piece of paper by Jack, "It was sent to Ralph this morning"
I read it quickly a quietly to myself
"Don't come for her, or even call the police. She is dead regardless, but I will play a game with you. If you win I will kill her quickly and pain free, if you lose you watch her die, I will contact you soon don't leave the house"
I subsequently found out that Ralph hadn't left the house. He was feeling this was somehow personal. But I wasn't sure.
"Is that picture a full video?" I asked suddenly not really knowing at the time what was making me ask that question
"Sure" Jack said turning to Ralph who decided to walk out of the room
"He has watched it several times, we can't find any clues, however we recognised the lectures voice and we have confirmed he is now missing from campus" Jack said quietly.
My mind raced something was telling me that they had missed something
Surely but then this was Jack, it wasn't like an amateur looking at this film, but a full time crime specialist.

©TheExpirement

However I sat myself down in the front and watched the film intently. It wasn't very long, but I asked for the controls, Jack needed to go and talk to Ralph so I was alone for ten minutes. I rewound the film and then I spotted it, the clue we had all been looking for. The room she was held in wasn't a room but a theatre set, I recognised it when I entered the lecture hall that evening, when Sabrina went missing before. I remember seeing the exact same set in the corner of the room. I dismissed it at the time as I thought it was there for the theatre group and nothing to do with Sabrina or her lecturer. I then found the zoom controls and zoomed in on Sabrina's face. Her bruises were I thought a little too staged, I remember having to help out with Fiona's friends. They were doing cuts and bruises for a lifesaving course at our local community hall, they asked for many volunteers, Fiona and I decided we would do the cuts and bruises and I remember being taught. This was staged, but for a reason I didn't know yet. I returned the film back to the end and as I did Jack came back in to the room. "Can I see Sabrina's room?" I asked

Jack seemed stumped at my question, but a voice, Ralph's voice said "Yes" quietly behind him I didn't have to explain myself, which I was pretty glad of at the time, as I didn't want to alarm anyone and I didn't want to give Ralph false hope either. I climbed the stairs and found Sabrina's room, Ralph showed me the way, before leaving me outside her room. Jack had been left downstairs, to concentrate his efforts on Darktronics issues. And that really is putting it mildly. I entered Sabrina's room and it was tidy obviously a cleaner had been in. The dark oak double bed had been made, her clothes had been neatly folded and a fresh set of pyjamas and towels had been placed on the left hand side of the bed. The room was full of different pictures, some of friends and family others of artists paintings. I wasn't looking for that, I was looking for a diary or something a clue to why this had been staged. "I wonder" I said aloud I entered her en-suite bathroom and behind the bathroom cabinet was a safe.

"There you go" I mumbled to myself

It wasn't hard to figure out the code, as my night of finding her on campus that evening had also given me that answer

Her bracelet she was wearing had a inscribed date and message. The date was the code for the safe, I was amazed that as the safe opened it wasn't empty.

I closed the bathroom door, I felt that maybe whoever was behind this may be watching. I somehow felt safer with the door closed.

I found a folded up A4 paper which was a script for a play entitled "Understanding Me"

I scan read the first few paragraphs which played out the scenes we had already been given a showing of.

My heart started to race as I wondered where this story would have in store for Sabrina.

I was pleased to see that the main character gets to run away with her lover and that it is forbidden. However, I also found in the safe an envelope "Dear Sabrina, Ralph needs you to move away now, he can't tell you yourself as he will die. You must meet with your lover on the first full moon night and run away as your play depicts. Trust me I am a friend not a foe " I read the signature it wasn't Jensen, but none other than Paul's. Under his signature was the same inscription and date on Sabrina's bracelet. Which I then knew that Paul had done this for Sabrina's safety, I put all the things back in the safe and replaced the bathroom cabinet. I wasn't sure what to do at first, but I then realised there was only one option and that was to talk to him directly then I rang Paul directly, whilst I know we didn't fully trust him, I didn't think he was capable of pulling of kidnap or murder. My heart and gut were telling me that there was a perfectly reasonable reason for this, it was just a matter of explaining it in full and making sure Jack and Ralph didn't kill him before we could ensure Sabrina was safe. I entered the lounge where Ralph and Jack were, Ralph looked up

"Anything?" he asked

"Yes, and your nephew will be able to explain everything" "I knew he had something to do with it" Jack said angrily, he arrived at the front door.

Jack wanted to kill him; Ralph looked at him as if he was the devil. And for me, I welcomed him in like some long lost brother. Paul did try to speak, but I asked us all to sit down and that we would go over what had happened.

"Paul please explain" Ralph asked, he was now calmer but still unsure.

I glared at Jack, to make sure he wouldn't do anything stupid. Paul who was wearing a blue t-shirt and blue jeans and white trainers sat down in the biggest of the chairs. He coughed and then began his story "We know that Sabrina was having an affair with her lecturer" We all nodded. "He encouraged her to act out and do experiments in all various things, I won't tell you what but she used to confide in me everything he did. Some things she loved others she hated. But she was cool with it as she never did anything fully that she hated. He too was cool with it and never pushed her. Until recently, it was about three weeks ago, she came to me in tears. I honestly thought they had split up and finally we would get her back. However, she explained to me how he had grown angry and that he was pushing her to do weird things but most of all she said that he was under orders."

"Under orders from who exactly?" Jack asked

Paul sort of acknowledged him, but just simply continued.

"I asked her to explain and once she had calmed down, she told me. He had taken photos of her, and it was with an old style camera proper film. So he had to go and develop it, she noticed he had left his mobile on his desk. So she had time to look at it, she found a text which was telling him what to do and how much he would get paid for doing so" He took a deep breath "She knew he was selling photos, but didn't realise it was all a plan. She didn't know who was sending it and before she could get the number he was back in the room"

Ralph motioned him to continue, he was looking more at ease. "I followed up on some leads, some friends on campus heard about him and I found who was buying the photos, but she then went back to him after confiding in me and he explained everything. Full details of who it was and why." He stuck his hand in to his jeans pocket and pulled out a scrappy bit of paper. "It was only the other night that she came to me with this" he handed it to Jack, who nearly bit his hand off with his snatch. "I told her not to panic, and I talked to them both, then they showed me a letter"

"One the same as the one in the safe?" I asked

He nodded "Yes, but I thought I would leave you two clues. The original letter was from Jensen."

"So where is she?" Ralph asked "I asked if they had a plan, and they said yes that they would act out their play, so that Jensen would believe she was going to die"

"But where is Jensen?" Jack asked

"I don't know, but what I do know, I found his minion waiting for Sabrina, I stunned him, he's currently in the boot of my car"

He chucked his keys to Jack, who promptly ran out the door

"I replaced him, hence I am wearing this"

On close up his clothes didn't fit and then he showed us a leather jacket.

"Jensen texted to ask had the deed been done, I said yes and he said that they had a play they wanted to act out and I was to do it, but of course change the ending."

Ralph stood up from his chair and breathed a sigh of relief.

"So what was your plan nephew?"

"Well I was planning to stage her killing, somehow let you guys know and we would pretend to grieve."

"Fine, that's what we do then"

I filled Jack in on the plan. He still wanted to beat the hell out of Paul, but he was impressed that the guy had thought of all of this on the hoof.

"Is Jensen watching?" I asked Jack

"Probably" he said and we put our plans in motion. Ralph then greeted us on the steps of the house as we were getting some fresh air.

"James, please can you stay over tonight, I want to talk to you about Sabrina"

"Of course, this is a terrible time for us all and we mustn't be alone" Jack gave me a hug as I walked in with Ralph.

That evening we were in the library, just like before, we were stood with our whisky in hand

"James, I don't want to get too sentimental with you"

"But?" I asked

"I want you to know that you can use this house as if it were your own. You are like a son to me now and it feels right that you can come and go as I please"

That meant a lot to me. I took it in, saying nothing at all. Simply sipping my whisky and we did a toast to Sabrina. Around four in the morning we were awoken by Jack bringing us bad news. "Sabrina died this morning, of a brutal stabbing. We didn't play his game, I am so sorry" Jack said he acted well but it was very sincere. Ralph called his doctor to give him something as he couldn't bare the pain. He was sent to bed and we played out the next few hours. There was only one thing niggling me, just how did Jensen know about Sabrina's and her lecturers play that part I needed answering, but first we had to play some grieving friends. The next few days were played out as if they had been fully scripted. I was moved in to

Ralph's home and finally got a chance to get to read some books in his library. Each day I was more than worried about Ralph as he wasn't eating or sleeping. He knew this wasn't true but something in his gut was worrying him. I had my own niggles, but I had to focus. I managed to get what I found at Finns and his Grandfathers to Jack, who was impressed.

"I don't think we are in any doubt that he made this personal" Jack said to me looking over the photos.

"Yeah but something really does bother me"

I said

"Oh, how did he get the play?"

I nodded, this is what I really liked about Jack he was on the same playing field as me.

"Well?" I asked

"I checked security at the campus"

"Don't tell me the lecturer kept a copy in his office?"

"Nope, Sabrina gave him a copy some months back and the guy that Paul caught, he was already following him came across it and took a copy, he was already following them both"

"Bloody hell" was all I could say

"Jensen has influence on all sorts of people"

"How is Paul?" I asked

"Worried that his plan isn't going to plan"

"Well hopefully we will catch this bastard"

Sabrina's fake funeral was due in a week, but Rock suddenly arrived at Ralphs home battered and bruised.

©TheExpirement

Chapter Twenty Four

I rushed out to the lounge from the television room, when I heard a scream. It was the cleaner who found Rock slumped on the door step.
I helped him up
Jack wasn't too far behind
"What the hell happened?" I asked
"I dunno man, he came out of nowhere"
Jack looked after the cleaner who wasn't too good with blood, which was now pooled on the door step. "Let's get you cleaned up and then you can tell me what happened" Rock sat down on a kitchen chair and he took a wet cloth from me and started mopping his wounds. He then took a moment to think about what had happened trying to remember each detail as he didn't want to miss anything. "I was cleaning out the finance store cupboard, they had several burn bags to collect, I was impressed as all but one had the correct paperwork. I took the last one as a good will gesture, Kaliey the finance secretary thanked me and apologised about the last bag" He mopped some more blood from his face, I found the plasters he winced as he stuck it on the cut above his eye brow. "I then went down to the burn depot, I put the three unopened bags on the furnace conveyer belt and waited for Karl to give me the thumbs up. As I did I checked out the other bag, sometimes you find freebies in these burn bags, I know I shouldn't but they burn all the free post it notes and pens and stuff" It was hard to disapprove of that I thought, but company rules are company rules. "I didn't find anything free, so I chucked the bag contents in to the blue bag beside the conveyer. That's when I noticed this"
He pulled out a photo from his rucksack
I recognised it immediately it was the same one Finn and his Grandfather gave me

©TheExpirement

"I then saw Karl signed all the paper work and then went back up stairs. I got a page to go to the science store cupboard saying there were no syringes. I was sure I filled that up only the other day, but I thought as it was from my mate May I assumed she had some information. When I entered the store room corridor that's when I got boshed over the head, I came to a while later and saw a man assaulting May so I rushed to her aid. He beat me twice over and gave me this, and simply said "Give it to James, or I will finish May" He then pulled out a white envelope. I was intrigued who it was from
"You did fine Rock, just fine"
I opened it carefully; I was already guessing this was Jensen. But I couldn't be sure.
I didn't think it could be a trap, until Jack stopped me he put his hand on my shoulder.
"Careful"
I then followed him, we went in to yet another secret room that I didn't realise was even there. But it was a replica of one of our labs. I thought well done Ralph for being so safe and secure.
I then moved back in to my training mode everything that I would normally do at work.
Jack smiled as he just let me work.
I suited and booted myself and then took the envelope in to the secure lab.
I carefully opened it using a pair of tweezers; it was clean there were no traps
I then opened up the carefully folded writing paper, this wasn't the usual A4 paper that we had been coming up with this was personal, I then read the scribbled writing on the paper
I turned on the speaker in to the office which Jack was patiently watching me
"Hey bud" I said showing him the letter

"Nice, you read it ?" He replied pressing on the speaker button in the office. "Sure, here goes, *Dear James and Jack, well done, most credit goes to Paul. His plan was genius, sadly though I held the trump card, I was watching Paul replace my man and well the rest was too easy I won't bore you with the details. Now you are probably wondering what happens next, you must trust me I will not go for Sabrina and her lecturer, for he will make an excellent father...oh I am sorry you didn't know did you. Never mind, time to run along now, you will hear from me Jensen very soon for the final challenge. Good luck*" Jack had gone pale, if he could see me now I also didn't feel good. Jensen now had the upper hand and we were all just pawns in his game. It was almost at the point of feeling like we had no more moves left. It wasn't like we had planned Sabrina's so called death in advance it had been done on the hoof. It was ringing hundreds of alarm bells for me, Jack left me in the secure lab, I was looking now for any evidence that could take us to Jensen's hide out and may be even find him. The one thing that really got my gut going was how did he know about everything we did. It was almost led me to wonder if someone within our group was a double agent so to speak.

I loved my gut, but at this point of my life I hated it, if it was going to be wrong for the first time today had to be it. I looked at my watch, it was gone four, I heard shouting, so I decided to log the evidence. My thoughts turned to Fiona, I wondered if she was okay and if she was able to sleep. I knew tonight with Jensen being so close to us.

I didn't think for one minute that the guy who assaulted May was Jensen, just another one of his minions.

That then led me down other avenues of thoughts and deliberations. I quickly scrawled down some ideas and then one by one I got my jobs done.

I joined Ralph for dinner around 8 that evening. He hadn't spoken to anyone really for most of the afternoon. He had rung Paul to ensure that Sabrina was still safe and this was now the conversation over dinner.

"She is safe," he stated as he ate a mouthful of mushroom risotto

"I am glad to hear that sir" I replied, I grated some more cheese on to mine, before taking a rather large mouthful "Yes, you know I thought it was rather brave of Paul to take her and that man to the Bahamas."

He never dared mentioned his name, the shouting earlier that I had heard was Ralph. I believe Jack had told him about a supposed baby on the way.

"I am guessing he financed it as well" I said, I didn't want to pry, but my curious mind was telling me to ask all the questions I could.

"Yes, which considering I thought he was going to do badly I am pleasantly surprised." He took a sip of red wine, it didn't matter these past few nights what we were eating, Ralph always had a bottle of red. I had decide to keep a clear head that evening, so I declined the offer of a glass. "I will ask her about the baby when they return" Ralph suddenly stated. I smiled, that was all I could do really. I sat my knife and fork down on the side of the plate and wiped my lips with the napkin. Ralph rang the bell, the chef as we liked to call him came out with pudding and as we tucked in Ralph looked up at me

"I know you are dying to ask me more" he said

"No, not all sir, I believe you have actually covered everything sir"

He smiled, I smiled we laughed. "Your right James, I shouldn't bottle these things up"

"I have never said that Ralph, but its true you shouldn't, it will do you no favours. If Sabrina is now safe, then we can concentrate on getting this bastard, as once we have done that if Sabrina is having

©TheExpirement

a child then dirty nappies will seem like a breeze" And with that we dived in to our apple sponge pudding with lashings of hot custard.

©TheExpirement

Chapter Twenty Five

I didn't believe for one minute that we could not beat this Jensen. We had too, I had to make this, and sadly I knew not all of us may make it. I had seen Ralph put all of his heart and soul in to this and now Jenson had made it personal and he wasn't about to let up either. All of us knew it, but I was sure I was going to protect not only Fiona but Ralph as well.
But now I needed sleep and that was just as important.
When the alarm woke me from a dreamless sleep I suddenly had a thought there was one way we could put the ball in our court so to speak.
"JACK" I shouted as I bolted out of my room, I was wearing nothing but a white t-shirt and checked pyjama bottoms
He turned to look at me, he was looking tired
"Yes James" he said
"Sorry, I had a thought how to get this f**** bastard"
"Sure, James, I can't help you anymore"
I was left stunned, speechless.
"What the hell?" Was all I could muster
Ralph then walked out of his room, he looked at Jack and shook his hand
"Good luck son, bring them home safe"
"James, get dressed, I will meet you in the dining room for breakfast"
Jack made his way out of the corridor and that was last I saw of him for a while. I did as I was told by Ralph, I assumed something had gone down in the night. I was worried, I made my way to the dining room, now dressed in my blue suit.
"Ralph" I said quietly, I could see he was completing something.
"James please eat then we will have a chat"

We sat and ate in silence, I wasn't up for a full English this morning, but if looks could kill from Ralph, I forced myself to eat my bacon and eggs.

It took a while before we had a chance to talk, there had been several calls to Ralph which had taken him away from the dining room. I wondered why Jack had disappeared but somehow I just knew I had to trust Ralph which as he was very much like my dad I did. It was blind trust, but there I was in his house being his surrogate son and it already felt like home. My thoughts were broken by his hand on my shoulder.

"Come to the room" Ralph said

"Sure"

I walked behind him, I assumed that we were going to the television room, and there I was wrong yet again. I really shouldn't assume anything.

He took me to a room which had plastered up on the wall all the evidence we had been collecting about Jensen. "Ralph this is serious"

"He has made this very personal James,"

"I know, boss but seriously"

"No need to call me boss"

"Okay, err Ralph. No that doesn't sound right"

"What sounds right?"

I decided that at this point it wasn't right to answer him so I decide to change the subject

"Where has Jack gone?" I asked instead

I saw his face change from relaxed to serious, but I could tell he was wondering what I would have said

"He has gone to get my wife"

"She in danger?"

"She's dead"

We sat there both in shock, at one point I thought Ralph was going to drop dead on me. He looked so frail, I wanted to hold him, to tell him that everything was going to be okay, but deep down I didn't know what was going to happen next so all I could do was keep calm and do whatever Ralph needed me to do.

I stood up and poured a glass of water from the night stand which normally held the whisky and handed it to Ralph.

He gulped it down and thanked me before taking a second

He then turned to me I could tell he was thinking something "Was this Jensen?" I said

"No, I don't think so, I think she was killed by someone else.." We both could hope that justice would be brought.

He paused, he then got up and came close up to me and said

"It's now down to you now to rescue Darktronics from this evil man. Jack will be back soon and you can have all these resources that I own James"

I stood there in shock nothing could have prepared me for this. I felt like I needed to run away and hide but it was time to be brave.

©TheExpirement

Chapter Twenty Six

The problem with me being in charge of all things Darktronics and the whole big rescue was I didn't have many of us left. Ralph was due to give a press conference that afternoon to tell the world about the death of his wife. Jack bless him was bringing back the body and wasn't answering any of my calls or texts. Paul and Sabrina I last heard were making their way back home the only good news there was there was no baby to speak of just yet, but the lecturer turned out to be quite good at business and Paul had some plans to make a semi decent man out of him. I was reading these messages whilst taking in the fact that I me James Kieran Folster was in charge of bringing down this bastard Jensen. Please do excuse the language, but seriously me?! What was Ralph thinking…. I know I know he's grieving, but there are plenty of other people more capable of bringing down a criminal super mind than me. Anyway, rant over I think… I was now sat in my office in Darktronics, I felt it was better that I was here. But as soon as I had entered my office there was a note from Rock. "Hey man, sorry I have been given some leave time, they don't want me freaking out about my attack I think, I am welcoming the holiday though dude. Sorry and good luck. Oh look out for a postcard. Yours Rock" I sighed when I had read that, I didn't have a man on the inside any more. That was until around about 1 when Finn knocked on the door. I opened the office door to see Finn who looked like he had a lot to tell me. He walked in wearing a grey suit and looking extremely smart. Whilst I wasn't expecting him to be wearing casual today he did look as though this suit was for special occasions and his shoes were polished.
"New suit?" I enquired
"No, sadly not, just one I use when I need to have a meeting"
My mind raced I didn't know he had meetings to go to

"Okay so spill what's going on?"
I said still stood near the door of my office with my arms folded.
"Look don't be mad, my Grandfather wanted me to find out more about Jensen"
"Okay" I said wondering what the hell was going to happen next
"Turns out he isn't working alone, or he is being funded by someone"
"WHAT?"
Turns out that Finn is a Darktronics auditor, he trained whilst working in finance.
"Don't want to know details, or how you managed to get this" I said as he handed me bank records of Jensen monies. He worked out that Jensen was being paid £10,000 every month
"Technically the money shouldn't be able to be tracked. The account number normally you end up being taken on a worldwide tour just from your desk. But seriously Jensen left us a trail."
Finn explained showing me the different months of monies; I was just about to ask where the money trail had taken us to when he showed me a record
"Look, he had an offshore holding account which contains millions, so Jensen has been giving himself a monthly allowance, probably just enough to get this job done."
I simply nodded
"The fact that he didn't hide this account shows he's an amateur at this game. So I checked some other records, he holds.."
Finn was about to finish off his sentence when all of a sudden the alarms and sirens went off in my lab. My heart jumped I looked towards my office and saw Dennis bringing in a box. I went through my automatic doors in to my lab, I was now wearing my protective suit. Finn was now my link between this box and outside. I was worried this was the beginning of Jensen's final plan?
I stepped carefully towards the box

©TheExpirement

I calmed my breathing down and thanked Dennis for the box as I carefully lifted it from him. As I began to analyse it I noticed that there was a finger print which for all intense and purposes looked like it had been made from blood. My stomach churned, I didn't want to know what was inside the box

I pressed the intercom

"Finn call crime, I need a fingerprint machine now"

He nodded

He called crime they were here in minutes, I was impressed normally we have to wait and waiting can sometimes cause your evidence to do some strange things, especially when they were the ones creating the package. But today was real, this wasn't some pretend package, this one I was worried about

Dennis then opened up his door and drove though the lab bringing me the mobile fingerprint reader. I took the copy of the finger print and put it in the reader

My heart sank when it found a match

"Finn, call Ralph"

I knew he shouldn't be disturbed but this was an emergency "What should I tell him" he asked back

"Tell him we have had a message concerning Phil"

I took some more evidence from the box and then I opened it

There was a head.

My head spun as I was trying to make sense of it all.

I recognised the face straight away.

Daniel Lewis the rugby fundraiser was dead and the suspect was none other than Phillip Dowing

Understandably there was a lot to take in over the last 24 hour period. For well all of us.

Ralph's wife had been killed.

Daniel Lewis had been murdered.

Jensen wasn't working alone.

145 –Expirement Series

And me little old me was now in charge of all the investigations and just to top it off either Philip Dowing was a murderer or a victim. Finn bless him was doing all he could to help me, when he realised what or should I say who was in the box, he sought out crimes, forensics and ensured that Lucy, Daniels sister wasn't in danger. Then just to top it off, the other member of my team Darren Michaels hadn't turned up for work at all for the last week. Was he dead too? My mind was racing, then I had Ralph on the end of the phone. He simply told me to proceed and to do everything I could. We had to find Jensen and then hopefully he would lead us to the overall criminal mastermind. I had a terrible feeling that something bad was just starting to happen and I wondered if we were winning or just playing a life threatening game. I grabbed a shower and then gave a statement to the head of crimes. He being Jonas Myers then showed me a text from Ralph which told him that he was to do everything he could to help me.

I thanked him and Finn.

"What do we do now sir?" Finn asked

"We find Darren"

I was worried as there was nothing to connect him to any of this. But we needed resource and Darren was one of the in crowd in the social groups in Darktronics. Daniel Lewis was really grateful for all his work when Daniel was trying to get everyone to participate in fundraisers. At times, if Darren was in everyone else was in. So I was told when I did some further background checks on my team. We grabbed a bus outside Darktronics. Finn looked really surprised as we boarded. I waited until we had sat down

"Seriously when did you get them tickets?" he asked me, I had managed to purchase two ten journey tickets, so that we didn't have to fumble for change, "I have my ways, Finn the key is being prepared. We can assume that we are targets, so being on public transport might just help us"

©TheExpirement

Plus I knew that this bus stopped right outside Darren's house. "You have to be kidding" I mumbled to myself

Finn who had grabbed a copy of yesterday's free paper looked up from the sports pages

"Guy with baseball cap and sun glasses" I quietly said

Carefully and quietly Finn took out a mobile phone, and took a picture

He then hid it behind the paper and set off a checker, which turned out to be a face recognition

"How?" I asked

"Jack" he simply replied

A match came back. We were on the bus with Jensen.

So much for trying a bus!

I texted Jonas and said what was happening, he told me to be careful and that he would send a team after us. It was a while yet before we would reach our stop. I wondered what Jensen was up too, Finn then wrote a text on his phone

"How did you know?"

I smiled

I pointed to the three letters in the paper G U T

He smiled back.

Jensen was sat in the front of the bus and had turned to the window when we had taken the window. Did he want to be spotted? Or was this a mistake by our criminal.

We were three stops away from Darren's house when he got off. Finn was tempted to leave, but I stopped him

"No, he has already made a mistake, let us go and check on Darren"

We arrived at the front door of Darren's house. We knocked on the door, there was some scuffling behind the door and the door opened cautiously

"Boss?" Darren whispered

"Yeah can we come in" I asked

©TheExpirement

"Yeah sure," he then opened the door fully
"Sorry I not been in," He said as myself and Finn walked behind Darren who was wearing a blue t-shirt and shorts
"Any reason?"
"Yeah I texted u man" he said I checked my phone
"Nope, didn't receive it"
Darren looked very confused at me
He motioned to two kitchen chairs which were placed by a breakfast bar. Finn and I sat as Darren then grabbed us some drinks and then his phone.
"Maybe it's your new number?" he then blurted out.
"What?" I asked
"You texted me saying if you need to call, here is my new number"
As finished my drink of orange juice he chucked me his phone
I then looked at the texts, indeed he had received a text telling him my new number.
I then read his text replying to that, it said
"Thanks James. I won't be in today as my brother is really ill in hospital and I need to visit him. I hope to be in tomorrow. Will keep you informed." My heart sank
"How is your brother?" I asked
Darren looked pale
"He's now in a coma"
That's all he could say, there was a knock on the door.
Finn bolted up from his seat. He then stopped either of us going for the door. Something was telling me that he thought this was Jensen.
I then saw Finn stealthy move to a point where he could see who was at the door without showing himself.
There was a guy with a baseball cap and sunglasses. He had a package.
Finn saw him put the package down and walk away.

©TheExpirement

Darren and I looked at Finn waiting for a signal.
He moved away from the window and looked at me
"He's put a package on the front door"
"Jonas's team should be on their way, I will ring him" I replied
"Jonas, its James, we have a rouge package on the doorstep."
Jonas soon arrived and there was activity on the door step.
As we weren't to move from Darren's kitchen we tried to work out who had sent Darren the text pretending to be me
Finn got out his rather useful mobile phone which he had convinced Jack to pimp up with security apps.
We did our best
"Darren, did you get any other phone calls or texts?" Finn asked him
"No, I had one from mum telling me about Riley my brother"
"Okay so how did your…Riley get so ill?" I asked
"He was in a fight.."
"Jensen" Finn then blurted out interrupting Darren
We both looked at him
"Explain" I said
"He was wearing sunglasses, he was obviously hiding something."
"He could have been trying to blend in"
"No sorry James, look.."
He showed me and Darren a newspaper article which he then read out loud as we couldn't see all of it on the tiny screen
"A young man in his twenties was brutally hit with a hammer outside the snooker club. Police are appealing for witnesses to come forward as a man wearing a black baseball bat and sunglasses was seen with the hammer prior to the incident. He was then seen entering a nearby fish and chip shop with blood on his hands shouting at customers and staff. If you have any etc. etc." Finn and I looked at the sketch from the police and it was Jensen. We had seen him this morning. I felt angry and Darren was looking even more pale

"You mean this Jensen was the one who has put Riley in hospital."
"Yes, I think it's a strong possibility"
"Finn get the group photo up"
"ah yes" He muttered, he then delved in to his rucksack he was carrying, he had a hard copy
"Is there anyone on there you recognise" I said to Darren as Finn handed him the photo
He looked carefully at each face on the photo. He was just about to say no when he spotted someone
"Let me just check something"
He then ran out of the kitchen and we heard him climb the stairs
"You think everyone on the photo is connected?"
"Possibly, but if not, he found Darren's weakness"
Jonas who had now cleared the package entered the house
Darren returned from upstairs and showed me a photo of his dad with Jensen and Jensen's father
I gulped, this really was personal. But I felt somewhat relieved that it was another lead.
Jonas then filled us in,
"I'm sorry to say that it was another body part of probably Daniel"
"Any note?" I asked
"Not that we can find, but more bloody finger prints; We will do some tests and fill you in later. Oh Jack is on his way home and Darren your brother is safe we have got full security around him just whilst we try and get Jensen." Little did we know Jensen was watching.
Darren decided it was best he checked in with his mum, to make sure she was okay.
"She is a strong lady, but she won't understand why there will be all the extra security"
"You go and then meet us back at Darktronics. It's not safe for you to be here."

©TheExpirement

He nodded and Finn and I jumped in the back of Jonas's car
He took us back to Darktronics.
I was impressed when we entered the crime lab. When it was made clear that Jensen was attacking Darktronics Jonas was brought in to bring the crime lab up to spec.
There were loads of people running around working, evidence being put up on the boards.
I looked around and then I heard a very familiar voice
"Get to the point" he shouted
It was Jack. I was very relieved to hear his voice
"Your back then" I said as I stood in the door way of the office he was in
He came over and gave me a man hug
"Yeah they let us come over with her body straight away"
Jonas then asked me and to come as he wanted to show me the results from the package I walked away, my thoughts turned to what Jonas had found in the box. "James, we found Mr Lewis's remains in the box. It was his limbs."
"Was there any more fingerprints from Mr Dowing?" I asked hoping that we had further clues. Jonas was about to answer when Ralph walked in the door

©TheExpirement

Chapter Twenty Seven

Ralph looked like he meant business. Jack was closely behind him. Ralph ushered myself and Jonas in to a room, Jack closed the door behind us.
"Right Philip Dowing has just contacted me" Ralph said in a serious tone. He then got out his phone and chucked it to Jonas who was pretty impressive with his catch
"Go, trace the call." Ralph ordered Jonas. Who promptly walked out of the room and as the door closed Ralph took off his suit jacket and sat down on the only chair in the room
"I am telling you he is in trouble, but my gut says that he might be in with Jensen" he then said looking suddenly tired "Seriously?" I asked
"Well either that or his investigations got him too close" Jack then advised
I was about to ask but then Ralph answered my questions.
"When we had trouble with Jensen I asked Phil to keep an eye on him so that we could make sure he wasn't going to do something like this"
He took a deep breath
"Just before you joined his team he had come to me to say that he had gotten in to Jensen's circle of friends." "We advised that he should keep a close eye but his distance as well" Jack then said
"So we now know he didn't keep his distance enough" I said sitting down on the floor
As I made myself semi comfortable against the wall Jonas walked in "We've traced the call to an old warehouse in town" he stated. Before any of us could speak he said
"My team are heading there now. The call seems genuine" Ralph stood up from the chair and walked towards Jack

©TheExpirement

They whispered something, I couldn't quite here. But whatever it was Jack had to leave and then Jonas soon followed as Ralph asked him to go watch the situation closely and I thought he said lock the door…
I got up from the floor and asked Ralph
"What the hell is going on"
"We are in here for our own safety"
"But we need to…"
"Yes I know, we need to bury my wife and to bury Daniel but James, Jensen is killing the people one by one, and if we don't stop him now"
"You think someone is on the inside?" I asked, I wasn't sure where that came from, but I had now asked it Ralph smiled "Yes, I do, but I can't tell you who I think it is. But the point is Jensen may have killed Philip and hell if he has then we could be next"
I gulped it was all starting to make sense, Jensen had made this personal, if Philip had gotten on the inside and too close then Jensen would make us pay for it.
"Why did you smile?" I then asked
"Because I am proud of you James, you are becoming the person I always believed you could be."
I sat on the chair as Ralph paced round the room, we were inside locked in a room with no windows and nothing to look at. Not even one of the crimes fancy coffee machines were in here and that was starting to get me.
Ralph spotted Jonas passing the door and knocked to get his attention, Jonas unlocked the door and still even though I was sitting closer I couldn't hear their whispers.
Three things were though now on my mind, coffee, Jensen and the third person, the real person running the show. As drinks thankfully arrived taking my thirst off my mind I focused on all the evidence that I had seen, my mind which was very much a photographic one

was focusing on the photos that Finn and others had shown me. I then remembered in detail Jeans conversation about Ruben Oliver. Could he be the person in charge, but since then nothing had shown up his name. Finn who had traced the money had hit a brick wall even though Jensen had been so sloppy. I finished my drink and found Jack and Ralph deep in conversation. I stood up from the chair and yawned. "Well?" I asked

"Jack has been looking in to if my wife was murdered by Jensen"

"Don't tell me you have found Ruben Oliver"

"I am stunned James, you really are making a good investigator" Jack playfully said giving me one of his brotherly hugs

I was wondering how he had found Ruben Oliver.

"I don't yet know if he is linked to Jensen" Jack suddenly said

"I was just about to ask that" I said smiling

"I know, but the problem is all we have is the photos."

"How did you find him?"

"The photo was left beside her body, with his face circled."

"But that.."

"His fingerprints were all over her hotel room"

"You know this is all starting to sound all too easy" I said, I wasn't sure why I had said that but Jack agreed.

We needed to do more to link all our clues

We then noticed Ralph wasn't in the room

"Where the hell has he gone?" Jack asked

We rushed out of the room, wondering where he had gotten too. I could see that Jack was worried, of course I knew that at some point we would have to bury his wife. My heart sank when we then saw Jonas's face

"Something wrong?" I asked

"Yeah, we have had another attack on Darktronics.

"Where, which building" I asked

"We can't enter it" Jonas said

©TheExpirement

Jack got out his phone
"Why not I asked?"
"Because Jensen has taken over all the cameras and security elements.
"He' not as stupid as we thought" Jack said who was still waiting for someone to answer
"Ralph, where the hell are you and what do you need from me?" Jack said
We heard Ralph giving Jack some instructions
Jack then pointed to Jonas to turn the television on
We turned it on...

©TheExpirement

Chapter Twenty Eight

We sat there in stunned silence. Darktronics cameras had been taken over by none other by Jensen Lyons
It was silent as we saw Jensen sat there smiling I jumped as Jack closed his mobile phone up.
"Ah hello everyone" Jensen then suddenly said
He adjusted his dark blue tie.
He then held up a clock
"You see this everyone, this is a clock set at the time I was sent away from this beloved institute."
He coughed and continued with what seemed to be a prepared speech
"Now what will happen over the next few days, will be some sad times for you all, because I have decided to bring down your beloved company and you will never know when it will happen. Just before I sign off, Jack you'll find Ruben's body outside Ralphs home, I didn't realise he would carry out the killing...but hey mistakes happen and you will be able to see that justice has been carried out"
The television went dead, Jonas picked up a desk phone
"Anything?" he practically shouted in to the phone
"Good, get a team down there now" He then said more calmly
He then turned to myself and Jack who was busy rooting in his jacket pockets for something which I thought would be important, but he was relieved when he found his gum.
"Yes Jonas, don't mind him" I said
We had been both distracted by his rustling
"Thank you James, we managed to trace his call and I am sending a team"
"We need to go and see if Ruben's body was really dumped at Ralphs" Jack said
"Yes, but Jonas before we go where is Philip?"

©TheExpirement

"Hospital sir, we found him dehydrated but holding a knife covered in someone's blood"
My stomach churned, I didn't want Philip to be implicated in the murder of Daniel but something wasn't sitting right.
"Keep me updated" I replied as Jack and I moved back outside
Jonas nodded and then turned to talk to one of his colleagues.
When we reached the car park Jack took me to another new vehicle
"What's this" I asked looking at the brand new four by four in front of me
"Shiny new and just been delivered"
I got in and you could smell the newness, little did we know then that this wasn't the one he had actually asked for. When we arrived at Ralph's house, we had already been beaten by a forensic team, which to be fair I wasn't that surprised at. I climbed out and was met by Sabrina, who was now very tanned.
"James, I am really glad you're here" she said
"What's the matter?" I asked as I could tell from her tone that she was very upset.
"Come with me James"
She pulled me away and I left Jack with the forensic team, we needed to know if the body was real and if it was Ruben Oliver. Sabrina led me in to the house, the same way that we would go to the television room and sure enough that was where we ended up. There I was met by Paul, who seemed very pleased to see me
"James" he said holding out his hand, I shook it, his was a very firm shake.
"What can I do for you Paul?"
"Well I need you to confirm something"
"Paul.." there was a whisper behind him, it was Ralph
"You should be back in bed" Paul turned to him
"IM FINE" he shouted at him

The last time I had seen him this angry was in the car with Sabrina, she now grabbed my arm. She was scared was it though of her uncle?

"Sir I am here to help, what can I do?" I said in a calm voice

"James, my dear James, you need to…" he couldn't finish his sentence before he fainted, I was held back by Sabrina

Paul called for someone I didn't quite catch a name, but what turned out to be his doctor rushed in and got him out.

Paul then followed, leaving Sabrina and myself

I turned to her, she was still holding my arm

"Why are you so scared?" I asked gently

"I think Paul knows something." She said

"What like something?"

"Like I heard him say to the doctor keep Ralph sedated so that I can run his company"

"But he knows that isn't his role"

"I know, but I am glad Jack got his new vehicle" she said suddenly changing the subject. "Yes, he is darn pleased with it"

"Ah James, I am glad you are still here, I wanted to know can you tell me all about the investigation?" Paul asked "No not really, you saw Jensen's video conference today that's all I know"

He smiled in his sly little way

"Now James, Ralph may think highly of you and I do too, but if you don't co-operate I think I may have to say make you go away"

"Oh really and why's that?"

"Paul please.." Sabrina pleaded with him

"Oh go away silly girl your trouble is nothing by nonsense, this is big boy games now and go and play with your dollies or something"

She turned away tears now pouring down her face

I let her go and she sat on one of the softer seats.

"Paul, don't think you're about to take over Darktronics"

"James" He said sternly and lifted his arm as if he was going to punch me
"Don't even think about it Paul" said a very stern voice behind me
"Jack, oh you have come to rescue James have we"
"No, Ralph has"
and with that Ralph walked in
"But I thought Paul you were there to look after me" Ralph said
"But Uncle"
"No Paul I realise you are in debt and that your trust fund is going to pay of those debts and well you just got greedy. No, I will send you to one of my dearest wife's refugee camps where you can learn that the simple things in life are best."
With that Paul was taken away looking extremely sorry for himself Sabrina jumped up and cuddled her uncle
"You did well my girl, now go your man awaits" he said kissing her on the cheek
"Huh?" I asked
"Sorry James, I thought Paul might play that card once I got wind that he was in debt. But hey you did marvellously and her man the lecturer he well is going to do right by her"
"Good, marvellous" I said smiling relived that this was nothing but a family feud.
Jack then made his presence known
"It seems like the body is really Ruben"
"Oh excellent, time to have dinner" Ralph advised as we then followed him out in to the dining room where a food was being brought out. I sat down and starred at my wine glass and wondered how my dear Fiona was.

Chapter Twenty Nine

The next morning soon approached, my night's sleep was disturbed with dreams about Fiona, I was worried. Somehow I needed to contact her and make sure she was okay. I got dressed and as I went in to the dining room for breakfast, I saw Jack pouring coffee and I managed to have a quick word "I need to speak with Fiona" I said quietly "I'll see what I can do" he replied gently I could tell on his face that he knew I was worried. Thankfully I could rely on Jack and by lunchtime I was very grateful. After my ten minute call with Fiona I was feeling more alive and ready.

Jack met me outside of Darktronics

"Thanks" I said

"No worries, I am glad I can be helpful" he replied smiling

"You're always helpful, so any news of the whereabouts of Jensen"

"Well that's why we are going on a road trip" he said

Before I knew it Jack's men arrived and we were settling ourselves in his still very new shiny four by four.

I smiled

"What?" Jack asked

"You have spent the morning polishing this.."

Jack laughed

I opened the glove compartment and there was a nice used cloth and some wheel moose. I shook my head pretending I didn't approve. I was actually quite jealous. We spent the next few minutes taking the micky out of each other. It was a brief restspite, we were in for the long haul today and I wasn't sure if it was going to last just for today. About an hour in to our drive, Jack turned in to a lay by and told his team to drive ahead.

"What's going on?" I asked

"We need to split up; I don't want all of us falling for Jensen's possible trap"

"So when are you going to tell me what Jensen left us?"
"Not yet, I need you to see what the team saw"
I read the text on his phone it was from Jonas
"Team hit, three down, but we need you to take a look"
I gulped, Jensen had left us a present and like Jack had said it could be a possible trap. I took a deep breath and was about to give Jack his phone back when I realised he was walking to a black estate car that was parked behind us. I didn't take too much note, but then as I looked at the back mirror I saw a face I recognised. Philip was sat in the passenger seat. What the hell was he doing here?
Jack opened the driver's door and jumped in, I decided not to ask
"Right let's get out from here" he said
Jack waited until the black estate car had gone and we pulled out of the lay-by.
We seemed to be following the black car, but then it turned off which according to the sign was going back towards Darktronics. I was confused, I didn't know why Philip was in the car.
Jack then made a sharp turn to the right. We were then back on a road we had been earlier on
"Lost our minders?" I asked
"Yep"
Jack wasn't giving much away, he was pissed off I could tell.
I looked at my watch we had now been travelling for well a good while. It was another three hours before we reached our destination. Jack stopped in what seemed to be just pure gravel. A few meters away I could see a warehouse in the distance. Jack grabbed his jacket from the back seat and jumped out of the car and slammed the door shut. I decided it was best to have a chat
"JACK" I shouted at him before he a stormed away too far
"What James" he said
"You can't go in like that" I replied

©TheExpirement

I stood my ground, I could see that Jack was pissed off, hacked off you name it that was how Jack was feeling
"I can't tell you James, I just can't"
"Look I saw Philip was in the car, he is calling the shots"
He laughed
"Thank god for you" He said
Apparently Philip had evidence that Jack's sister was somehow involved.
Now at this point there was no time for him to explain in full that would come later. "Okay right, what are we expecting here?" I asked Jack who had now calmed down enough
"Well Jonas said there were three packages, all containing a clock"
"Some kind of puzzle?"
"Yeah maybe"
We entered carefully Jack led as he was carrying his gun
"Over here" he said
As I entered the warehouse door all I could see were clocks on shelves, they look brand new. I couldn't see much else due to the darkness. There were no windows and it smelt stale "Hold on" Jack whispered
"Jenny" he then said
I moved closer towards Jack and a young woman was crouching in the corner of the warehouse
"Jack" she replied
They embraced
"So you are involved?" he asked her straight out after their hug
"No Jack, here look I was sent this"
Jenny is an event manager for a local newspaper. She organises big events the likes of supermarket openings etc. However, a few summers ago now I remember how she barged in to Jack's office when we were scoffing down doughnuts.
"Seriously boys you two will be on diets"

"Yo sis love you too" Jack had replied in between a bite of an iced doughnut and a jam one.

I laughed as he then somehow asked her what she was doing there

"I got this massive event in London"

This had made her one of the best event managers. Since then she has been consulting the newspaper and working in London. Jack hadn't seen her in months until this moment in some warehouse where all I could here were ticking clocks. She pulled out a folded piece of paper "Read this...Oh Hi James"

She then said as she gave me a hug and a kiss on the cheek. "So you were sent here to meet a guy called Jensen who was looking to rent this place"

"Yeah problem was, he placed a load of money in front of me, of course we don't do business like that, so I tried to get away, but then he showed me his gun and well here I am."

"Did Philip show you pictures?" I asked Jack

He nodded, it was a massive set up

"Any ideas on these clocks?" I asked her

"Yeah we delivered them to a watch event in Southampton these are the exact ones"

"Don't touch" Jack suddenly said as Jenny was about to reach for one to show me their company logo to prove her story

Jack walked up to her and gave her a reassuring hug

"I believe you" he then said to her she smiled

I liked Jenny she was self-assured, she was married to a Mark Finlay who is a navy officer. Him being away on tour fell in to her event patterns, and she always used to boast to Jack that it kept their relationship fresh.

As we walked towards to the door of the warehouse, I was behind Jenny and Jack and I saw what she was wearing, a regular black fitted t-shirt, blue jeans and trainers.

"STOP" I then shouted at them both

©TheExpirement

Jack was the first to turn round

"What James?"

"Lift either foot up" I asked Jenny who waited for her brother to nod

I delved in to the inside jacket pocket and found a swab I brushed it on her trainer and then took a closer look at it.

"We need to see what Jensen was making" I then said.

The substance that I had spotted was none other than linseed oil. Jack took a look at the swab and agreed with my findings and right on cue we both turned to Jenny and said

"Show us where you have been"

Firstly Jenny took us outside to where her and Jensen were talking, then she showed us where they fought about the money. At neither site could we find traces of the oil. But I did note that where they fought about the money they were in line with the road, that was where the photos would have been taken.

I made a mental note as I then ran to check up with Jenny and Jack who were heading to a side door

As we entered there was again nothing but a single clock in the middle of the room.

Jack ordered Jenny out of the room "Out now" he shouted I stood behind him, he carefully walked around the room. It wasn't as big as the other was and there was no shelves, nothing showing that anyone had been in here. Then as Jack approached the single clock in the middle of the room I saw the yellow stain

"At the bottom of the clock" I said

"Clocked" he replied

"Hope you didn't mean that"

He laughed then he put on a glove, that he had tucked in his trousers.

He pulled an evidence bag out and placed what seemed to be a folded note paper in to it. I then went outside and found Jenny sat on a makeshift wall.

"No trap then?" she asked

"Hopefully a clue"

"You think he is watching?"

"Probably"

Jack then opened the four by four and propped open the boot. The gadgets were amazing in the boot, laptop screens, forensic kit everything you could wish for.

He took his time and then he spoke

"Well it's definitely Jensen and he writes, don't worry Jenny isn't involved. Only Jack and James are to arrive at the Old Cavern"

"Anything else?" I asked

"Nope"

"You know where that is?"

"Yeah. But Jenny we need to get you to safety"

"Sure, my Matt is due home tomorrow, the base is near here"

We were now very tired and hungry, so we drove Jenny straight to the barracks.

Thankfully we got her in safe and sound

"See you boys soon" she said waving goodbye

I could see that Jack was more than relived to leave her in safety but there was an air of sadness.

We drove for a little longer until we found somewhere to eat. That then was our first night in the four by four.

©TheExpirement

Chapter Thirty

The night in the four by four was actually quite comfortable. I just wasn't sure why we couldn't have just rocked up in to a local hotel but I forgave Jack when he pulled up to a restaurant for breakfast.
"I am starving" I said as I jumped out.
After full English I was done, I couldn't move
"I need a walk"
"Not yet, I need to check if it's all clear"
"What?" I asked I wasn't sure. My gut was telling me that Jack hadn't told me everything
Jack had gotten up from the booth that we had been placed in. I was impressed; the restaurant was modern yet traditional at the same time. I was taking a look at the framed photographs; they showed the history of the place. But I was taken away from my thoughts when Jack walked back in and ordered two lots of pancakes from the waiter who was busy cleaning glasses. I noticed Jack was a lot happier
"Hungry?"
"I did ask for a takeaway""
"Guess we are off then" I replied
"Well in a minute, but I am guessing I owe you an explanation"
"Would be nice to know"
He smiled
"As you know Philip turned up yesterday saying that my sister was involved. Now I didn't realise that he didn't know where she was"
"Until when"
"Today, he texted saying that Jenny hadn't been found yet. So I sent him to London, to hopefully get him off our back"
"But why no comfy bed, not that the seat wasn't comfy?"
"I thought we were being followed. I couldn't be sure"

The waiter brought over the two takeaway boxes and the bill. We paid in cash leaving no trace. We said our goodbyes and left the car park. We were back on the road again. As we approached what I had hoped would be our final destination, the Old Cavern. I was worried that as he had used Jenny. Did he know about Fiona, I shook my head to try and clear it of these sudden fears. The Old Cavern was an impressive site, with the front covered in ivy, it boasted tradition. I was looking for clues that maybe Jensen had left us, but there was nothing obvious. Jack put down the window letting in some fresh air. He took his time in picking a spot, I saw two lads kicking a ball but they seemed harmless as we finally picked a spot in the big gravel car park. I took a breath and got out of the car, Jack rummaged in the boot for a bag. He gave me one, it was a business bag, we were now as he put it "IT consultants" luckily I knew a thing or two about the old computer. As we entered via an old wooden door, there were a few couples sitting in the corners of the bar, come restaurant. As we walked towards the bar, the young lady stood just near the till on our side the bar "Hey the Lyons party?" she asked

"Yes" Jack said

"Come with me" we followed her through another doorway and to a more laid out restaurant. We were shown to a table where there was an envelope in the middle of it. "Can I get you anything?" the woman asked

"No thanks"

She walked away not looking too pleased.

Jack stopped me from sitting down, he then got out his gloves and picked up the envelope

"I think he is truly playing with us" I said extremely quietly not fully trusting that he wasn't listening to us

"I'm guessing this wasn't what we were expecting?"

"No, I was expecting to have to blend in, hence the covers, but hey he's too clever for us" Jack said as he then opened the envelope.
It was a series of photos from Darktronics, the first being in the science lab, the next few were from the fire department the rest were a series of rooms that would need further investigation.
I too then put on some gloves and picked up one of the photos trying desperately looking for a clue.
The waitress from earlier then appeared behind us
"I'm guessing you are the police or something" she suddenly said
"What makes you say that" Jack said
"Oh you seem the type."
"Anything we can do for you miss?" he replied wondering why she was bothering us
"It's just he told me not to give you this"
She handed Jack a business card
"What else did he say or do"
A young man then appeared with some drinks, non-alcoholic sadly but they were welcome none the less, even though I really could have done with a pint.
We then sat down
"He came in here like some mad man, constantly laughing and using his phone"
"My boss the landlady told me to keep an eye on what he was drinking, she knows I can handle myself but even I was worried"
She took a sip from her lemonade and then said
"I can't remember what he said exactly, but he had three pints by this point. He wasn't drunk, maybe tipsy but I thought he had said he could make me rich and famous. I ignored him and just made sure he paid for his pints. I was glad when he left, that was two nights ago. I didn't need to lock up that night, so I went out to my car about twelve, as I pulled out of the car park, I drove a little ways

down the road, when I noticed something flashing on the passenger seat."

She paused taking a gulp of her drink

"I pulled over to the layby ensuring my doors were closed, I then saw this phone ringing, so I answered it, it was him"

"Did he threaten you?" Jack asked

"Yeah he said if I didn't take some money and make sure you got these photos I well I won't tell you what he said, then someone appeared at the layby with the envelope and said Jensen sent me. My instructions including the business card which he said for me to keep"

"You heard from him today?"

"No sir, he said he would be watching"

"What made you talk to us?" Jack said whilst looking for security cameras

"I told the landlady and she told me to talk to you, I think she said she could stop any signals for a while."

Jack and I then checked our phones, it was true, any signal was being blocked. I was impressed

"Okay if he rings, ring us" I said as I gave her my phone number

"Sure, thanks"

The landlady appeared and told us that the signal was back up. We thanked her and made our way out of the Old Cavern. As we got back in to the now not so new and muddy wheeled four by four, Jack gave me the business card. "Hopefully we are just one step ahead of him now" he said before we drove off in silence. It was to be yet another long drive before we reached the destination. The destination on the card, "Why do you think he gave her the business card?" Jack asked

"Maybe it's being tracked?" I said thinking we had just suddenly played in to Jensen's track

"No there is nothing on it" he replied

"But he will find out she gave it to us"
"No bro, I made that copy"
I didn't dare ask how, I just had to keep my faith in Jack, he was the only person I was trusting right now. Of course not forgetting my own gut

The destination was a business park in the old part of a town. It was fourteen miles away and the way Jack was driving it didn't take us that long.

We arrived in to the outskirts of town the sign to the old business park had been vandalised but Jack managed to see it just before nearly missing the turn. He pulled in and found somewhere to hide us. It was now time to play cat and mouse. Jack took out his phone and rang the number on the card

"Are you frigging serious?" I mouthed silently to him
"Trust me" he replied in the same manner
I sat there and waited
"Ah Mr Lyons please"

Jack placed the phone on speaker phone and we waited hopefully for Mr Lyons to appear. I tried not to make a sound, we couldn't hear anything

"Mr Lyons will meet you in the car park" the lady said
"Thanks" Jack replied
He then grabbed the phone and jumped out
"Come on" he said to me
He then got out a walkie talkie "He's making a run for it"

We then started to run, I was trying to keep up with Jack who was really legging it.

As we ran from where we had parked over to the office a white car nearly ran us over it was Lyons, he made a sign at us as he passed us.

Then I noticed Jack was lying on the ground, holding his leg
"Jack, you okay?"

©TheExpirement

I said rushing over to him
"Yeah I think it's just a scratch, damn it where's the walkie talkie?"
I looked round and I found it on the verge just outside an old office block that looked really run down
"here you go" I said handing it to Jack who was now sitting up
"Juliet Mike do you read?" he shouted
"Yes I do read, we have him"
Was that it was it all truly over? I sat down next to Jack we didn't feel like celebrating just yet, we were too worn out for that. Jensen was arrested and the process of finding out the truth had only just begun. When we heard from Jonas that Jensen was detained, Jack and I walked along to the office that we found to be his base. The office was full of papers and boxes and drawings. On closer look we saw detailed plans of all his attacks and his computer was full of emails on his plans with Ruben Oliver. I was relieved now that we could bring this man to justice. Jonas had taken him to the Darktronics holding cells for interrogation. Jack turned to me in the office "Well, we can get Jean and your Fiona back now"
"Yes, we can and can I go home?" "Of course you can, I'll get your stuff back for you." Ralph was delighted with the results of that day, we were now stood in his office.
"The last few months have well been nothing short of a nightmare"
He said stood by his desk
We could tell from his face that things had certainly taken its toll. Sadly though the process with Jensen was going to take a lot longer than anyone had thought, for starters he wasn't talking
I remember sitting in on one of Jack's interviews with him
"Come on Jensen, tell us about this blueprint"
Jack laid out the flat evidence bag, which contained a blue print of the forensic lab of Darktronics
He sat there in his white t-shirt and his grey prison trousers. He didn't seemed bothered

©TheExpirement

"Okay, so let's start with the basics"
He smiled as Jack said it
"Oh something funny?" Jack asked
He carried on laughing
A laugh that sent cold shivers right through my heart, as I took my leave out of the room I could see Jack getting more angry by the second.

Chapter Thirty One

Jonas arrived that afternoon with some more good news
"We have found the home of Jensen"
Jack and Jonas rushed out of the office so that they could process yet more evidence.
I smiled, I turned to see Ralph stood there
"Sir" I said
"James, I think it's time we went and got our girls back"
I had never heard him say that before
"Jean and Fiona I think will be pleased to see us" I simply said not trying to push him on his statement. We needed our friends, we needed to bury those who had gone and the next few months would be another emotional ride that we were hoping to control.
Ralph took us to his car and we drove to meet our girls, I was impressed how relaxed Ralph seemed on the journey up
"I hope we haven't messed their plans up" Ralph said
"I am sure we have, they probably will make us pay" I replied
We laughed, it was so good to laugh
We arrived, to see them waiting outside a very posh hotel
Ralph put down the window
"Well good evening Ralph, James" Jean said
"We have plans for us all" Fiona then said
My heart skipped, my mind was racing, my darling girl was stood there and all I wanted to do was pick her up and hold her tight.
Jean handed Ralph a token, it was for the hotel car park. As we drove in to the car park Ralph said
"That means we have messed up their plans"
We burst in to more laughter as we exited the car, it was nice to be walking in the warm evening, the breeze was gentle.
We were still laughing as we met the girls in the hotel lobby,
I grabbed Fiona by her waist, holding her tight as we kissed.

I then noticed Jean and Ralph had a kiss too, I was happy for them both, it was about time we had some happiness. That night we spent the evening drinking cocktails, eating in a posh restaurant, then the girls showed us around the city, both of our girls well I should say ladies were wearing evening dresses, as it got cooler Ralph and I had to man up so we handed our jackets to them so that they could keep the chill off.

I looked at my watch, it was two in the morning when we were doing this, but there we were the four of us just well enjoying life. We entered the hotel about four and got a few hours' sleep before we had to take the journey back home, home how I longed for my bed. Before we took the journey home, Ralph had messaged me to meet me at the bar. It was serious, as it was "Don't let the girls know" I could tell, there was something wrong, Fiona stirred as I got up "Where you going?" she asked sleepily "Oh Ralph has a secret mission for Jean, I just need to go help him with the final something" "Oh good, she loves him dearly" she then said I was good at making up stories, thankfully Fiona as off guard that morning as usually she asks me so many questions that my stories fall apart. Part one so far so good, I went down stairs and met in him in the bar

"What's up?" I asked him

"Jack rang, they found another set of boxes"

"What?" I asked

"They were found near your home James, and Jensen killed himself last night"

I cursed

"What the hell do we do now?"

"I am waiting for Jack to tell us"

Then his phone rang

"Jack, please tell me it was something we missed"

©TheExpirement

"I'm afraid not, we need you and James back now, and keep the girls in the hotel. They are safe there."
My gut was in knots, I was terrified so was Ralph
"Look we were meant to be burying my wife tomorrow"
"I'll tell Jack" I said, I rang him back
Moments later we were back in our respective rooms, Fiona was now up
"Don't tell me, we can't go home"
"No I am sorry, I thought this was over"
She was scared, I was petrified
Jean and Ralph knocked on the door

I could tell Jean had been crying her eyes were red
"Right now, let's go and have breakfast, we must be strong" she said holding Fiona's hand
We went down to the breakfast area in silence. The nightmare had re-awoken itself. After breakfast, we walked in to the hotel car park and I held Fiona's hand tight and Ralph was hugging Jean as we said goodbye.
"Stay safe" we all said and Ralph and I took the journey back to Darktronics. The journey home was one of worry and the complete opposite of our more buoyant journey up. Ralph turned on the radio as it was my turn to drive; I was worried what Jensen had left behind him. Was this just something we missed? Ralph suddenly turned the radio off
"Not a fan" I said
"No, but also I need to ask you something"
"Go ahead boss"
He yawned
"Look let's get some coffee and then you ask me the question"

The services were not too far away, but it was long enough to let Ralph rest his eyes. As I concentrated on two lorries trying to overtake I wondered what was Ralphs question.
I smiled as he looked at rest as I heard him snore slightly. I turned on the indicator and Ralph awoke
"The services are just here" I said
"Time for some caffeine" he said stretching
I smiled, and turned in to the car park.
As we got out of the car, my legs were aching the car park was fairly busy but we made a bee line to the coffee shop. After the short walk my legs were now working properly as we ordered our liquid caffeine
As we sat I could tell Ralph was thinking
"You need to ask me that question boss?"
"Yeah, I err I don't know what to do"
"Well is it this whole Jensen business I'm not sure…"
"No, don't worry it's not that, its woman thing"
"Oh okay, is it Jean?"
"Yes I love Jean dearly, I love all the jewellery she wears, the way she does her curls in her hair"
He paused
"Sorry I am babbling, but I can't help but wonder if its…"
"To soon" I said
He nodded
"Only you know what the right time is and I believe she loves you back"
He went on to tell me how is wife was seeing someone new and that their marriage was on the rocks, but I was impressed with his loyalty. We continued our journey and arrived with Jack waiting for us outside the office.

Chapter Thirty Two

Jack took us in to his office; this was a novel thing, it was rare for me to actually enter here. He usually made himself at home in other peoples offices. I smiled it was tidy, but I was soon focused on the issue at hand.
"Do we know were these boxes came from?" Ralph asked Jack
Jack who was now sat behind his desk at his computer, tapped on it
"Yeah, here look"
He turned on a television screen up on the wall
It was a map of the country
"We found them here which was around the house, the cctv then allowed us to track the parcels"
He then clicked on a remote and a red line appeared around the country
"Looks like Jensen left us a good bye present" Ralph said
"Yeah, when we found the first box, he just laughed and then before you know it he's dead"
"How did he kill himself" I asked
"We think a poison bomb inside him" said someone behind us
We turned to see Jonas at the office door
"You have the results?" asked Jack
"Yeah, we found the package inside his gut" he replied
"Oh that's disgusting" I said
"It seems like he had planned it all" Ralph said
"So what's next?" I asked
"I think we need to find out what's in the boxes?" asked Jonas
"What we don't know yet?" Ralph asked in a very serious tone
"Sorry what Jonas means is that most were empty, they were like dummies, then we found a few which are being analysed now."
Then the alarm in the main Darktronics lab went off.

©TheExpirement

Jonas had run out of the office, towards the firemen who were entering the building. Jack stopped us moving, he radioed over to Jonas
"A fire had broken out in the main café, as soon as I had arrived the firemen had come out and had said it was a false alarm." Jonas said

Jack turned to us and said
"False alarm"
Something in my gut was saying this was only the start.
The fire alarm as it turned out was false, it was faulty. I was staying with Ralph and Jack arrived the next morning
"Good Morning Gents" He said as he arrived in the dining room
"Good Morning Jack" I replied
Ralph wasn't saying much
"I'm guessing we will have to move the funeral?" Ralph asked who was sitting at the table who moved his still full breakfast plate.
"Yes I am afraid so, we don't want anything to happen sir" Jack replied
"So what are we doing?" I asked
"Well the boxes are being analysed by your team James as we speak, we think that.."
His phone went off, my gut churned
"Okay thanks" he said then putting his phone back in his pocket
"Good news?" asked Ralph who was now sipping coffee
"Yeah it turns out that the boxes had indeed been sent whilst we were trying to capture Jensen"
"So it's possible we are just tidying up after Jensen then?" I asked
"Yeah I think that is the case James, but I am now getting more confident that we can move Felicities funeral to the end of this week" Ralph looked relieved, it also meant that Fiona and Jean could return.

I just hoped that this really was the end, Ralph instructed Jack to continue with the investigations just to tie up loose ends. As for me, well I went back to work to help my team finish analyse the boxes.

As I entered Darktronics there was a sense of worry and grief. A lot of people respected Ralph and his wife and her death had hit them hard. I was asked when the funeral was about a dozen times as I walked towards the lift entrances. When I entered my office Finn, Lucy and Darren were in the lab busy working on one of the boxes. I was impressed they were looking like quite the professionals. I was even more impressed by Lucy, she had been naturally devastated by her brother's death, but getting Jensen and bringing him to justice was her focus. Darren was looking good too as the doctors had advised his brother was getting better slowly. I stood at my desk and read the reports and found that he was trying to send us down different avenues. But nothing new was coming forward. I decided to leave my team to it and went for coffee and doughnuts, I had some reports to write up as well and for a minute or too it all felt like things were back to normal. The rest of the week, Jack spent his time investigating all the evidence, and was tidying loose ends. To make sure of their safety Jean and Fiona were going to arrive the night before, so that Jack and his men could ensure that the hotel was safe. Even though it was hard I decided to stay with Ralph, I was worried about him. It was the morning of the funeral, the funeral cars outside were being prepped and Sabrina was trying to convince Ralph to at least eat something.

"Sabrina, go and see if the cars are ready" he said to her, he was calm "Okay Uncle" she said, she passed me at the doorway "I tried" she whispered

"Don't even think about it James" Ralph turned to me and said "Don't worry, I wasn't even going there"

I carried on and ate my breakfast; he was at least drinking orange juice.
I grabbed a couple of apples and slipped them in to my jacket pocket
Jack then arrived in the doorway
"We are ready" he said
We got in the cars and set off, we then joined the hearse as we drove near Darktronics, all employees were stood solemnly outside, some holding flowers others just stood in silence.
Ralph had ensured that the service would be shown to the employees, we had a big lecture theatre and other television rooms to allow those who wished to watch. Ralph turned to Jean and said
"Seems everyone is here"
She smiled at him, I held Fiona's hand tighter and then we saw the far building blow up.
It was if everything was moving in slow motion. I jumped out of the car as it had stopped
Jack was there
"GET EVERYONE AWAY FROM THE BULDING" he shouted
His men moved shuffling people away, Ralph had also gotten out of the car
Jack then pulled me aside
"Look, you need to get to your lab, a box has been delivered"
"What about Fiona"
"Don't worry I will get her safe"
I then made a run for my lab, I was literally running, I could feel all my muscles ache.. "Calm down" I was saying to myself
I looked at my watch is was still early in the morning, I couldn't believe it, as I got in to the relative safety of my lab my watch said eight.

©TheExpirement

Chapter Thirty Three

The box arrived promptly at 8.00. The sirens were sounding in my lab as I walked carefully up to the box. It had been carefully wrapped in brown paper and stuck with glue; the address was handwritten so I was careful not to rip any evidence as I didn't know if this was for real or a test. My heart and gut were telling me this was for real; I didn't want it to be, not today. Not today of all days. I took a deep breath and pressed the yellow switch on the console in front of me. Finally the sirens had stopped and my office filled up with a team collecting the data. I could see my boss pacing behind the group of scientists; he was worried I was worried. I carefully took apart the box piece by piece, studying everything as much as I could. I looked over to my office and I saw the angst on their faces, the lab, my lab was under attack.
Then I saw the reason for this box... a clock stopped at 8. I held it up to my boss who was stood silently watching.
He nodded. We were under attack full attack..
I couldn't believe what was happening
"Can I get Finn, Lucy and Darren in here please" I shouted over the tannoy
No-one answered
Finn then appeared at the lab doors, I buzzed him in
"Where are the others?"
"I think Lucy was in the building that blew up" he said quietly
"Darren?"
"I'm here sir, sorry I was helping them bring the bodies out"
"That's fine, are you both okay?"
"Yes sir" they said in unison
We continued to analyse the box, it was full of evidence.
As I let Darren and Finn analyse the contents of the box, I decided to look at the box itself

©TheExpirement

I then noticed a couple of things that were making me squirm deep inside
"Get me Jack please" I asked
Jack appeared a few minutes later, this time he decided to enter the lab as he could tell what I had found wasn't to be broadcasted
"What have you found?" he asked
"Possible copycat" I simply said
I showed him a bloody finger print on the box, similar to the ones that were on the boxes containing Daniels remains
I then turned it back over to see the mark that our security mail team make
"But that's when Jensen was already dead" he whispered
Finn and Darren, were still busy working on the clock they hadn't found anything unusual until
"Hey guys you might want to see this" Darren said
Jack and I walked over to them, I then saw the clock make and a newspaper article
"Isn't that the date when Jensen killed himself?" Finn asked
"Crap, get me my team" Jack shouted
A few minutes or so later I was stood outside my office, I needed air, all along Jensen had someone on the inside, I had made Darren and Finn swear that they wouldn't say anything about the date. I just hoped that I could trust them. I decided to go and help with the clean-up of the building that had blown up. Sadly my first sight was of Lucy's body, I was then told later that she had been in the same vicinity as the blast and badly burned from the resulting fire. My mind raced back to the moment we heard the blast, I then realised I had heard several blasts.
I quickly looked for my phone
"Jack, where did you store those other boxes?"
"What the ones that were dummies?" He asked
"Yeah, I think they were the bombs"

©TheExpirement

He then checked with his guy, they had indeed been put in the building.
We hung up and I raced towards Ralph's office
"Jean, Ralph" I said entering it
"James" they said
"Can we go back to your home, we need to run some CCTV footage"
"Sure"
"Not so fast" said a dark voice behind us
What are you doing here Philip?" Ralph said in a serious tone
"Well to finish the job, I was asked to do"
"Oh and what's that?" Jean asked
"To set off more explosions and to give the send-off Jensen really intended"
"Are you going to kill us all" Jack who had been one step of us already, was apparently already looking over the CCTV and found that it was indeed Philip Dowing who had entered the building this morning and set the bombs to go off. In the meantime, myself Jean and Ralph were facing a life and death situation
"Maybe I will kill you all, if I feel you are worth it" he said smugly
"Do as you wish" Ralph suddenly said
Jean looked at him, I saw him move his right hand twice it was out of sight from Philip
She calmly turned to Philip
"Now if you don't mind, I need to go home" She said picking up her bag and making her way to the door
"I'm sorry Jean, but that's not possible" Philip said stopping her in her tracks
I moved towards Ralph slowly, "You two can sit down and stop moving" Philip shouted at us
We did as we were told, in between the seat was a gun and well neither of us were afraid of using it
"So please can I leave" Jean continued to say

©TheExpirement

"NO" he shouted right in her face
She stepped slightly back "Well then fair enough have it your way"
She made a move and stabbed him in the chest, he fell to the ground and she well killed him. I had to turn away, I hadn't seen anyone kill anyone before, as for the dead body well let's just say my gut didn't thank me for being there. Ralph, Jean and I then made a run for it, we didn't know if the office or building was going to explode or not.
The whole of Darktronics was evacuated.

Chapter Thirty Four

It was now time to take stock of all the things that had been happening, it had been a massive rollercoaster of a ride and finally just for once it had stopped.
Fiona had wanted us to go away just the two of us and she meant flying somewhere, but because we didn't know if Jensen had left us any surprises Jack had advised us not to fly as he couldn't pre-check where we were going, but thank fully Jack had given us the all clear for us to go away in this country. Investigations were naturally continuing to make sure that the right people were all behind bars. Or dare I say it dead. It turned out that Philip Dowing was one of his sleepers and there were a couple of others that had been undercover so to speak within Darktronics. Over the next few months, we buried Felicity, Daniel and Lucy. All the other employees who had died in the fire and explosion were laid to rest. It was one emotional rollercoaster and I needed it to stop. There were still families arranging funerals, the toll of the dead reached in to the 60's, I didn't dare ask the teams how many had life changing injuries. Ralph had ordered us not to return to work until Jack had given the all clear. We spent our days with Fiona's mum and dad and enjoyed re-decorating our house, for a fresh start. It was my first week back, as Fiona was now three months pregnant it was decided by everyone that it was safer for her to be at home. For a while she was a caged animal, but when I realised that all was going to be fine, I allowed her to do some jobs we had planned. I had always been a worrier but she wanted me to let her be herself. When I had found out that, she was carrying my child I was being extra sensitive. She understood, I was soon put back in my box when she lost her temper. I don't recall over what, but I realised that it was silly of me to cage her like this. We had been in the safe

house and been away from each other for too long and the horrors we had seen had been too much. So I had to let her be, otherwise I could have lost my Fiona and child. That had made me see sense and I remember giving the list of jobs to do, which she saw as a massive present. We kissed goodbye that morning and for the first time in a long time we felt normal. I took a deep breath as I for the first time walked back in to reception. Just beyond the armed guards, which had now doubled, Ralph stood there with a big smile on his face. I went through the checks and felt relieved when the receptionist said "A very big welcome back Mr Folster" I smiled and thanked her very much. It was nice to be wanted back and it was nice to start feeling normal again. Ralph greeted me just by the sliding doors

"Good Morning" I said offering my hand out

Instead Ralph dropped formality and hugged me

"Morning James, welcome back" he then said

We laughed, oh how good that felt to finally laugh again

As we walked past the wall of remembrance, my eye caught sight of all the new hooks that were ready for the people who had recently gone. It was a realisation of just how bad the last few months had been.

I took a deep breath as we walked in to the corridor; we took the lift and then went up to Ralph's office.

"Wow" I suddenly said as we walked in the door

"Great isn't it" he said

His office which used to have minimal in it was now cosy, with a soft seating area to entertain guests, and his desk was now untidy.

"Sit down" Ralph said opening up a new cupboard

"Thanks" I replied putting my stuff down by the new leather couch

He then walked over and offered me a selection of soft drinks

"Posh" I said looking over at his now open mini bar

"Yes it is, it's all thanks to my new PA" which turned out to be a close friend of Jeans

I was glad that things had begun to change around here. We had lost a lot of dear friends and we needed our luck to change. This was a simple step in the right direction. Ralph and I then caught up

"So you going to be a dad" he said

"Yeah, it seems strange, after well everything" I replied, I must of look worried

"Sure its worrying James, but seriously don't worry you'll be fine" he said

I smiled, it was refreshing, Ralph had three children Raymond, Zac and Kaliey all of them were now living in different countries. I noticed a family photo up on the wall

"Ah yes, the crazy three, all taking after their dear mother and going on their own adventures, Kaliey though will be over here soon as she has some news" Ralph said beaming, it was nice to see him smile.

"Right then sadly we must talk work" he then said coming out of his thoughts about his family

"Yes sir, I was wondering what my job will be" I said sitting up straight, I was hoping that the job I would come back to would be something familiar rather than something new.

"Well I think you are now able to train others, so we will give you an apprentice for six months at a time" Ralph said firmly

"An apprentice sir?"

"Yes, I think this company needs fresh faces in the testing department, but to ensure safety I think we need to get them testing before we go for real, if you follow me Mr Folster"

"Yes I do sir; do you have a programme ready for me to follow?" I asked

"No, I want you over the next two months come up with one, when you are done and we have agreed we will then let loose our first

apprentice, that way you can be there for Fiona, and for goodness sake take the first two weeks of summer off and take Fiona away somewhere"
"Yes sir, I will be off to the travel agent as soon as I can"
"Jack is waiting for you James, don't let me down"
And with that I picked up my bits, shook Ralphs hand and bid him goodbye. But just before I left the room, I turned to him and asked, "Sir, is it okay to call you Dad when we are away from work"
He looked at me and simply smiled. I returned home from work feeling quite chuffed; Fiona had left me a note on the kitchen table.
"In bed, not been well, dinner is in the fridge"
She had been suffering with a cold and it had been a surprise finding out she was expecting.
We had been in total shock; I still remember it like it was yesterday. We were sat down in our room, it was just after our final funeral that we had attended together, we had tried to go to everyone, but it had been a great strain on us all, so from then on we shared the burden, but even that got too much at times.
"You okay my dear?" I asked not knowing if she was coping with all the horrors we had seen
"I don't know, it's been so stressful" she replied looking at me with tears in her eyes
I cuddled her tightly
"We'll be okay now" I wasn't sure myself, but there was no way I was going to have my girl stressed out. I was tired and wanted to sleep, but my thoughts about all those that had died was keeping me awake, I needed to calm down somehow
Fiona yawned and stretched as she stood up from the chair
She had been notably different over the past few weeks; I had assumed it was all to do with the horrors.
She then walked in to the bathroom saying "I'm going to have a shower"

I put on the television to keep myself awake, all our stuff from the weeks away were still unpacked, I began to open the odd suitcase and started putting the clothes in to piles.

As I sat back down, I was flicking through the channels when Fiona came out of the bathroom with a massive smile on her face and yet tears running down her cheeks.

"Hello daddy"

I wasn't sure how to react at first, but then as it dawned on me I suddenly realised just how amazing it felt. I was going to be a dad, and we were going to be parents. After all these horrors I was over the room, I went over to her and kissed her. It made me smile thinking of that moment, even though we had been through a lot. It was a wonder that we got through it all. Anyways I was feeling quite chuffed I had managed to book time off for me and Fiona to have our week away. The boss Ralph had promised us that we could have a week away on the house. It was very generous considering we could of gone anywhere, however we decided to go to the Lake District. Jack and I had a plan and that was all that was worrying me at the moment.

©TheExpirement

Chapter Thirty Five

The next day Jack and I flew up to the Lake District and the business had brought our cottage, they decided it made sense to have a base, as some people would be working this way.
I remember walking through the streets and finding a cottage, I could even picture Fiona here and I whilst I didn't want to dare dream about bringing our child here, so not to jinx anything I could picture family holidays here. I was over the moon when Jack had arranged the purchase with the owners. Luckily it was empty, Whilst Jack and his minions went about sorting security I went in to the nearest local town.
There I saw it and there I brought it.
Now I was feeling really chuffed
But as I came out of the shop I heard a clicking sound, it sounded like the clock that had been in the box, I jumped hoping that I wasn't being too obvious as then I noticed it was only a tourist taking a picture of the shops own sign, phew these few months had indeed made me nervous.
I smiled at the photographer who simply smiled back, I wondered if they had noticed my jump. I took a deep breath which calmed me down and I went for lunch in the local pub and there I met Jack.
"Yo dude, you get what you need?" he said as I sat next to him
"Yeap, just got get some courage now"
We laughed
He had already got me a pint of my favourite bitter and we sat and chatted for bit
"Reminds me of when we first met" Jack said as we were handed our pie and chips by the waiter
"Thanks, and yes Jack it does" I said
We tucked in to our food and my mind took me back to when we met back in 1998

©TheExpirement

It was an old fashioned pub like this one with a fire roaring in the corner, I had gone in there to get my dinner as I couldn't be bothered to cook that evening
I smiled at the bar tender who was a young brunette and ordered my beer and food

"No chance" said a guy who was propping up the bar as she walked out of sight
"I'm sorry" I said
"She is already taken"
"Ah okay, and you are?" I asked
"Jack McGiver"
"And is it you who has taken her?" I replied
"Well firstly I shall ask you your name, and then I shall tell you"
"James Folster"
"Well Mr James, nope, she is taken by the other waiter"
I smiled and walked over to a vacant table and sat and drank my pint of beer.
After a while and once I had finished my food, Jack came over to my table
"Fancy a game of pool?"
"Sure"
We played pool and then we walked home,
"So I was expecting you" he said as we were clear of the pub entrance "Oh, Darktronics are you?" I asked
"Yeah, here to formally offer you a job, starting next year?"
"Cool." I replied I had several offers from them and when you were approached that meant they were extremely serious about you.
"Your good at pool, come and play here" he said handing me a business card. I went on to play in a league and Jack was captain, we became good friends and he was a welcome face at Darktronics

©TheExpirement

when I started. Back in the pub in the Lake District we were on pudding
"Shame they haven't got a pool table" Jack mumbled
We hadn't played in years, we both had to take our leave from the pool league due to our jobs. "Yeah, shame, never mind, have to start heading back anyway" I said looking at my watch, we had been there a few hours, we were picked up and driven back to the helicopter pad where our lift home waited. Now I had to stop worrying about how I was going to propose to Fiona and to keep it all a secret.

©TheExpirement

Chapter Thirty Six

We arrived back from holiday engaged and with a strong feeling that things were going to get better. We had a wedding and a baby to plan for, it was nice to have normal things to look forward too. Jack had reassured me that things had been fine whilst we were away. I was pleased to see our house looking well just homely and Fiona was looking forward to finishing off some jobs.

The next day Sunday, Fiona was positively beaming when she walked in from the garden early afternoon; it was our last day before work, it was a day to savour. The sun was shining and she had wanted to start to grow her own vegetables and make a child friendly garden area.

"You are looking pleased with yourself" I said wondering if she had done more than just planting vegetables. I tried to stand up and peek out of the window, but she stopped me

"You know peeking at surprises means forfeits young man" she said cuddling up to me

"Just feel good today" she said

"It would seem so young lady" I replied as she then moved on to my lap

"So I have finally put up those shelves in the nursery" I said quite proud of myself

"Oh mummy has to check this" Fiona said getting up and quickly moving towards the stairs

"Hey no need to check" I said hoping that my efforts were up to 'mummy's' standards

I laughed as I then ran quickly up the stairs

"Not bad daddy" Fiona shouted not realising that I was now behind her

I took a moment looking at my beautiful wife to be

"Time for daddy and mummy to have a treat then" I said

©TheExpirement

"ooh Chinese daddy?" Fiona asked enthusiastically
I nodded
It was a nice to be calling each other mummy and daddy as we had to get used to being parents, something that was going to take a massive change.
I went back down stairs and found the takeaway menu and rang through our order we had our usual and I decided to order extra spare ribs, I was feeling extra hungry.
Fiona then joined me on the couch as we waited for dinner to arrive, it wasn't long before it did.
As we tucked in to our chicken and mushroom soup and extra prawn crackers and don't forget the extra ribs, I got up from the couch as we decided to relax and eat rather than formal dinner. I walked in to the kitchen and poured some water for us both when the phone rang. For some reason my gut lurched, maybe something then was telling me that all this horror wasn't over, but I grabbed the phone, but Fiona had already done so in the lounge. As I walked back in, I saw her face and I nearly dropped the glasses of water, my dammed gut was always right.
I steadied the glasses on a side table and listened to the conversation
"Dad what's wrong?"
I couldn't quite hear what her dad was trying to say
I was worried.
"Okay we'll make our way over" Fiona said and hung up
"They received another letter, but it's about mum" Fiona told me
I was worried, Fiona was holding something back
I sat down next to her and asked
"Hey, what's your gut saying?" I asked sternly
"It didn't sound like Dad fully" Fiona said looking really worried
"What do you mean?" I asked
"I mean it sounded like an impression of him" she said

I grabbed my phone out of my pocket and decided to ring Jack, there was obviously someone trying to spoil the party. Jack had warned us there maybe a few people who might of liked all the horrors towards Darktronics.

"Should we go?" asked Fiona who was near to tears

"Don't cry, no we should wait, I think Jack will be best placed to deal with this" I said trying to keep Fiona relaxed.

I had tried calling Jack, but the phone was constantly engaged, the longer it went on the more I worried.

Fiona was now laid out on the couch trying not to worry if there was anything wrong with her parents.

We had tried calling several times to her dad and mum but there was nothing.

Then finally Jack called me back

Jack then phoned me back

"Hey Jack"

"Fiona got a funny call from her dad, but she said it was like an impression"

"Yeah don't worry James, we were listening"

"You were checking on us still?" I asked

"Yeah we thought we'd keep an eye on you, look man I was worried, I don't want anything to hurt your kid and Fiona"

"Thanks Jack, you're a good mate. I think. Look Fiona's parents"

"James, you were good to wait…Patrick and Samantha are fine, there is nothing wrong here"

"What do we do?" I asked, my mind was racing was this something new, a joke a sick one at that or just someone playing with us"

"Wait there, don't answer the phone or door and I will text you with a code when I reach you" And with that we waited again Fiona was relieved that her parents were fine, but she understood that our lives, our unborn child could be in danger.

"Why would Jack keep an eye on us still?" she asked as we turned on a music channel.

"I think he wants to be extra sure" Now there was not much else to do but wait.

I woke to a text coming through on my phone two hours later I received a code, I rang Darktronics and confirmed the code. Jack appeared at our front door. I was relieved to see him, but I was surprised to see him so quickly

"Helicopter"

"Wow, they must really blow the bank"

"Yeah, but hey well done for waiting"

"It was Fiona's gut feeling"

He gave Fiona a big hug, Jack was going to be Godparent to our child, he was very much part of our lives.

Jack and his colleagues checked our place out and tried to reassure us that nothing bad was going to happen.

Jack stayed over so that we would feel safe, but in the morning there was a letter on the mat I opened the letter and my heart sank as I read it out loud

"Dear James,

Well done for passing these challenges I have set you.

Question you must now ask yourself is the baby yours?

Don't worry you'll hear from me soon.

Regards R."

I could feel the rage building inside me and I need to punch something. I nearly broke the wall, I was so angry and Jack had to restrain me

"We will get them" he said

Little did we know we were being watched.

©TheExpirement

197 —Expirement Series

©TheExpirement

Chapter Thirty Seven

The day was Thursday when we had our son; Frederick Jack was born in the early hours and weighed in at a very healthy 7lb 5oz. I remember ringing Jack, Ralph and then Fiona's parents and telling them the good news. They were all over the moon and couldn't wait to cuddle him. Cuddling him for the first time was for Fiona and me the most special moment we have probably had in our entire lives.

As for parenting Fiona was a natural, she had decided that she wasn't going to follow all of the parenting books exactly but use their advice when her instincts weren't strong. For those of you wondering, I did my part I got up early on weekends to calm Frederick down or change his nappies. Jack who was Fredericks Godfather popped over in the fourth week, he had already brought him loads of gifts, but today he just brought himself. Sadly someone else, who at that point had a challenge for me, was again going to make our lives a misery; I was in the kitchen when I noticed there was a package at the back door. The back door was slightly ajar and I saw a clear plastic bag.

My instinct was to call Jack and have this placed locked down, but I decided I couldn't and I decided to just read the note that was attached which simply said "Are you the dad?" Again with this question, it hadn't been too long ago when we had received the letter from R asking the same question, Jack who had tried his best to track the owner had found some rogue admirers of the late Jensen Lyons and he had found that they were going to continue his evilness. So once they were safely locked up we had at that time assumed we had resolved this issue.

My stomach churned, it was now a month since my darling son had been born; we had been hopeful that we had seen the last of this evil ness. However, we suddenly had more proof that someone else was behind this, I put on some gloves and took the bag and the letter and put it in to my office which I quietly did not alerting anyone else to the issue just yet.

I took a deep breath and simply smiled and walked back in to the lounge.

I knew Jack could tell something was up, but on a serious note I wondered if we were being watched and that made me jumpy. The day was Thursday and these Thursday's were not about to get any better.

That evening, Jack and I were enjoying a nightcap and as we sat talking I heard a noise coming from the kitchen. Fiona was already in bed and Frederick was sound asleep, I nearly jumped out of my skin.

"What's the matter?" Jack looked at me extremely concerned.

"I need you to read something" I replied

I took him into my office and showed him the package from earlier.

"Look try not to worry, I am sure this is just some follower doing orders not knowing that Jensen is dead"

"It bloody better be Jack, I can't be sitting here thinking someone opened our door with no noticeable break in and well my son Jack."

"I know," he hugged me I needed the comfort. I needed more than just a hug I needed to know who had done this to our family.

The wind continued to batter the back door which was what I had heard earlier and just before Jack and I turned in for the night he checked the door and noticed that it had been slightly damaged, something that I had clearly missed.

"Look, don't worry, I'll fix it." He laughed and rummaged in one of the drawers I prayed he hadn't found the posh cutlery but he had found an old screwdriver and he managed to realign the lock. I wasn't convinced, but I to be fair, I didn't hear a thing again that evening.

©TheExpirement

The next morning, Fiona was up early feeding Frederick. So was Jack and he cooked us a full english. I was impressed, it was now Friday and well, I felt somewhat relieved for some reason, and I felt good. Nothing else had happened and Jack had taken all the evidence away for analysis and I felt comforted that I had a weekend coming up with my family, just the three of us.

It was back to work on Monday for me, Fiona had a few more months off, but a package arrived on Friday afternoon for her.

"Expecting something?" I asked to carry in a box which was marked from our local bookshop

"Yes thanks, " she smiled and grabbed the box from me; Frederick was asleep and just watching him sleep melted my heart.

I turned to see Fiona looking at a set of books which were a mix of textbooks and exercises.

"Not work?" I asked full well knowing that she had been in touch with Jean her boss and our dear friend.

"Research and training" Fiona replied, looking at the front of this thick looking text book which said analysis of fire scenes.

Fiona wanted to keep her eye on her work, and part of the training was an exam, which was based on theory of fire and how you can analyse the evidence. Jean had agreed that when she wanted to return from maternity leave that she could become a teacher of analysing evidence. I was impressed as this wasn't something I realised they did, Jean had the developed a set of modules for secondary school all the way to university about fire evidence analysis and how important it was to learn from all fires. It was now going be Fiona's job to teach other colleagues on the evidence analysis.

I picked up one of the books which contained several exercises, a page was marked in the corner and I turned to it.

There was a picture of Darktronics and the fire that had been made from Jensen's evil. Jean had put a note in, "We have to learn from

this dark evil, be strong through this part"
I thought that was kind
"Everything alright?" Fiona asked
"Yes, it's a good book, I'm impressed."
I focused back on my son and we spent the rest of the day with a walk in the park and we fed the ducks.
I wondered what was ahead of us and then I got a text from Jack.
"Seems like Ruben Oliver is alive, will see you at Ralph's on Monday have a good weekend."
I decided not to tell Fiona and we filled the weekend with as much fun as we could.

©TheExpirement

Chapter Thirty Eight

I arrived at Ralph's house first thing Monday morning. I wanted to be at work, assigning new challenges to my new apprentices. That was a good job, I wanted to challenge them in new ways, and my plan was to have them work in Science for the first six months, then three months in Crime and then the last three months in the fire. Their second year would be spent in the area that they were good at. However, no, here I was having to deal with this evil man Ruben Oliver.

I took a deep breath and opened the door to the big house of Ralph Mearlow. It from the outside just looked like an average big house. Of course it did look rich, but average, inside though there was a lot of richness. As I entered the front room which was massive and contained a dining table I noticed a new set of paintings on the wall. They were a mix of portraits and landscapes; I looked closely and saw Z Mearlow as the signature.

My thoughts were disturbed by footsteps coming towards me, it sounded like high heels and as I turned to the sound I saw Sabrina, Ralphs niece walking along.

"Good Morning James, " she said

"Good Morning, you are looking lovely today" I replied, giving her a kiss on the cheek she was wearing a red dress and lots of jewellery

"Thank you, I am off out now, I believe Uncle and Jack are in the television room"

"Thanks, have fun"

It was nice to see her happy and relaxed. I continued to look at the paintings and then I heard the telling footsteps of Ralph.

I turned and started walking towards the far door which I knew would lead me to the television room.

"Ah, James there you are" Ralph said as I opened the door

"Sorry, was taken in by your son's paintings"

"Yes they are good"

"He is very talented."

"Yeah, you can meet him when he comes home"

We walked the rest of the way in silence. Ralph seemed calm and relaxed. I thought it would be hectic, if this Ruben Oliver was really alive, we would have everything in lock down.

As I walked into Jack was sitting down and was sitting there in just jeans and T-shirt, he wasn't looking himself.

"So James you received a text on Friday" Ralph said

"Yes, sir, I was told Ruben Oliver was alive"

"And can you tell me who sent you that text"

"Jack"

"Indeed."

"Jack, what's going on?" I asked

"I didn't send it."

"Okay, so someone is playing with us again, " I said, folding my arms, looking at Jack for just a glimmer of hope.

"Yes, now the thing is James we don't know who it is."

"Are we sure Ruben is dead?"

"Well, yes, but..." Jack mumbled

"But what?" I asked sternly wondering what the hell was going on.

"There were two." Said a female voice behind me.

"Jean, how are you?" I asked greeting her with a kiss on the cheek

"Very well thank you."

"Goodness yes. So can someone explain what we know about this Ruben?"

"I will, my dear" Jean said, taking her seat

"Now do you remember Rory?"

"Yes, the poor guy who shot himself"

"That's the one. He and his twin went to school with Ruben. Now it was always strange that they had identical burns. Turned out that Ruben had done something very chilling to both of them, he had

burnt them both. Whilst I won't go into details, the fire that was later set in their room was to make it look like an accident. No-one questioned it, because the boys were too injured.
Now Ruben seemed like a loner, but I remember seeing him in the school grounds, talking to someone."
She paused.
"I believe it was his twin brother."
"So does he have an identical?"
"Not according to their birth records. Daniel Oliver was born three minutes after Ruben and from the announcement in their local paper, it simply says Mr and Mrs Oliver are proud parents of two twin boys Ruben and Daniel."
"But are we believing the records?"
"Well, yes, as that's all we have to go on"
"Do we have a photo of Daniel?"
"Nope" Jack said grumbly, "Okay, but surely they would have gone to the same school"
"Yes they did. But Daniel never appeared in any of the photos, it was always Ruben." Jack then said
"Okay, so are we assuming this is just some case of revenge."
"Yes, we are in now, but the package that you received leads to Ruben"
"or Daniel?"
"True."
The truth was we didn't know yet if the guy that had been killed by Jensen was Daniel or Ruben. Now we just had a maniac on the loose and we didn't know quite literally where to find him.
I sat down for the first time that day and found myself wondering what hell was about to be unleashed on us now.
We had to find clues and we didn't really have anywhere to start as far as we were concerned all of the clues led us to a dead body.
How I longed for just a normal day.

©TheExpirement

"Okay, so what do we do next?" I asked, wondering if someone had a cunning plan.
"To be honest James, we just might have to wait."
"For the love of…" I shouted
"James, dear" Jean spoke sternly interrupting my explosion of anger
"Sorry, we waited last time and it cost us our friends' lives."
"I know, but even our leads have run cold" Jack said, looking a bit more lively, Ralph had gotten us coffee and we needed a pickup.
"Okay, so we know he questions the parental legitimacy of my son."
"Right, so does he question his own?" Asked Ralph

We were thinking on the same lines.
"You think his parents aren't his parents?"
"Indeed, or something like that."
I could see Jean thinking, she then turned to me
"So if he is questioning that, we must assume that he has issues with Fire."
"Okay, so we need to be focused. We need to do our research of this Mr Oliver whichever he is, we must find him before he does damage." Ralph said
Jean then picked up her bag and kissed Ralph and was about to leave
"Oh Jean, Fiona says thanks for the books and the note."
Jean then turned to me
"No problem, dear"
I just hoped that no-one would get harmed like before. I had my son to protect and I wasn't about to let this Ruben Oliver bloke do anything nasty.
Ralph was busy talking to Jack and I looked at my watch, I thought I should be getting back to work but Ralph had other ideas. He turned to me as Jack walked out of the other door to the side of the television screens.

"So James, I need you with me today, " he simply said
"Okay, I will need to let my team know"
"They have been told that you won't be in"
"Where are we going?" I asked, not sure what Ralph had planned for me, but nothing could get the feeling that Mr Oliver was going to ruin everything.

We walked through the house, and whilst it was feeling like home, I still could get lost quite easily. We reached the library and I was still taken aback by the number of books that he had and I suddenly remembered a book I should have returned by now. He must have been reading my mind.

"Don't worry about the book James"

All I could do was smile.

He was looking for something in his old oak wooden desk, it was a key but it too was wooden. He then went up to the far left bookcase and just like we've seen on film a secret (well secret to me) door opened up from the bookcase.

"Welcome to my own lab" Ralph said

"I am not surprised" I replied

There it was a full lab, just like we had back in Darktronics, everything I needed. He had others in the house so I was very intrigued as to why he had it stored away.

He didn't say a word as we walked through the automatic doors, the bookcase door had shut behind us; the lights came on as we walked down a short corridor which was cold but felt clean and sterile. I wanted to ask all the questions that were racing around in my head, but I couldn't. I just somehow knew that he was about to give me some answers.

©TheExpirement

Chapter Thirty Nine

"Welcome to my den, or man cave as Jean puts it" Ralph said as we had entered another room which was at the end of the corridor. So that was the lab, corridor and now a massive room covered in photos, newspaper articles, you name it, it was here.
"What the.." I said staring at the walls covered at what I would initially call evidence.
"I know a lot to take in, but don't worry we have all day" He said sitting down in one of his nice leather office chairs.
"So explain to me what you see James"
I calmed myself down, there was a lot of information to be processed.
"Okay, so on this wall we have all of Jensen Lyons antics, then this wall" as I walked to each section I looked closely and explained what I saw
"Here we have Jack and Paul, then there's little old me and the late Philip and to finish we have the lovely Jean."
"Excellent, so now let's think of the why" he said smiling
"Well you are in charge of one of the most important companies in the world, having a close circle of people is key and keeping an eye on them is just as important as filling out the paperwork."
I was impressed, he had notes on each of us beside the photos
"What I am not quite understanding is why you are showing me"
"James, I am dying."
Quietness came over the room, not even the sound of us breathing could be heard.
Then the shock came and I felt cold and then the questions filled my head.
"How long?" was all I could muster
"Well we have some years, the doctors told me this morning, but they can't be sure. I have a rare cancer, and yes for many years we

have been trying to slow it down for now I am in remission but they say it can come back with a vengeance at any time."
"Does anyone else know?"
"Yes, Jean knows, my children know and now you."
"Sorry to hear it Ralph"
"Thank you James, I am sorry that I had to tell you in such a brutal way I suppose."
"This is why this is secret?" I suddenly asked
"Yes, they did their tests in the lab on me, so that it could be kept hidden away from the public eye so to speak"
"But this room?"
"Dedicated to finding the right people and keeping an eye on my enemies"
He looked up at the wall about Jensen; he was indeed an enemy of Darktronics and therefore Ralph.
I took a seat in the other big leather office chair, it was extremely comfortable and I was taking in all what I had been told when he handed me a book.
"Take a look" he said
It was a dark red book, kind of like a photo album the sort you get for special occasions. Inside as I opened it up there was a paragraph handwritten
"To my dear son, make sure you have a great adventure and look after yourself, Yours and all my love Dad"

Then as I turned the page, it was a mixture of handwritten notes and photographs, paper cuttings.

It was the timeline of the creation of Darktronics, all his hard work that had gone in to the making of the company was all written down.
"Take a look at page 246" Ralph said smiling and looking thoughtful
As I turned the page, it was my dad and Ralph smiling together, I

took a deep breath it was an amazing picture. But then something else took my eye

"What is it James?" Ralph said

"I just realised something"

"You took this picture when you were first diagnosed"

"Ah you spotted it?"

"Dad is hiding your hospital wristband"

"He noticed it just in time, but it just sticks out"

Then it dawned on me, why Ruben and Daniel might not have been seen together.

"Daniel is ill" I spluttered out

"Sorry?" Ralph asked

"Think about it, why else would he miss the school photos. His brother was hiding his brother's illness; they must look similar if not identical."

We sat there in silence, then Ralph grabbed his mobile and threw it to me, "Phone Jack" he said

"Sure, I will get him to test the body"

Jack thanked me for the news and said he would look and get the tests done as soon as he was back.

He was working off the grid today for Ralph, I wasn't about to get involved in what he was doing as I was sure I would be told if it was needed.

Ralph was now rummaging in the filing cabinets and found some papers, I wasn't sure what was coming up next, but I was surprised.

"This James, is a copy of my will"

He handed me the will and I read it. There was my name against the Darktronics business.

"But…" I started to say I was in shock, Ralph was now pouring out two whisky's. I needed something just to steady my nerves.

"Yes, I have children, three wonderful children that have never wanted or need this business. I will let you decide James, I need you to accept today, we can never speak of this again." He was quite stern when he said that, this was serious. The man that had become my second father was dying, he was handing the family business over to me and all the trials and tribulations that went with it to me. I was scared, I was excited, all the emotions were flooding my brain then Jack rang us back.

"Hey Sherlock" he said laughing

"Okay, enough with the compliments" I replied as Ralph hit the speaker phone button

"It would seem we have Daniel in the morgue, we have found his medical records, he had alopecia and severe eczema."

"Blimey, so what made us realise he was Daniel this time?"

"We found the medical records and we have just found that the finger prints are copies of Ruben's whose are on file, and DNA well that matched too, so Ruben must have done something to his brother."

"Okay, so we now know Ruben is alive and well."

We hung up. It was hard to comprehend what exactly Ruben was trying to achieve. Had he killed his brother?

My attentions turned to the other pressing matter at hand, Ralph looked at me, he could see that my mind was very much on overtime, wondering what the right thing to do.

We had been in the office for some time, my stomach was beginning to growl and I hoped that Ralph hadn't heard it.

"We can have lunch as soon as you have decided" He then said laughing, I thought he was serious, but then lunch appeared in a dumb waiter which was hidden in one of the shelving units, just beside the door way.

"So tell me if I take on Darktronics what are the terms and conditions" I asked as I tucked in to my bacon and lettuce sandwich.

"Well its simple, run the company, the board does not have control over you as you will own all of the company, the only thing to worry about is if they give you a vote of no confidence. But they can't do that for five years."

"Five years?"

"It took my father's original business five years to get up and running when he first took over, so when he created Darktronics, he ruled that five years gives you time to get your feet under the table, learn the business and get the confidence of your workers."

"And your children won't come and bash the door down for their inheritance?" I had to ask it was a bit brutal but I was making a massive decision

"No, because Zac has taken on the art company over in Italy, we brought it for him for his 18th but now he runs it and said that when he has children they will take over that company. As for Kailey, well her fiancé is now running my wife's veterinary business in Africa and they are about to settle and have a family, and for Raymond well he is head of the Darktronics School in New York. I did ask him about running the business and he seemed very interested, but then he won funding to start up the Darktronics University, I had a chat with my lawyer and the board and they nominated you."

He passed me a signed letter titled Nominated Vote of Confidence Darktronics board. I was proud, and it sent a shiver down my spine.

"So what do you need me to do" I then said, finishing off a nice iced doughnut and a glass of lemonade.

"Sign here" he said

"Dad, I am willing to accept this grand offer" I said as I signed the form. There it was done; I was to be the owner of Darktronics. I just hoped that Ralph that I now called dad every so often, was going to stick around for a little bit longer. Because I knew, I still had a lot to learn.

More than I could have ever imagined.

I looked up at Ralph, who had a tear in his eye, he too was proud. He had found his heir and I was over the moon that he had enough

©TheExpirement

confidence in me to run this business of his behalf.
We hugged and then we finished our drinks and he topped up the whisky.

©TheExpirement

Chapter Forty

Yesterday seemed like a dream, the rest of the afternoon was learning all about Darktronics and what plans Ralph has for the company. It was a steep learning curve for me, but I took as much as I could in and more importantly I became even more part of Ralph's life and he told me more detail about his illness. I also learnt a little more about myself, but that for me is something I shall keep to myself just for now. I am now sat in my office in Darktronics. My new team of apprentices are currently in the fire department today and are learning actually how to fight fires. Scary stuff if you ask me, but they all seemed to be looking forward to it.

Since yesterday's revelations, I could not tell anyone about being given Darktronics, it is a secret, if I let slip I lose the lot. And soon enough my thoughts turn to that evil man Ruben Oliver. We were confident he is not lying in our morgue and that is his brother, we now need a bit more detective work to find out if he has left us any more clues.

I look over my notes I have been scribbling down as I go, I wonder what will happen next, then I get a knock at my office door.

"Hey Jamie" I say as she walks in, she is from the fire department

"Hi James, I've been asked by one of your new team members to bring you this"

Jamie hasn't been in the fire department long, she is wearing full fire kit, I ask "How are they getting on with the fire tests today?" She simply smiles, and gives me their package, I am impressed, and they have met their deadline.

She leaves the office and I open up their assignments, they are all there and I begin to read.

I hope that they are doing well today, they have had mixed results so far, but I am pleased with their progress.

The rest of the day was taken up with the assignment markings, a

©TheExpirement

few odd packages were sent to my lab then I got to go home. Fiona and my dear son Frederick were in the lounge, Fiona was reading more of her textbooks, and Fred was wide-awake playing with some toys.
I wanted to tell Fiona of the greatest gift I had ever received that is of course after my son. However, Ralph did explicitly tell me I could tell no one not even my nearest and dearest.
Fiona knew something was up, but when I said it was between Ralph and me she understood that I really could not tell her.
Even though we had a lovely, evening together I could not shake the gut feeling that tomorrow was not going to be the best day.
I arrived at Darktronics late, it was raining, and after being up all night with Frederick I had rushed breakfast and realised that I could beat the traffic with the bike. No chance not in the rain, then as I came in through the main reception I nearly slipped, luckily for me the big rug with the Darktronics logo on it came to my rescue. I managed to dry my slippery shoes on it and found myself walking a bit more steadily through the corridor up to my office. Rock the cleaner and one of my best friends, had already been to the café for me and got me my coffee and iced doughnuts. Fiona had last week been on at me about this extra food, but today I needed it. I found solace in the coffee and doughnuts, only to find the computer system was down. It was as IT support put it a "Routine downtime, sorry its taking longer than we thought". Then just as I thought things couldn't get any worse they did. The phone rang, it was Ralph, he too was in a bad mood. "Can you get to my office asap" he sternly said, I knew he wasn't in a mood with me or more like I hoped he wasn't, but it was really going to be one of those days where everyone was in a bad mood.
As I got to his office, the door was already open, I stepped in as there was no-one around
"Ah James, please sit down" said Ralph who was suddenly behind

me causing me to jump a little.

"Good Morning sir" I said as I sat in the chair nearest his desk.

"I see you were late today"

I was about to explain, but he continued

"We all were, and as you can see all IT systems are down, which I think we can take as a warning."

"Oh is this Mr Oliver?"

"We don't know yet, but one of our crime people are checking our professional hackers, just making sure we haven't screwed up the upgrade again"

"Indeed, good idea"

"Now, the other issue is we have had an overload in packages being delivered overnight"

"What you mean unwanted packages?"

"Yes, like the ones you used to test, I know already this week we have sent you the odd one as we were getting strange packages again. I think we might be under attack, so I need my best people on them today and so your lab when you get back will be locked down and you will be working in there until we can clear the worst of it. I am sorry James, because of the IT you really are going to have to go back to basics. Just remember safety first, if you are not sure, we will get Dennis to blow them up out in the bomb disposal yard, but I need the evidence."

I took a deep breath, then I realised the day it was Thursday. Sadly I just knew too that Ralph was right, we were under attack and whilst we believe it was Ruben Oliver's doing we had to assume nothing and find the evidence we needed.

So I went to the café on the way back to my office, whilst the coffee and doughnuts had done I knew I would be in there for some hours, so I went and got a breakfast a fully cooked one. This would now keep me going to way passed lunch. We weren't allowed food in our lab for health and safety reasons, the only thing I could have in there was the water bottles and by the time I got in to my lab there were six of them already filled up and ready for me on the side of the labs console.

Back to basics rang in my ears that meant I had to assume anything was in the packages from bombs to poisons to well anything you can think of.

As I changed in to t-shirt and jeans, I texted Fiona to tell her that today wasn't a good day and that I loved her and Frederick loads. She replied quickly with her love you back and saying that she had every faith everything would be okay and that Jean was there with her.

Thank you Ralph I thought, he really did care about us all.

I then put my lab suit on and entered through the automatic doors, I was then fully sprayed down with a cleansing shower and Dennis my robot brought in the first package. It was just an ordinary plain brown envelope, the address was typed and I thought that it wouldn't have too many surprises. Thankfully, I was right, it was okay it was just a letter that was complaining about the way Darktronics vets were currently doing business and how they didn't look after the people enough whilst they were waiting for their animals to be seen. I wondered if this was Kailey and her fiancé business. So after checking for anything malicious I put it in the paper tray and pressed the buzzer for the next one.

The next one, was a little more interesting it was a dark blue box, it had newspaper articles stuffed inside of it and in the middle well was a dead mouse. I was not impressed, I love mice, I would have them as pets if Fiona would let me, but we have promised ourselves a pet rabbit when Frederick is a little older. Anyways the dead mouse was yet another complaint at the vets, I wondered if this was an attack on the vet business. I repacked up the mouse and sent it off to be dealt with, and I opened up the newspaper articles, they all had the same day on them, they were personalised papers the sort you can make on the internet. I put them to onside and then took on the next package; again it was another piece of mail which was another complaint, this time it was about the crime lab, then the next few after that were complaints about the Darktronics School.

I then realised what the pattern was, the day which was printed on all the packages were Thursday and then as I sat at the computer inside the lab area I also noticed another pattern they all had the same post mark. Now this wouldn't necessarily be the case even within our mailing system here we don't use the same post mark. The post system gets packages and post from all over the world, if its assigned to the Darktronics HQ, or Crime, Fire and Science. If any of the other sub businesses are sent here then we give them the HQ postmark and send it over to them. If it's for any part of the Darktronics businesses here then we give it our own postmarks which belong to each sub section. This allows us to audit, so the school one for instance should have been the normal post mark from the local post office, Darktronics HQ and then the school one when they received it.

I was now concerned, I believed that someone had just redirected all the post. They wanted to overload our system.

After typing up most of the evidence I then got the next package, this sent shivers down my spine. It was a clear plastic bag with a DNA kit inside. Also attached was a hand written letter.

"Dear Mr Folster, I hope this finds you well. I realise from your Doctors notes that you have not been to check with him the DNA profile of your supposed son. I realise this is a difficult choice for you, but I am going to make this simple, do it and you will find out the truth. Do not do it and you live the lie. Also the longer you leave it the more evidence I will send you. Yours R"

Well Ruben, you have my attention was all I could say, I pressed the buzzer and in walked Ralph and Jack in to my office.

©TheExpirement

They were looking at my computer, when I was able to get in to my office. I knew that there were plenty more packages to deal with, but I had to tell them about this one and my other findings.
"So you know I pressed the 'this isn't a test'"
"Yes, sadly I cant even spare your team to help" Ralph explained. This was very unusual.
Jack was still busy looking at my computer
"That's fine, its just that I have noticed a couple of trends, it seems someone has diverted our post, we are getting the normal complaints and not just for HQ but for the school and the vets. I noticed they all have the same postmark. Where they have a day printed they have Thursday on them."
"Good lord" Ralph spluttered out in a bit of shock.
"I believe Ruben has also sent me this"
I held up the DNA package and then handed to Jack who was suddenly listening in.
"That's the same as what was delivered to your house" he replied looking carefully at it. Ralph frowned, he apparently did not know about the one to my house.
"Yeah, and so if it's Ruben, something must have happened on a Thursday and now he is overloading the system" Ralph was about to speak when my phone went off, it was a text
"Where did you say my team of apprentices were?" I asked Ralph
"They are testing packages."
"Okay we are under attack, lock Darktronics down now." I said forcefully
Jack then read the text aloud after grabbing my phone out of my hand.
"Opened package in lab, Found a poison, dealt with it as per textbook, however, in medical as face is burning...Troy texted by Nurse Mayweather"

©TheExpirement

Ralph rushed out of my office and before we knew it Darktronics was on lockdown.

Chapter Forty One

For the rest of the day we were on lockdown, Ralph said that there must be a connection with Ruben and the fire and of course the day of Thursday. Once he had placed Darktronics in lockdown, he sent Jack off to check my apprentice over, I was worried about Troy and I wanted to know all the gory details. But then to my amazement, Ralph was changing; in to his jeans and t-shirt, we found these a lot cooler under the lab suits. Then he grabbed the other lab suit and put it on, he turned to me.
"Well let's get through these other packages James, I too would love to go home today"
We stood there working together for the first time, it was good, he was just as meticulous as me, Dennis the robot came in every so often with new bottles of water and updates of what else was happening around Darktronics.
Three hours in and we had come across more complaints and a lot more post for the vet business over in Africa. I also learnt about another new team in Darktronics which I never knew existed.
But that wasn't up for discussion right now, we were elbow deep in sewage, yep someone bless them had decided to send us a bucket of sewage. I was the one with the longer pair of gloves so, yeah you guessed it I was feeling around making sure there were no hidden surprises. We never knew where that one came from; a message came in from Kailey that they were expecting some samples, so not to throw all of them away, but sewage was definitely not on the list.
We were now sat in the office, we had reached midnight, the worst had been cleared and it was Ralph and I who were still working away, so much for going home today. The medical teams were working on Troy who was doing well, but it was still early days.
This we had decided was a test a massive test. I got a phone call from Fiona letting me know that Jean would be staying over with

her and Frederick so I could rest easy that she was being looked after. Ralph smiled when he too heard the news, and turned to me and said
"Want to have some fun tomorrow?"
"What about all the evidence?" I asked trying not to yawn at the same time.
"That's what the rest of the workforce are here for and you and I have earned a day off. Lets get home and clean ourselves up and get some well-earned rest."
"Yes sir" then I yawned and stretched and Ralph just burst in to laughter.
I laughed too, it was funny seeing him laugh this much
"You do make me laugh James, come on before you fall down"
He texted Jack on the way to the car and found that he was too getting some well-earned rest and that he would have a report for us tomorrow.
"Good, we will text him our locations tomorrow"
"Will we not be in work?" I asked
"Nope, I need your expert help"
"Okay" I said yawning yet again
"Sorry" I managed to get out
"No worries son"
That was the second time this week he had called me son, the first time was after I had signed the papers, he had said how proud he was to have me as a son. I smiled and the motion of the car sent me to sleep.
The next morning I was woken by the smell of bacon coming through the corridors, my door was slightly open. As I awoke I found a glass of fresh orange juice by the side of my bed, I drank it one I was incredibly thirsty as I sat up from the bed there were a pair of slippers, as I was putting them on the smell of the bacon got stronger. My stomach growled and I walked out of the bedroom

and turned left down the corridor, following the smell. As I reached the kitchen, I saw Ralph cooking in his pyjamas.

"Good Morning James" He said, smiling as he got some eggs from the fridge

"Good Morning, and may I have it poached sir" I said in a funny polite voice

"Of course, now sit down and have your breakfast" he replied in a very fatherly manner

I laughed and did as I was told, as I sat down I wondered what today would bring

"So then dad what are you going to be doing today?"

"Well, firstly we eat our breakfast son, then we are doing to do the whole man thing of DIY"

I laughed out loud, this was going to be interesting.

We had breakfast, which was cooked to perfection

"I didn't realise you were such a good cook" I said whilst finishing off my cup of tea

"Well Jean and I are spending more time together and we like to cook, so I thought I should practice. Now come on, time to get dressed, we need to go shopping. Meet me at the top of the stairs in fifteen minutes"

I did, we were still on the top floor this was the first floor kitchen, I quickly got washed and dressed, I met Ralph at the top of the stairs. He then motioned for me to go in to a room, there was an empty big room. But it was very well decorated with fresh paint, there was a dark red feature wall at the end, then the rest of the walls were cream.

"This is going to be Jean and my master bedroom"

"Excellent, so we are doing what today?"

"We need to put up the bed which is being delivered this afternoon and we need to go and buy some other furniture."

That was our day quite literally, we drove to the furniture store and

©TheExpirement

Ralph was browsing an oak wooden wardrobe that wouldn't look out of place in Narnia, when Jack entered the store.
"Ah you found us" Ralph said even though his head was firmly in the wardrobe and wouldn't have seen Jack enter the store behind him.
"Yes sir, now we need to talk"
Ralph mumbled something and then took out a notebook and wrote something down, he ripped it out of the notebook and handed it to a conveniently placed store helper and it all suddenly dawned on me that this was all orchestrated.
"Great" I said out aloud
"And the penny drops" Ralph said with a big smile
"Okay, so if we are not really doing DIY and shopping then what the hell are we doing here" I asked really confused
"No really we are, just we needed a safe place to talk" Ralph said putting his arm round me
Jack though wasn't saying a word
"Okay, so lets go and try a new sofa" Ralph said when I realised that Jack was far, far too quiet. We sat on a very comfy leather sofa and Jack sat on a giant bean bag and at one point I thought he looked a bit green, I was feeling extremely concerned and was about to ask a question when Ralph started talking
"So, I asked the store to close for a day the people you see around us shopping are actually agents from Darktronics. They if you like are my bodyguards, we haven't yet found out why Darktronics was attacked yesterday, but we do know that someone did divert all the post to our headquarters as a test."
He paused, he held up his hand to stop me from asking questions
"We found another letter from Mr Ruben Oliver saying *"Dear Darktronics, because James will not and has not followed my instructions you will all be tested. Enjoy the post"*
I sat there in silence, he had made this personal but I did not know

why, Jack forced a smile to try and make me feel better but now it just felt like this was all my fault.

I just felt like it was, the amount of guilt and poor Troy was seriously injured.

I closed my eyes for second to stop myself from freaking out.

"So do you want me to take a test?" I asked bluntly

"I don't think it will stop him" Ralph said

"But we have to try" Jack advised

"But this will kill Fiona, she will never trust me again"

Jack looked angry

Ralph just glared at him

"I can tell you two have already been at loggerheads over this."

"Yes, we have" I admitted.

"Look son, seriously I don't think it will stop him, but he has made this personal to you and yet with the burning of Troys face apparently Jean went and saw him and saw that it was very alike to what the twins suffered. I think that there is more to come"

"He wants to find the weakest of us all" Jack said

At that point we were all resigned to the fact that we were under attack by this Ruben Oliver and whilst we had found an enormous amount of evidence we just didn't and couldn't find him.

The store helper then came over to Ralph and handed back the piece of paper, Ralph read it and said "Yes thanks if they can put it in the truck outside that would be most helpful"

As he then followed the store helper I noticed the logo on one of the bodyguards hooded tops, it was the Darktronics logo but underneath it said "D.I.U"

This was the unit that I never knew we had until now, Darktronics Intelligence Unit was what it stood for so Jack told me on the way back to Ralphs house. They were set up for incidents like that Jack was one of the first recruited, you start out in another department and you learn as much as you can, you never tell anyone you are part of the unit until you are brought out on a job like today.

I was impressed, surprised and at the same time overwhelmed by the fact that I could actually be running this place one day, I still had tons to learn.

The rest of the day was as it was said this morning, "DIY". However what wasn't mentioned this morning was the beer, things seemed to go a bit better the more beer we drank, that was until Ralph put a nail through his thumb and a semi angry looking Jean walked in to the hospital A&E department and took us all home.

It was fun and I enjoyed every minute of it, but in the back of my mind, I couldn't shake off the feeling I had in the store that morning. Was I to blame, was I really the father of my child and now doubt serious doubt had crept in and I spent the evening having to hide it from my dear Fiona and son.

The next morning with a cracking headache I took the bus to work, it was time to go back in and see what was next in store for me.

I opened my office door to find Jack looking how I felt

"Hangover" we both said and smiled

"What can I do for you this fine morning?" I asked him whilst drinking another pint of ice cold water

"I wanted to know if you thought about doing the test"

I could tell this was breaking him as much as me, I took my time I carried on a drank the water and took some tablets too.

"To be honest I don't know, I want to because if it makes him stop then great, but what if the test breaks me and Fiona and he then carries on a kills one of us I mean who knows whatever I do I am in a lose, lose situation."

He nodded, I understood why he wanted me too, but this time I had to ask Fiona and that wasn't going to be an easy conversation.

Chapter Forty Two

There were no more fun days for us men; Jean hadn't let Ralph out for a while because whilst the nail in his thumb wasn't anything too serious it was the hangover and his mood that apparently had upset her a little. As for my being let out well Fiona wasn't too fussed as long as I was still getting up on my turn during the night, but work had hit its usual busy period and to be fair playing a bit of pool down the pub was enough for Jack and I.
The weeks went by without incident; Jack did not push me about the test because he knew I would know the right time to talk to Fiona about it. In addition, with it all going quiet on us, we were feeling a little optimistic that Ruben Oliver had maybe turned his attentions elsewhere.
This was until I arrived home on Wednesday; Fiona was worried sick about taking her test the next day.
"Darling you will be find you have studied loads"
This was her evidence exam, this was one of the hardest exams she would have to do, because it was theory and it was based on chapters that had a lot of history for us and the company.
"I know, I just.." Fiona began saying looking like she would burst in to tears yet again
I hugged her tight , we had decided to give her the space Patrick and Felicity had taken Frederick for the next two evenings. This was so that we could give Fiona space to worry about the exam and for me to take her out tomorrow night when it was all over. Perfect.
Fiona snuggled up to me on the sofa that night as we kept things easy, we had written key messages on index cards and she had done as much revision as she could physically do.
The next morning, I made her breakfast in bed and found out her lucky bracelet. She smiled and thanked me, I then left for work. She had another half an hour before she was due in. At the front doors

of Darktronics I was greeted by Jean
"How is she this morning" she asked kissing me on the cheeks
"Fine, better than last night"
"Good, I am sure she will be fine"
We went our separate ways and I went to my office and spent most of the morning clock watching.
I found myself lost in assignment reading from my apprentices, they were turning out to be a very useful asset to the business. My phone then rang, it was Fiona saying that she was finished and would go home to have a bath and relax. I smiled that meant the exam had gone extremely well; we just now had the agonising wait for the results, which was a whole month away.
After reading the assignments, I went down to the hospital to see Troy. I was impressed he was making amazing progress and he asked me to sit by him for a while. His mum bless her had been smothering him and he needed someone else to talk to.
"I want to come back, when I am up to it," Troy said quietly.
"Sure just don't rush it. We will have lots for you to do," I said with a smile.
He tried to smile but I saw him wince in pain.
I sat there for a while longer and read from his favourite car magazine to him, I was terrified as he went to sleep and his monitor started bleeping, it was only to say his heart rate had changed, the nurse came in and did some checks calmly and then went back out to in to the corridor. I said my goodbyes and followed the nurse, I caught up with her
"Hi, can I ask you a question?" I said hoping that she was not going to say, "You're not family"
"Yes James"
"Okay, thanks how long do you think he'll need?" I was wondering how she knew my name, but then I saw the Darktronics logo up on the wall and as we reached her station, I noticed a piece of paper

with names on it for Troy's room.
"Well we cannot be fully sure, but don't expect him back at work for at least a year"
"I'm not; he asked me if he can come back"
"It's the physiological factor we have to worry about Mr Folster. As I had a patient came back just the other week with more issues than his burns."
"Thanks, that was very helpful, look after him" I replied
"We will."
As I was just about to exit the station I saw a bunch of flowers which said "Troy" on it
I reached over to see who they were from, I saw the signature and turned to the Nurse and said
"Can you get me security?"
She looked at me and knew I was serious without hesitation security was on the end of the phone.
"Hi, can we find out who delivered these?"
"Yes of course. But can I just confirm who you are?"
"Yes, sorry I am from Darktronics my name is James Folster and my apprentice Troy was burned by this man who has signed these"
"Ah yes James, this Mr Oliver, Ralph put him on our watch list, come to our security office and we will take these, thanks Nurse Helen. " he said as he picked the flowers up
"I'm Gavin by the way, I run security here for the nurses"
"Well nice to meet you Gavin I'm guessing you are always busy"
"Yes.." we were interrupted by a young nurse walking past and giving him a smile
"It's a tough job James but someone has to do it" Gavin said laughing, we had now reached a set of lifts, as we went up to level 4 I wondered who was working for Ruben Oliver as I didn't think he would have the nerve to show his face here.
The room was full of monitors, a phone, a desk and there was a

©TheExpirement

kitchenette off to the side. I didn't think it was too bad
Gavin placed the flowers down on the floor, and then took off his fluorescent jacket and made his way to the kitchenette. I heard him fill up a kettle as I sat on one of the empty seats; the other two were covered with papers and other bits and pieces. I turned to watch the monitors and saw the nurses' station where we had just been, the view was perfect I just hoped we could get enough evidence. I felt a chill go down my spine as Gavin walked behind me
"I just have to ring the wife" he stepped out of the room closing the door
I kept quiet as I tried to listen, something wasn't feeling right
"I have the package" I heard.
I stayed calm when Gavin walked in.
"So then lets rewind that cctv for you" he said chucking off the papers from the seat
"Did you notice them when you arrived?" he asked
"No, I arrived about two hours ago" I said trying not to panic
"Sure, I will set this to go back two hours and get a cuppa, would you like?"
"No thanks, I am fine"
Phew no chance of poisoning me.
"No worries, but I am gasping " Gavin got up from the chair chuckling to himself. I thought it might get quite lonely up in here, but then as I looked around it reminded me of my office in some ways.
A few minutes later Gavin came back out with a mug of tea, he put it down and I saw that the mug had crayon drawings over it.
"Children?" I asked
"Yeah, my youngest is four, I got this for father's day" he replied proudly
The cctv had now gone back, we then played it and sure enough about five minutes in a courier arrived, not our guy the flowers

were taken directly away. This happened several times, then it hit me
"Nurse Helen came in to Troys room just before I left, she wouldn't have been able to receive or take them anywhere"
Gavin smiled and said "here you go"
Sure enough he had fast forwarded the recording to that point, a young man wearing a blue denim jacket, a grey baseball cap and dark blue jeans. He even looked up at the camera.
"Can I get a copy?"
"Sure, already done." Gavin had already made a recording as we had been watching it.
I thanked him and then left. I was sure there was not something quite right, it all seemed a bit weird.
I couldn't shake that feeling, but I texted Jack and said I would drop the disc over and then I would go home.
As I went back to Darktronics, I wondered who the guy was and why did it not feel right in the security room with Gavin.
So I texted Fiona and said I would be home a bit later, she didn't reply so I just thought that she was asleep.
I walked up to Ralph's office as Jack said he should be there if not leave it there and he would pick it up a bit later.
I left it there, I heard raised voices coming directly from Ralph's office, and so I left a note for Jack on the PA's desk.
I went back to my office and set about running a search, we had access to all employees and other organisation employees. I set my search running for Gavin; I just needed to know who he was and why none of this felt right.
I arrived home and little bit earlier than expected, I heard Fiona on the phone as I walked in
"I am not sure, he'll be home soon" she said, I had assumed at that point it was to her mum or dad to decide on when we were picking up Frederick from them.

©TheExpirement

Then I came in to the lounge, she was holding a very familiar package
I gulped.
"Hi" I said
"Hey, err someone left this at our doorstep"
"Okay may I look"
"Nope, I think you already know what this is" Fiona replied sternly
"Was there a note?" Of course there would be, Ruben was now forcing my hand.
"Yes, I shall read it to you. *Dear Mr James Folster, many thanks for contacting the DNA testing centre. We have sent you the DNA testing kit, please ensure...then it says make sure your son has not been in contact with the following...*"
"It's not what you think"
"Oh, and what do I think"
I let her calm down for a second or two
Of course quite rightly she believed that I had contacted the centre to see if my son was indeed my son. Now it was time to explain what had been going on
"I need to show you some evidence" was all I could say
"Sure"
I showed her the evidence on my smartphone, it was handy having access to our databases. I just did not think I would be showing it to my Fiona.
"I couldn't say, I know you would never cheat and I knew we didn't need this."
"Don't you ever decide not to tell me when it concerns our child" she shouted
"I am sorry"
We kissed and we stood there for a while just hugging and she let her emotions just pour out. It had been a stressful day.
I received a text from Jack saying he had gotten my disc and that

my office computer was bleeping.

I replied and said thanks, but there was no way I was checking the computer now. So I turned off my phones and made the evening a very special one for my dear Fiona.

Sadly the next morning we awoke to the house phone ringing, it was Fiona's dad saying nothing to worry about and could they return Frederick an hour earlier than planned. Fiona said yes and then as she put down the phone.

"I forgot to tell you, I was telling Jean yesterday when you walked in"

"Did she know?"

"No, she didn't, but she sounded like there was something familiar about the centre on the letter."

"Thanks, I shall look in to it." I then looked at the alarm clock on the side, I was already running late, but I decided a few more minutes wouldn't hurt.

I rocked up to Darktronics a whole two hours later than I should have been

But to be fair no-one seemed to notice, then I remembered as I clambered up the stairs to my office about Jacks text saying my computer was beeping

"I wonder what it has found" I said to myself

As I entered I saw the computer "Match Found"

Then my gut churned it had found it not on the hospitals database but the police database. Gavin was a well-known criminal. He had not long been let out of prison.

Whilst processing this news and before going to Jack, I decided to see if Nurse Helen was real. Yeap you guessed it she was not, I just hoped Troy was alive.

I rang Ralph's office and was told to get up there as soon as I could. I went straight up.

Ralph welcomed me straight in to his office

"I assumed it was urgent" he said

"Yes, sir I went to visit Troy I think he might be in danger"

He was straight on the phone ringing the hospital

"Thanks, we will be in touch"

He looked up at me, I could tell this might be bad news.

"He's alive but critical"

"Thank goodness"

"Yes, now tell me what you know."

I told him everything that happened yesterday and what greeted me when I was at home. I told him that Jean had found the logo of the DNA centre very familiar. As I was about to finish Jack and Jean walked in to the room.

©TheExpirement

Chapter Forty Three

Jean was looking worried; I hadn't seen her looking this worried before. "What can you tell us Jean?" I asked.

"James, I recognised the DNA centre because my sister works there"

"You think this isn't a coincidence"

"James, I think we are beyond coincidences." Ralph replied.

"What do we do, well Fiona and I have decided we are not having the test"

"It seems we are too late" Jack suddenly advised

"Huh?"

"My sister contacted me when I told her to check for your name, it seems Mr Ruben Oliver has done the test for you"

"No, that's not true, how did he get our DNA"

"We don't know James, Jack has his team over there now and well I cannot believe what this evil man has done." Jean advised

"Well that's fine, do whatever you have to do, but Jack I don't want to know the results."

Ralph and I were left alone in the room, Jean went with Jack to the DNA centre.

"James, I know this is going to be the most awkward question I am ever going to ask you."

"Don't ask it" I said sternly

"James,"

"No seriously I don't want to know anything, this is eating me up"

"But, you are your Fredericks father and that's true. But if he places someone else in the frame, maybe that will help us."

"Fine, but I don't need to know"

"Okay son, now you best get on home, Fiona has been given her results early"

"You serious?"

"Yes, we decided that it would help your situation"
I raced home; I prayed that Fiona had passed.
"Honey, did you pass?"
I then felt a bang on my head and my world went dark.
When I awoke I was tied up to a chair, as I came round I could feel the bump on my head. Its sore very sore and I feel like I want to be sick.
As I get my bearings I hear voices, one of which I recognise
"Gavin?" I whisper
"Hey James, how you doing?" he says as he walks towards me giving me another unwelcome punch across my face
"What was that for?"
"Just doing my job"
I tried to nod, but my head was killing me and for not answering even though I did not realise I needed to I got another punch to my face. This time I felt my nose go crack and I felt the blood trickling down my face.
"Seriously" I mumbled.
I saw his arm get ready for another punch, but someone stopped him.
"Take him to our Doctor" She said
"Yes ma'am" Gavin replied.
I was untied from the chair and pulled up, then pushed out of the doorway. I could not see much, my eyes were starting to swell up. I felt fresh air hit my face and I took a deep breath, Gavin laughed, "You won't feel that ever again"
As I was being walked across this courtyard I looked for clues, but these were old warehouses and the stench reminded me of cattle, but I couldn't be sure.
We then walked up some stairs, they were concrete, and I kept tripping up, as they were not very level. Gavin then undid my handcuffs and sat me in a chair in this old room, which looked as

©TheExpirement

though it was clean. The bleach assaulted my nose as Gavin once again cuffed my hands.

The doctor as everyone referred to them, was wearing a suit and a mask. He picked up a needle from the table and without warning, injected it in to my nose. I screamed as it went in, a few minutes later the pain from my nose subsided. He had injected it with anaesthetic and thankfully, it was numb. The doctor did not speak to me, and was busy washing the blood off my face when the woman from earlier came in. "How long doctor?" I did not hear the doctors' response but she seemed satisfied and promptly walked out. Gavin then undid my cuffs and then Gavin gave me an Oxygen mask. "Laughing gas, you'll need it"

I duly took it, a few seconds later my nose was put back in to place. Then after a few minutes to get rid of the pain, Gavin pulled be up from the chair and gave me a fresh set of clothes to put on. As I got dressed, the doctor tided up and left.

"Come on time to go" Gavin advised me

"Where are we going?" I asked,

"To see someone very special"

This time I was bundled out with a blindfold on me, obviously we were going somewhere where they really didn't want me to know where I was.

I found myself sitting in the dark on a very soft seat. My hands still cuffed this time in front of me I tried to feel around but there was nothing.

"There is nothing you can do Mr Folster" said a voice

"Who are you?" I asked, it was a man's voice and I wondered if this could be Ruben

"Someone who knows the truth" he replied. He had a very deep almost rough voice.

"Truth about what"

"Your son"

236 –Expirement Series

"What, what about my son is he okay?" I panicked I hoped he had not hurt my son

"He is fine, his mother was told that you have gone on very special assignment" he replied. Then a recording of it played in the room. "Hi Fiona this is Sally from the Darktronics reception, James wanted me to message you that he and Jack are on a special operation." I recognised Sally's voice, I tried not to panic, this meant they wouldn't be looking for me.

After a pause

"Thanks Sally" Fiona replied and then I heard Frederick cry. My heart sank, this was the first time I felt as if I wouldn't see my dearest son again

"Don't worry I don't intend to kill you Mr Folster"

"What do you intend to do?"

"Teach you a few lessons."

"I don't understand."

"I know but you will."

©TheExpirement

Chapter Forty Four

I was alone for a while not sure how long as I was still blindfolded. As I waited, I could hear different footsteps, the room I was in sounded hollow of all sudden. Then I heard someone scrape a chair and someone whisper "Quietly"
My thoughts turned to this morning, all the clues were running around my head not making any sense.
Then it was my time to move, Rubens minions were obviously clearing stuff out, then I was moved. I recognised Gavin and in some way, I was relieved, at least I knew what he was capable of doing. I let myself be moved and I was still blindfolded.
"Where are we going?" I asked
"To your next meeting"
I stayed quiet, again trying to listen for clues but there was nothing, but the floor turned to gravel and was very uneven. As we crunched over the gravel, I heard others walking towards us.
"Ah Mr Folster, thank you Gavin that will be all"
As I heard Gavin step away, the man who had greeted me spoke to me again.
"Mr Folster please come this way" he took me by the arm and pulled me and then pushed me in to a car.
The blindfold was now off and I could see I was being driven very fast down a dual carriageway, but I did not recognise it. Then we stopped suddenly was put in to another car, this time with tinted windows and I was now surrounded by muscle men and even though I could have made a move but I probably would have been dead before I reached the door.
It was not long before we had a reached the destination, which surprisingly was a hotel. I took in the name The Hound and Wolf as I was bundled out of the car. I was not sure if I was meant to see the name, but I tried not to focus on anything so that my handlers

would not get spooked.
As we quickly went through the reception area, which was tidy, clean, and very posh, I was taken to room.
I stood in what effectively was a lounge, it had a big flat screen television on the wall to the left of me. Two leather chairs and a sofa surrounded a coffee table, which was wooden and had a carved flower decoration in the middle.
A man who I did not recognise was stood by the windows, he was dressed in a three-piece suit, cream but he wore no tie. He looked tired as he waved the bodyguards away. His face was rugged and had clearly had some plastic surgery done. "Mr Folster, I must apologise for the way my bodyguards behaved"
I nodded, I did not say a word.
"You must be hungry" he then said very calmly
"Yes I am, but for answers Mr.."
"I am Ruben, Ruben Oliver" he offered his hand. I did not offer mine.
"I understand Mr Folster, you feel badness towards me"
I couldn't say a word to him. I was angry and he wasn't helping with his rather smug look.
"Please sit, if you wish. Do you recognise this hotel Mr Folster?"
"No, I do not"
"Yes, it must have changed since you have been here as a child"
How did he know where I had been as a child, this was starting to really get annoying and more scary than ever.

"Don't panic Mr Folster; I am not going to kill you. Also you can be assured that your family are not at risk,"
My stomach rumbled and in the silence, he smiled "Seriously we must eat." He picked up the phone and ordered room service. To be fair the steak sandwiches he ordered were a godsend.
As I sat and ate we hardly talked I did not yet know the point of me

being here, except he had some evil purpose.

"To be honest with you James, I did not quite foresee all this hurt. Whilst that may surprise you, the mere boy Jensen Lyons was shall we say a loose cannon." I did not want to show my anger and rage about Lyons, there were numerous times I had nearly lost those who I clearly cared about, I wasn't about to show any weakness.

"Now Mr Folster, you may ask me a question,"

I thought about it for a second, I wanted to be confident and yet not too clever.

"Why are you focusing on the DNA of my child?"

We sat there in silence; he put his hands to his mouth his piercing blue eyes are focusing in to space. This was interesting how he was about to answer the question, I knew in my head that he would not answer it truthfully but my heart really needed the truth.

"You will understand one day, but this is not the day I answer that question"

I sighed,

"You see Mr Folster, I cannot give you all the answers, but do you have any other questions?"

"When can I go back to my family?"

"When you have completed this particular part of your challenge"

"Okay so what the hell do I do now?"

"Well Mr Folster" looking at his watch

"It's time you had a good sleep and rest, how is your nose?"

I was, taken aback by his question it was almost kindness.

There were things that night I dreamt about which I will not make public. They almost haunted me until I hit the mini bar that Ruben had advised was free for me. Therefore, after a few I felt the pain in my nose disappear and sleep was soon upon me. In the morning that came far too early, I awoke when breakfast was brought in. I welcomed the hot food and lots of coffee.

A letter was on the breakfast tray and it had my name on it, there was no leaving without reading it and I had checked to see if I could get out, but it was as if Ruben had brought the whole hotel. I recognised his minions everywhere.

After my second cup of black coffee, I read the letter it said,

"My dear James, I hope you slept well. To get back to your family (I hope in one piece) I would like you to take the keys in this letter and drive to the following house. 142 Mansion Place. The car has an in built satellite navigation in it will show you how to get there. Take care Mr Folster I look forward to our next meeting"

I took my time in the shower and to be fair I was impressed by the full wardrobe of fresh clean clothes. I found a holdall at the bottom and a wallet full of money. My personal items were nowhere to be seen but in the wallet was a picture of my son that brought a tear to my eye. On the back Ruben had written, "For him"

As I left, the car was waiting for me in the car park, I knew I would be followed and my curiosity was wanting the answers, so I did as he had instructed.

I drove for about three hours, the roads were mostly country and windy, they were hard to navigate and occasionally I had taken a wrong turning, but the sat nav was soon shouting at me to turn around. I did not want spook my minders come bodyguards, but there was hope when they asked me at one pit stop. "I do not know where it is either, but we will only get spooked if you head for home," one of them said. One thing did haunt me slightly; there was no sign of Gavin.

My mind raced as I entered what seemed to be the last lane I recognised it, I then saw the house and even though the name meant nothing, my heart sank this was my late Grandmothers house.

©TheExpirement

Chapter Forty Five

The last time I had been here was when I was ten. It was a very difficult time for my father and me as we had arrived three days before she died. I remember being excited as she always baked my favourite cake cherry and vanilla sponge. However, when we drove up the same road as I did today, we saw an ambulance outside. I had decided not to get out as I was ten and whilst I remember being curious, I did not want to see my Grandmother ill as it scared me. My father Jonathan let me stay in to the car and I did not see my Grandmother alive again.

The house now stood in the excellent condition that my dear Grandmother had kept it in; I knew that from my father that the house had been left to his cousin who had been like another son to them. My father had the other part of the considerable estate, which his cousin was able to buy out. I remember visiting only once after my Grandmothers death, but this was the first time as an adult. I took a deep breath and stepped out of the car, there were no sight of my minders, and I took in the sight of the old house with the garden still as spectacular. I took a moment to smell the roses and I saw the old sundial at the end of the front lawn, which I remember running around. As I walked up to the door, it was no longer the solid oak door, but a modern dark blue. The door was unlocked and I walked in to the hallway. As I child the smell of the cake used to fill the hallway and I used to run down to the kitchen for a big hug with my dear Grandmother. There would be no running today, the hall smelt of death and destruction, gone was the old wooden look and just plain old magnolia had been painted on. I was not sure, whether my mind was playing tricks on me or if this was the reality of Ruben Oliver.

As I walked in to the lounge that was the first door in the hallway on my right, the old wooden stairs, which actually still looked like they had been looked after, were on my immediate left. I dare not go upstairs yet; I did not know what was in store for me in the lounge. The sat nav in the car had told me that the lounge was my final destination.

As I entered long gone were the big grey soft fabric sofas that were so comfortable that as soon as dad had sat on them, Grandmother and I had left him to sleep. I hit the new rock hard wooden chair and looked at the boxes that were in front of me. There were six of them in all; brown file boxes were heavy as I tried to move it closer to me. I jumped as the old style phone in the corner rang breaking the silence. I rushed over to the far left corner and picked it up, I then noticed a big old painting on the wall it was familiar but I could not place it. "Hello James" said Ruben on the end of the phone "What do you want me to do?" I asked I got straight to the point; I did not really want to spend too much time here if I could help it. "In the boxes are some pieces of the jigsaw, you may even find some answers to your question. However, I need you to find someone for me."

"Who?"

He paused

"My sister" he said before hanging up the phone.

I was taken aback by this, I did not realise he had a sister.

I sat in the lounge and found an old beanbag stored in the cupboard under the stairs, I also found the kitchen had been fully stocked which I was grateful.

The beanbag was a bit musty but it was more comfortable than the old chair they had put in.

I opened the first box and sorted the photos from the documents; I did not take in the photos until I had found some sticky tape and put it up the now peeling wall. I took a look back but as I turned the opposite wall the painting was haunting me. Then I realised who it was, it was my Grandfather then as I looked at it I remembered there was a safe behind the picture.

I knew Ruben was probably watching so if this were anything to do with my family then Ruben would probably use it to harm my family or me. I took my deep breath, took down the picture, it was not as heavy as it looked. Then I saw the silver key pad, I wondered what the number could be. I sat on the floor next to the picture trying to think of any number, and then something on the painting again took my eye. I looked at my grandfather and remembered that my dad used to look at the picture a lot when he was on the phone doing business. I then saw what my dad was always looking at; a picture behind my grandfather was of a holiday they had taken years ago. That holiday date was the number. As I opened the safe there was a simple white envelope inside, I took it and sat back on the floor. As I opened it my stomach churned, I carefully started to lift the opening of the self-sealed back and then I found myself ripping it as I realised the quicker I knew the quicker this all should be over.

Inside was a folded letter, it was on cream paper that you could see the fine lines, it looked important. As I unfolded the letter, the logo on the front made my stomach churn. It was DNA centre that had become our focus. I read carefully and aloud

"Dear Mr Oliver, I am writing to inform you of your DNA results. I firstly must apologise for the time it has taken us to retrieve this information. However, I am delighted to inform you that we have found your father. Please find attached a copy of your fathers' record and the current known details.

I thank you for your patience"

I turned the page over and froze; nothing had prepared me for the name at the top of the second page. Ralph Mearlow.

Time stood still for me.

Then I heard footsteps, and my world went dark.

©TheExpirement

Chapter Forty Six

I honestly had thought when I awoke the next day that someone had hit me. However, there was no sign of anyone being there or damage to me. It was as if someone had ordered me to sleep and it had put me straight out.
My stomach growled for food as I wandered towards the kitchen, my mind was still foggy so fond memories were not protruding by brain this morning. A scrawny looking piece of paper was on the kitchen table. It simply said "Use phone if you need more food"
I smiled and turned to the big American fridge that stood proudly in the corner of the kitchen. Cool air hit me as I opened its door and soon enough I was tucking in to some well-earned breakfast. As I gulped down the fresh orange juice, I wondered if this sister of his was still alive and if she was, was she older or younger.
Once my belly had been filled, I chucked my plates in to the dishwasher and sat back in the lounge, my make shift evidence wall looked a mess. I needed to become detective, I wondered if Ruben would allow me to ask him some questions. I scribbled the question on a piece of paper and held it up to the non-conspicuous camera in the far left corner. It was not long before the telephone rang it was Ruben.
"Yes of course you can ask questions." He sounded quite polite but I did not hesitate
"I was wondering, do you know if she is alive and would she be older?"
"Yes to alive but I do not know if she is younger or older than me, that's where for once my memory fails me."
"Thanks" I replied
I was about to put the phone down but he spoke
"I see you found my father, I did not realise you would be so quick. And so you may realise she is my half-sister"

Then the line went dead.
Therefore, if Ralph Mearlow was indeed his father then it was time to go hunting in to his past.
However, the make shift evidence wall screamed for my attention and there I began my work.
What was there was now gone, I replaced it with a picture of Ruben and Ralph. I added on others such as his brother. I then drew stick people on A4 pieces of paper to put in Jean, and then Ralphs other family.
With string marking the connections, I soon had what to others may look a mess, but to me it was organised and one that could easily have brought down my world and Darktronics as we knew it.
After grabbing my sixth coffee, I wondered what lay in the boxes that were still stacked.
However, I stayed focused which helped as I wrote down all the possibilities. One of which on the third day of going through paper after paper. A possibility that Fiona was indeed Rubens sister which made me feel sick in the stomach and heart breaking, was this why he had been challenging me? Could this be the reason for it all, or was she some mastermind behind this and I was a pawn in her chess game. My brain started to tell me it was the caffeine talking but my heart was telling me something different.
Then I thought of my dear son and that's when I put a massive question mark on the possibility and moved on.
I had no real idea how many days I had been away, but the boxes stacked up with dust and the place wasn't looking particularly clean, but then the phone rang.
"Hello James"
It was Ruben again, I wondered what challenge he had left for me, I knew I had to leave at some point, even though being here felt like home.
"What can I do for you?" I asked, I was not feeling anything towards

Ruben, I just knew that he had set me this challenge.
"Well I think it's time for you to leave. I suggest you get your notes, are you ready to leave Mr Folster?"
There was no chance to reply as the phone went dead. The red light of the camera in the corner of the room shut off. I breathed a sigh of relief, I hoped that I was going to see my son again, that was the one person I was truly missing. In the remaining time, I made my notes I also got a chance to rummage in the top box. It was full of old photos, and then I heard the knock at the door. It was Rubens minions and I was dragged out of the house in to the awaiting car. The photos and the rest of the boxes would have to wait.
As I got in to the car, or I should say pushed in to the car, I couldn't help but wonder if this was the start of something good or bad.
I belted up and then Ruben turned towards me from the driver's seat, it was just me and him in the car.
"Hello James, I think it's time you went back in to your old world. Now you realise you must finish what I have asked or I will take everything you know away from you bit by bit."
I nodded, I wanted to speak but something stopped me.
"Yes, I think you have enough leads now. You can ask for my help at any time. But seriously James don't trust anyone"
And with that he drove me back.
I was sat in the cell for over six hours before Ralph and Jack burst in.
"Where have you been?" I could hear Jack asking me
"In here" I mumbled
My head throbbed again
"We have searched all over for you" Ralph said helping me stand up. I had not realised I was on the ground, but it was all part of Rubens plan to make me look I had been held in captivity.
I asked if Fiona and Fred were okay and thankfully, they were.
I had begun to wonder if how they found me, but I decided not to ask questions and left Ralph and Jack to clean me up.

©TheExpirement

My face hurt, my bones ached from being on the ground and being kicked, but I relaxed in the shower. I was now at Ralphs; they for some reason had decided to take me there instead of home as the hot water blasted over my head I thought let the interrogation begin.

©TheExpirement

Chapter Forty Seven

I went to the main dining room once I had finished having a shower. I remember Ralph muttering to me that I looked hungry, but today for once; I did not feel too hungry.
However, I did as I was told, as I walked down the corridors, I found myself wondering who was going to start the interrogation.
I knocked on the door but there was no answer, to be honest the whole house seemed quiet, too quiet. I tried the door handle and found that door was actually slightly ajar so I went in. To my surprise, there was no one in it. Maybe I had taken a wrong turn and had entered the wrong room. As I turned to go out, I felt a hand on my shoulder. I took a deep breath as my gut was telling me this wasn't right.
"Everything is fine Mr Folster"
My heart sank, what did Ruben want now, all I knew was I had to continue my investigations under everyone's nose and report back to him via back channels.
"How can I help you Ruben?" I replied not wanting him to answer
"James you seem scared, come let us sit"
We sat down at the wooden dining table which was all laid out for lunch. I wondered what had happened to Jack and Ralph.
"I didn't realise for some reason that Jack would have prepared so many questions for you" Ruben started talking, I wasn't really listening until he put a load of papers in front of me. They were definitely Jacks scribbles.
"Okay, so what, I wasn't going to tell them anything"
"I understand, but you see I cannot and will not take any chances. So this is why I am here and you are just going to have to let this play out and your so called kidnapping will be forgotten"
"So called" I couldn't help myself
"Yes okay, but at least Mr Folster you understand why"

©TheExpirement

I didn't really, but I just played along by nodding and waited for my next instruction.

He looked at his watch, it looked familiar to me but I couldn't place it.

"Now the others will wake up in a minute, I must tell you what to say. "

"How about you came here to see how I escaped?"

He laughed,

"That's actually a good one, but then why not take you again. No here you are, here is your script."

"He placed it in my hands" as we were sat opposite

"I will be in touch soon Mr Folster, good luck and please remember who you are dealing with"

I was left feeling annoyed, I should have beaten him right there and then, however I did not have the energy.

It wasn't long before Jack ran in the room and found me tied to the chair with a gag. Ralph was soon behind him.

Once Jack had untied me, he asked

"Who was it?"

Jack took the piece of paper from me

"Read it aloud Jack"

"I see gentlemen that your boy is back in town, however please take his kidnapping as a warning to you all. I sadly couldn't stick around for a chat as I have business to attend to, however I have taken what I need so thank you. Good day, Ruben"

"What the hell did he take"

Jack looked around the room, but no one spotted anything missing.

"Did you see him with anything James?"

I shook my head but racked my brain for clues. Then lunch arrived and we picked at the food as were not particularly hungry.

"No one is missing a watch are they?" I asked

"No" they both said in unison, the watch may have looked familiar but it was not what he had taken.

As we sat in silence, only the clock on the wall ticking was the only sound we could hear. I stared out of the window and wondered what was next for us.

That's when it hit me.

Jack was possibly the father of my child.

Fiona could be the sister of Ruben that he was looking for.

However, I doubted this out of all the facts as he could have easily got her DNA.

Ralph was potentially the father of the Oliver's, and I was the one who had to play it out or some would say go with the flow.

Jack got up from his chair and paced around the room

"We pride ourselves on our security and yet you get kidnapped, all what happened before and now this."

"That's what he has taken"

"What is it James?"

"Trust"

The pair of them looked at me as if I was speaking a different language, so I explained.

"You said it yourself Jack, we pride ourselves here in Darktronics on security. Even though science is under deniably the force that drives us, security though is our true definition."

I stood up, I was finally putting some of the jigsaw puzzle pieces together.

"So your saying that Ruben is trying to break in?"

"Not quite Jack, what he is trying to do is kill the core. If you look after every disaster Darktronics have faced, most of them we get clients, we don't lose them. Because unless and forgive me when I say this, but unless we are dead we rebuild and ensure that our clients are safe."

"But if he breaks us, i.e. the driving force behind it then no one will ever trust us" Ralph said finishing off my explanation

©TheExpirement

Jack continued the pace, but I was suddenly feeling very hungry and tucked in to some rather nice looking ham sandwiches.

"That's all very and well and good, but what the hell do we do?"

"Jack you ask a very good question, but firstly we must get this young man back to his family"

"Quite right, but Ruben will not stop until he gets answers" I said in between crisps and a second sandwich.

"Fine, but you must slow down or you will get indigestion. Jack go to the television room run through the cctv let see what goons he brought with him today maybe there are some weak spots. As for you James, ride with me to your house as I need to explain something."

I jumped up grabbing a can of drink and followed Ralph out of the door, but just as I got there Jack came up to me.

"Take care of yourself"

I replied with a man hug whispering "You to"

©TheExpirement

Chapter Forty Eight

As we got in the car, I felt a sense of relief that my friends had not grilled me, however I would have preferred not being tied up.
We drove in silence for a while which gave me a chance to just well enjoy the country side, that's when I realised we were going round the long way to my house.
"Worried we are being followed?"
"Yes and No James, you are very astute, pull over at the lay by"
Ralph replied to me and then shouting instructions to his driver.
I got the feeling I wasn't home and dry yet about the grilling.
As we pulled in to the lay by Ralph un did his seat belt and turned to me.
"Now James, I know you know more than you are telling us, so tell me do you think I am Rubens father?"
I was shocked was this some play by him to try to make me fess up about what had happened to me.
What I said next was crucial.
"Did you get me kidnapped?"
"Touché James"
There was a short pause before he began talking to me.
"I knew Ruben was up to something, not so long ago he started sending me letters from his school days which said that his father was his step dad and this he wanted to know who his dad truly was. The strange thing was that there was nothing really threatening about the letters, until one day he sent me a DNA kit. I wondered what on earth I needed this for, when the fourth letter arrived."
"Don't tell me one of your kids isn't yours?"
"Correct, but the mad thing is I always knew. My dear late wife had told me that who the child's father was and that he didn't want anything to do with it."
"So why send you the kit?"

"I replied saying that I did not see the reason for the kit and saying I already knew about my child's parentage. I hadn't heard anything for days until a letter arrived saying I was the father of Ruben and Daniel."

"So he thinks you're his father and because we have the father son bond he sees me as a threat"

"I think so James"

"Why are you telling me this?"

"The truth is I offered your services and so yes I got you kidnapped"

I felt sick, truth was out there I wanted to get so angry and to be honest I didn't want to speak to him or Ruben ever again, but I knew deep down that if I didn't none of this stupidity was going to go away.

"But I didn't know what he was going to do"

"So what service did you actually offer him?"

There was nothing but silence.

I could feel the anger building up inside me not knowing how I was going to explode.

Ralph then went in to a side door pocket and pulled out a letter. Handed it to me and said

"Read this and I'll give you a moment" in doing so he stepped outside with the driver leaving me alone in the car.

"Dear Ralph, I cannot call you father yet as it is far too soon. Therefore, you know that your dear wife slept with my step dad when you were off playing golf. I did not assume you would take this as a surprise but more as a focusing of the mind. You see I need to borrow James to look in to my family history for me so that I can present my findings to you when I meet you. I will also be giving him enough of a clue so that you can work out who I have been working with in your close circle. I believe this person has had far too much fun and let us just say their contract for me is ending. If you agree then make sure he is home alone and I will do the rest.

You only have my word that he will not die on this occasion. Yours Ruben."

This had been all a set up.

I was angry, annoyed, and now all of a sudden I could not trust Ralph.

I decided to put the letter back in to the side pocket. I then got out of the car where I found Ralph and the driver talking about some woodpecker they could see.

"Well?"

"I don't know if I can trust you"

"I would never have told you James if I didn't trust you"

Now that was true.

"You think Jack is the person he is working with"

He nodded and said, "It seems like we have a mole here too"

All of a sudden, the driver looked pale.

I turned to see what Ralph was now getting out of the boot. It was a handgun with a silencer on it.

"Tell us everything you know and I will spare you"

The driver looked nervous and thought about running, but I decided not to let him past me. As I really could do without seeing someone get shot.

"I cant if I do he will kill me in worse way that you do"

And with that all I saw was his body fall to the ground. I was in a bit of a daze really, we moved the body after taking his wallet and phone.

"What makes you suspect Jack too?"

"Well when I was kidnapped that's all I heard was about Jack being the potential father to my child."

We clambered back in to the car, this time in the front.

"I am sorry James, I do hope that is not true for you. You are a great father. Now let us look at to whom he was talking to"

We opened the phone and found several messages to his wife, but there was nothing too suspicious, had we just killed the wrong man?

Ralph handed me the phone whilst he checked his wallet. I decided to read the messages again but this time the sent messages.

"In lay by awaiting further instructions"

The last message was a load of little pictures.

"I think we have to break the code"

Ralph smiled when he took out a card which to the untrained eye would look like a store reward card. But to us it was to decode the messages.

After some working out we realised that the final message said.

"Jack advises you to record conversation, then to meet Ruben at the house"

We looked at each other. What did we do now? Was it go home to my Fiona and dear Fred or was it confront Ruben.

As I was about to point of the obvious when a car pulled up alongside us, it was another one of our drivers.

She got out of the car that drove off promptly.

As she got in to ours, Ralph turned to her and asked "How's the weather in town?"

"Clear sir, but rain is due in"

And with that we were off.

Chapter Forty Nine

As we started to arrive in to more familiar surroundings, I started to wonder what lie in wait or if was just enough to test us and spook us. Was Jack working for Ruben or was Jack trying to spook Ruben. Not a clue
Not even my gut was giving me a clue, so I took some deep breaths and they slowed my heart rate down considerably. I was worried, but Ralph was a picture of calm.
To help the build-up of anxiety I watched the passing of trees and roads, and forced myself to try to spot wildlife. I had not even counted a magpie when we arrived outside my house.
Ralph turned to me and spoke bringing me out of a trance
"We go in as normal, you first and I will play the caring boss"
I smiled, "Are you not?"
We giggled like little boys in the playground; it was a gentle reminder that we were better than this hurt and pain.
I got out the car and walked up to the door, I rang our doorbell, not knowing if anyone would come.
Silence.
"Everything alright?" Ralph whispered behind me
"Seems a little quiet"
I replied then looked through the letter box
"Shit, we need to break this door down"
"Why?" Asked Ralph in a sheer panic
I couldn't tell him straight away but Jean was lying down unconscious in the hallway of my house.
We started to bash the door, then my neighbour came out of his house
"Everything alright James?"
"Err no, sorry Mike I have left my keys.. you know how it is?"
"Haha yes, hold on I think I may still have the spare set"

Mike had been given a set, when we first had Fred, as Fiona was very much suffering from baby brain and was getting forgetful.
"Here you go"
"Thanks, I owe you a pint"
He smiled and went back in doors.
I opened the door quickly, Ralph running passed me to get to Jean
"She's alive"
"Shall I call an ambulance?"
"No need came a whisper"
Jean woke up, and gave Ralph a big cuddle.
"You were playing dead?" He asked
"Yes, now I will explain what's happened. Sorry James, can you get us some tea. I think we will need it"
I was relieved that Jean was okay, she had a few bruises on her but nothing to worry over. She was getting a enough fuss from Ralph. We were all sat at the kitchen table, holding our mugs of tea waiting for Jean to recount her day.
"So my dears" she began after taking a good gulp of the tea
"I thought something was going on, when the new driver was ordered. I was down in the crime lab at the time dropping a few fire things to be analysed when I saw the lady run out. As soon as I saw the car I knew something was up. I then walked up slowly past forensics and the car pool area when I bumped in to Jack. He seemed shocked to see me, we said hello and carried on our way. I hadn't quite put two and two together until later on."
She took a pause drinking more tea.
"I went back up to my office, when I heard his voice coming from someone's radio. I was able to hide behind one of the buildings so I could listen. All it said was "Driver taken and Ruben is on route"."
Ralph sighed,
"I had ordered a new driver as the guy we had was working for Jack"

©TheExpirement

"Don't worry dear it wasn't her, she was fine it was the security guard on the car pool."
"He had eyes everywhere," I added,
"I don't believe it," Ralph muttered. He was angry and I could understand we had all trusted Jack.
Jean stayed silent for just a while.
Then after a knowing look from Ralph she continued her story.
"I then saw Jack leave, but he did not take his car. I noticed he fumbled for some keys, then huffed and went back in to the car pool area. No one to be seen where you could ask for keys. So I decided to take my chance. I went in and once again, he was surprised to see me. "Sorry Jack we mustn't keep meeting like this." He smiled. "Need a car?" I asked and he nodded. Take this one, I was only dropping it back" He thanked me and he drove the rental that one of my fire students had for their weekend course."
Ralph smiled.
"You had a tracker on it, our way of knowing the students get to the correct destination and
as a safety measure". They smiled.
"So you tracked him back here"
She nodded
"So tell me, how did you come to be inside the house?"
"Fiona and I already had a meeting set up. I was just an hour early. Just remember James that what I tell you from now is pure fact."
I nodded in thanks.
"I pressed the doorbell, and waited. I could hear muffled voices. It was Fiona and Jacks, I could hear him saying "Why is she here", "I told you that she was due, you have panicked and now we are going to have to deal with her, wait here and I will handle it". She came up to the door and welcomed me in. "Sorry to be a bit early", "No worries Jean, now I promised you cuddles with Fred, he's upstairs in his nursery" I went upstairs, Jack at this point was nowhere to be

seen, I suspected he was hiding, not wanting to show his face. It was when I went back downstairs after seeing Fred and there they were discussing what they were doing next."

Ralph at this point had got up from the table and was pacing. I think we all knew what was coming.

"They had been discussing the fact that Ruben was on to them and that they needed to go away. It sounded like they were going far away. Fiona asked where, but Jack simply said, "Where we can raise our child and be family". That is when he saw me and panicked. He went for me, but after a few punches I pretended he had landed one and that's when I played unconscious or as you said it dead"

I felt sick.

I had not wanted this to be true.

Fiona had done the very thing I had been dreading, cheated on me. Now I was angry.

©TheExpirement

Chapter Fifty

My anger was just boiling inside me it was as if Jack had now become Ruben. Come to think of it were they in this together. At that point in time I didn't care. My whole life had once again been turned upside down, inside out and right now I was just plain angry. For the rest of that day all I can remember is Ralph and Jean making sure I was alright. Jean packed me some clothes and anything else I might need.
I sat on the stool in the lounge holding a toy that I had brought my son...his son. I felt sick, I wanted to beat him until he felt the pain I was in.
Then Ralph grabbed my arm pulling me up. "Come on lets go"
I had wanted to go upstairs but they wouldn't let me and in a trance I left my house.
I think I was given a strong sedative or something as when I awoke I couldn't remember anything.
I was led in bed in my room at Ralph's house the windows were open and the curtains were moving with the light breeze. It was sunny, I smiled. I always felt better on days like this.
After awaking and showering I felt a little more like normal. Not sure what normal is but I sure felt like it. I walked in to the dining area and was greeted by Ralph.
"Hey you are awake"
"Yes, I slept like a log"
"I know, we kept an eye on you"
"How long was I out for?" I seemed panicked by the way he said "I know"
"The doctor gave you something to help, you have been out for two days"
I was shocked, but felt relieved that I was being cared for. It was then when I remembered the anger and why I was here. But I felt

relieved that I wasn't on some street drinking myself to death. After dealing with the shock of being sound asleep for two days, I ate like a horse. Jean who had now joined us gave me a motherly look. I slowed my eating and just smiled.

The obvious elephant in the room was Jack and what he had done to my life. Ralph though kept things to the business and that whilst I had been out sleeping Ruben had tried to contact Jean.

It was then I realised I didn't have my phone. When I asked for it, Ralph passed it to me and said that I had several missed calls. When I looked at the number I recognised it at once. It was the landline in my grandmother's house. This was Ruben and I was guessing because I hadn't contacted him, he was now trying other ways to get the information he wanted.

"Do you think its Ruben?" Ralph asked as we sat in his lounge

"Yes, I do. But we could do with knowing if he thinks I am dead or if he knows well everything"

"Hmm this is going to be one hell of a game to play."

"Well at least we know one of his end goals"

"We do?"

"Have we heard from Jack?"

Ralph shook his head and seemed annoyed that I hadn't answered his question. It wasn't the time to tell him about a probable sister. But I gave him an answer.

"We know Jack got spooked and if you remember that Ruben said someone's contract is coming to an end?"

"You mean he his hunting them down?" Ralph said standing up and starting to pace around the room.

"Well there is only one way to find out." I said, taking out my phone.

©TheExpirement

Ralph looked at me. I think we both knew then as we had all along, we had to let Ruben call the shots and today was not the day for changing the plan.

I rang the missed call number. I refused to call it my Grandmothers phone as the memory of walking in to her house and giving her a hug was far too painful to relive right now.

"James, I have been expecting you."

"Well sorry I have been a little unwell."

"Yes, I know what happened. Now tell me are you fit enough to go on a road trip?"

I paused.

"Yes you may put this on speaker Ralph will indeed need to know as he is going to help you."

I did as I was asked.

"Now, as you have both worked out Jack has been working under my influence. I have to say to his credit and yours Ralph that it took me a long time to find a way to crack him."

"Just please tell us what we need to do Ruben." Ralph was getting agitated, he did though seemed slightly relieved that Jack hadn't just given in to him.

As for me, well the jury was still out.

"Okay gents, you have by now probably guessed that I would like Jack dead. It is up to you to bring him to me or for you to have dealt with him. He also has ten million of my money and well I would like it back. I don't think I have to tell you the consequences if I do not get a satisfactory result." I was about to ask what he wanted to do with Fiona. But he had read my mind.

"As for Fiona and Fred, we'll let them go and start a new life somewhere, but James I know how angry you must feel so it is entirely up to you."

He then asked me to take off the speaker, he asked me if I had told Ralph about the investigation for his sister. When I answered no, he

©TheExpirement

was relieved and asked me to put it on hold until I had found Jack. After I hung up, Ralph was on his phone, not long after I was then seen by the doctor who gave me the all clear. I think it was either the care that Ralph showed me or a last ditch attempt to get us out of this horrible task. However, this was our mission in life. To find Jack and get the money. Worst of all we may have to kill him and that sounded good as it was being fuelled by my anger.

Chapter Fifty One

I wasn't sure how long it would be before we received all the information that Ruben and his men had found on Jack. Ralph had already set us up with supplies and we decided to work out of Jacks work hide out. We were just about to get in the car and there was a delivery. Inside the folder given to us were a few prints outs but the other was a usb.

In the car, Ralph wanted to enter it in to his netbook. I stopped him "Don't" I said

Ralph looked at me, his face asking me why but he wasn't speaking "I will explain in a bit. Driver please stop off at this store." I grabbed an old business card from my jacket and handed it to the driver.

Ralph sat back in his seat, I could tell he trusted me. What was now certain was we had to and only really trust each other. Today was going to be a long day and this week was going to feel like a year. Keeping us together was going have to be a joint effort.

The driver pulled up outside an old warehouse building, the silver barbed wire fence needed replacing and there was an old rusty sign saying "Trespassers will be killed". I stopped the driver and Ralph from getting out. No-one was dying today.

I got out and walked over to the fence, there was a gate with a coded padlock on it. I entered the number and entered. It shut firmly behind me. Either I was going to die right here, or I was going to be let in and get what we needed.

The camera above the warehouse door was now firmly pointing at me. I knew that if they suspected anything I would not bed leaving here alive.

The door then opened. I walked in and was confronted by a hatch and another camera. There was nowhere to go. The camera then whirred and a tv screen came to life in front of me. I didn't even see it, making me jump.

©TheExpirement

"Don't be scared James" said a distorted voice
I sighed with relief.
"Okay what do you need"
"A brand new laptop. Three of your finest hand guns and the usual."
"Always a pleasure"
Deep down I knew at any point Ruben could double cross us, hence the need for weapons. Whilst I didn't want anyone getting killed it was necessary. As for the usual, I won't go in to that just right now, but to sum it up, it was my back up plan.
After waiting about 20 minutes the hatch opened and my goods were in there. One brand new boxed laptop and on the unexpected bag a note saying "Here's a free bag" smiley face.
I was amongst friends here right now, albeit an old friend who I hadn't seen in a while. But I felt relieved.
I opened the laptop bag and the handguns were in the bag and so was the details of my back up plan.
I turned and walked back out in to the fresh open air. I would have to tell my friend that they needed to get some air freshener in that place, it needed freshening up.
I walked back out of the gate which I had to put the exit code in to and put the bag and laptop in to the boot.
Getting back in to the car, Ralph hadn't really moved from his position of staring out of the window. I buckled myself in and gave the driver a signal to go.
We arrived at Darktronics about an hour later, I asked the driver to take my new laptop and bag down to Jacks hide out.
Ralph who had sat in silence didn't even question me going to my lab. I raced up there knowing that time was of the essence. As I entered it, everything had been left untouched. I grabbed a few bits and some papers that I thought my help. For some reason I had a sudden overwhelming fear that I might not ever see my lab and

office again. It had been my safe haven for years.
I closed the door. No time for sentiment.
As I started to walk back down the corridors, my phone buzzed. It was Ralph and as I answered it the driver responded. "We will see you outside the front doors." I began to panic.
I wasn't worried about the message as that was expected, not knowing where Jacks hide out truly was. But the fact that Ralph wasn't speaking to me.
I was going to have to crack that nut sooner rather than later.
The driver did indeed meet me outside the front doors along with his mate. I smiled it was a guy I recognised from the crime lab.
"Ralph is down in the office starting to sort out boxes."
"Is he talking?"
I prayed they would both say yes.
Instead they both laughed.
We didn't say much else. However, the guy from the crime lab went straight in to the room where Ralph was indeed sorting boxes. The driver held be back for a second.
"Look I know we laughed but I am worried about Ralph."
"How so?"
"It has been a while since I have seen him in this sort of mood."
Ralph tapped on the window and waved for us to come in. Story time would have to be a bit later on. I whispered to the driver, "Tell me later."
He acknowledged and we went in to see what Ralph had found.
Inside one of Jack's boxes was some neatly folded maps.
"They are not maps they are blueprints." Ralph had spoken, but I guessed this wasn't going to last long.
"Does it say where for?" I asked, hoping that it would be nicely clear on the blue print.
"No, but it does look like a mansion."
"Not yours then?"

©TheExpirement

Not even a smile. Only from the driver.
I then booted up the new laptop. I asked for the usb stick and just before I plugged it in, I booted up a little black box.
"What's that?" The driver asked.
"A signal blocker. I am trying to buy us some time so that Ruben cannot track our every move."
Ralph was now sifting through another box. Looking for ideas, clues.
As I opened up some of the files I found one with the blueprint.
And a address.
"Let's go." said the driver
Then we looked at where it was. Deep in Switzerland.
"I don't think we can get there just this second."
"Do you really think that they would be there?"
"No"
"But…" the driver was about to say and then I opened up another file. Which contained another set of blue prints.
"How many boxes do we have here Ralph?"
"20"
I sighed.
"What are you not saying now?" the driver asked.
"20 files are in this folder. Which means that he has already been here and copied all the files."
"Great, so back to square one."
Ralph was once again back in his position of watching out the window, deep in thought.
"No I think we are off to Switzerland after all."

Chapter Fifty Two

We doubled check what I had suspected that all the files on the computer were indeed exact copies of the boxes.
Ralph still wasn't talking and me and the driver had started to figure out a way to get us to Switzerland. Then the guy from the crime lab who had gone out to get food suddenly turned up looking like hell.
"What happened?"
"Ruben happened."
He handed over another folder.
I opened it, whilst the driver looked after the guy from the crime lab. I never did find out his name, as that was the last we saw of him. I understood, being spooked by one of Ruben's goons was enough to put anyone off.
In the folder were three plane tickets and a hand written note from Ruben
"Gents, well done you have found that I have already done the hard work for you. Now your plane leaves at midnight and I think that as I am in a very generous mood that is when your week begins. See you soon and good luck. Ruben."
We had a few hours to get to the airport that was enough time to get ourselves together.
The driver had seen the other guy out and had ensured he had safe transportation home. It was all we could do in these times. As for Ralph he was looking at the plane details and was looking at some of the other blue prints.
As for the driver well he and I had some talking to do.
"Hey come with me." I said to him and with that we left Ralph in the room.
"I don't think it's safe for us to be out here." The driver said.
"Well we know Ruben has been here already and if he wanted us dead."

©TheExpirement

"He would have done it already."
"Look I wanted to ask you about Ralph, but firstly what is your name, I can't keep calling you driver."
"Thomas Davidson at your service."
We shook hands and smiled.
"What do you want to know about Ralph?"
"You said earlier it's been a while since he has been in one of these moods."
"Yes, it was years back. I mean he is a quiet private man where there isn't a day where he doesn't have quiet time. But this is deeper than that."
"I thought it wouldn't have been that long ago considering all the things that have happened here in his empire of Darktronics."
"That's very true James. But now it is starting to get very personal. Many years ago when he was setting up this business after his dad. Someone had tried to take over, someone quite close to him at that time. Not anything unusual, but it was when they made it personal."
He paused.
"I was hired then as a driver, my training was going well and I was chosen along with three others to train to become Ralph's main drivers. We had been told at the start that if anyone stood out this was on offer. Little did I know that it meant more than driving. However, back then I was young fit and well healthy and eager to impress. I was doing two sessions a day in the gym when I noticed Ralph was watching me, or so I thought."
As he took a deep breath, I could tell he was reliving this in his mind as if it were yesterday.
"Three weeks that continued, I then noticed on the Thursday of the third week.."
"Did you just say Thursday?" I asked raising a hand apologising for interrupting him.

©TheExpirement

"Yeah why?"
"It may mean something, sorry please continue."
"There was a woman who had also been in the gym. When I racked my brain I realised that she had always been in there at the same time as me. Ralph that day confronted her by the weights and then had the room cleared accept for me. I was left watching Ralph and this woman argue. I remember her saying "Don't worry Ralph, daddy won't be too hard on you." I didn't at that time know what it meant. I was in a bit of shock as she was then knocked out. Ralph called me over to come help him take her out."
"Dare I ask what happened next?"
"Well I have no idea what happened to her, but as for me he briefed me in what she had done. She had threatened one of his children, who were very young. As you can see he regards you and even Jack as his kids so I think he is just reliving that hell."
"You don't happen to know the name of the woman?"
"Err let me think, oh yeah I remember Katherine was her first name. If I ever think of her second I will let you know. But why the question about the Thursday?"
"Let's just say that too is ringing some alarm bells."
All I could wonder was if that Katherine was the sister or even Rubens mother. I couldn't think, I had to put that aside but it was useful information.
I thanked Thomas and I went back inside whilst he enjoyed a well-earned cigar.
Ralph had packed up the laptop and most of the blueprints.
I thanked him and he just nodded.
I was worried about him. I checked my watch and realised it was now time to go, especially as we needed to eat.
Our driver, sorry I mean Thomas decided it was probably safer to go to one of the drive thru's. We had a mix of chicken and burgers and it was all too welcome.

©TheExpirement

We parked up in one of the strangely quiet airport carparks. Ralph got out to go pay and we didn't stop him.
Thomas turned to me
"He has a gold card for one of these, so hopefully its not going to cost us much. But James we are in this together. He was quiet for days after that Katherine disappeared and do you know what got him talking?"
"No?"
"A morning paper came through with highlighted pages direct to me. I took it to Ralph and he jumped for joy."
"What was on the paper?"
I asked, but then we both jumped. Ralph knocked on the window. It was time to go.
As we walked in to the terminal building, we waited near the stairs whilst Thomas checked us in. As we only had hand luggage this was going to be a quick process.
Then I remembered the handguns.
Thomas ran over from the desk and asked for the bag. I felt relieved he had remembered them too. They were taken out of the bag by airport security.
Had we just lot them I thought to myself?
When we got through security, Thomas turned to me and said
"Don't worry about the stuff, its safe we will get it at the other end."
Now we waited for our gate to be called.

Our gate was called and I looked up there it was dead on midnight. As we walked over I noticed how no other passengers were coming with us. Surely not I thought to myself, had Ruben put us on a private jet. It made me wonder how much money he had and where he got it all from.
In turn we handed over our boarding passes and then walked

©TheExpirement

through one of the gate tunnels. A fairly young man welcomed us on to the plane.

"This is swanky." Thomas said behind me.

It sure was, the plane wasn't like your average plane. Gone were the rows of seats replaced with fine leather ones in groups of four and twos. All with tables.

We were shown to our seats and we prepared for take-off.

"This is very posh Ruben." I said out loud

Ralph who still was deep in thought closed his eyes as we taxied round to the runway. It wasn't long before we were up.

After we had reached cruising altitude the captain had given us the clearance to stretch our legs if we needed.

Ralph who had now opened his eyes looked pale, but seemed calmer once he had a drink inside of him.

I moved over to the four seater that was empty, as Thomas who had sat next to me was sound asleep and I didn't want to wake him. My mind was going over too many things for me to be able to switch off and sleep.

Plus this wasn't a long flight, it was only a couple of hours. I knew that I probably should have slept, but then I didn't know what was waiting for us there and that was one of the things that were keeping me awake.

Ralph joined me as I read some more of the blue prints, it wasn't making sense to me. Had Jack built the mansion?

"You know you should be sleeping." Ralph said to me.

"I could say the same thing back, but we both know we have far too much going on."

Ralph smiled.

"Do you think Jack is really there?"

"Well Ralph all I can say is we are not far from finding out. I think deep down he is here as this was his best option. However, I don't know what Jacks end game would be. If Ruben knows where he is then why not just hand over yourself."

"Because Ruben doesn't want that."

I was about to disagree. But Ralph carried on.

"It's about you and Fiona and Fred. Ruben has for the past god knows how long fixated on the fact you are not Fred's father biologically. Sure Ruben wants Jack dead, but that's because he just seemed jealous of him. But he wants to see what you are going to do when faced with the reality that your best friend betrayed you."

That gave me a lot more to think about, whilst I had a hundred questions to ask I had welcomed the insight and for now that was enough. I sat back in the seat and tried to enjoy the rest of our journey.

We arrived at Sion airport which I later looked up to see that it was one of Switzerland's quieter airports.

Thomas was handed our packages as promised as we walked out in to the fresh air. I had wanted to come to Switzerland on holiday, but that seemed like a distant dream. We were about to get a taxi when a car drew up.

The driver introduced himself as one of Rubens employees. We were driven to a hotel which wasn't too far away. We were shown to our room and literally it was a room, no time to be shy now.

The driver had given Thomas keys to a car which turned out had directions already in its satellite navigation to the mansion.

We gave ourselves time to think of a plan, which to be honest wasn't much. Ralph had gone back to his quiet self, Thomas admitted that his true skill was only driving. Great I thought to myself.

"Something is bugging you." Thomas advised as we all checked our handguns.

"Yes. Why do we need a week?"

All three of us stopped, it hadn't dawned on us one little bit. Why a week, if Jack was really here in Switzerland. Why a week.

©TheExpirement

"Son of a …"

"Ralph?" I asked

"It's a diversion."

"Sorry what now?" asked Thomas who looked very confused at this moment.

To be fair I wasn't following the statement of diversion either and probably looked very confused.

"By whom exactly?" I asked hoping this was going to be simple.

"Yeah if you can spell this out in simple terms that would be helpful." Thomas interjected.

I tried not to laugh at that comment, but it would have been helpful.

"I think Ruben knows that Jack isn't here. Either it's a diversion from him to say that he has Jack and therefore we are about to find out what we are made of. Or Jack has put us on a diversion so that he can attack Ruben without us interfering."

"That makes no sense." Thomas blurted out and it actually sounded quite angry.

"No there is another option." I said

Ralph looked at me, he wasn't angry but I could tell patience around here was thin. So I didn't waste any more time and said:

"Ruben knows Jack isn't here but the trail has gone cold, therefore the week is time for us to follow the trail and find out where Jack is."

Ralph nodded in agreement.

"But we are all agreed on one thing." Thomas said sounding only slightly calmer

"What is that?"

"We are all going to find out what we are made of."

A few minutes later we are out driving towards this mansion. I couldn't help wonder what lay in store for us. Of course what we hadn't taken in to consideration was that we could have all been killed and Jack and Ruben take over Darktronics. God my imagination was running wild, it was getting hard to concentrate. But then we were there and a very unassuming run down building was in front of us.

We parked outside and went in through the front door which was practically off its hinges. I think the trail had just gone cold..ice cold.

As we walked along the corridor, I had my handgun ready pointing in front of me. I didn't want to shoot, but needs must in these dark times.

We had agreed to clear each room just like they do on many cop shows that between us we had seen many a time.

But when we went in to the lounge, we realised why Ruben had brought us in on this hunt.

In front of us were four dead bodies, blood everywhere. No sign of Jack or Fiona and thankfully nor Fred.

When Ralph who had clearly been watching too many cop shows, had gloves on and was checking the dead men's pockets.

"Ruben's goons." He then shouted as me and Thomas had gone from the lounge and checked out the dining room.

"Bloody hell." Thomas said as we found another one of Rubens men hanging from the chandelier. It was quite a frightening sight.

He had been tortured was our best guess from the wounds we could see.

Slowly we decided to check the other ground floor rooms. No sign of anyone alive, thankfully we didn't find any other bodies.

As we were checking the kitchen, I saw Ralph come out of the downstairs toilet holding a piece of paper.

"Found something." He said

I was about to ask what then we could hear sirens.

"Time to go." He said

And we that we ran out of the house and back in to the car. We didn't really know where we were going but Thomas decided to get

us back on the tourist routes so that we could blend in a little.
"Shall I go back to the hotel sir?" He asked after we had driven for a few miles.
"No, we have a new address. Just stop off at the next available stop."
I wasn't sure what he had found.
Thomas had found us a little spot in a carpark, behind some coaches.
Ralph took out the piece of paper.
"I think it's a clue from Jack."
"What does it say?" Thomas asked.
"Go to the airport, travel 10 km north and take the second exit."
I looked at the piece of paper.
"It's Jacks handwriting."
"I know, but he normally leaves more of a clue." Ralph said.
"Well we didn't get to check upstairs. Maybe they had to rush out of their too."
Four police cars then raced past us, it was a timely reminder that we could have just been framed for the killing of what we believed to be Rubens men.
Thomas wasted in no time and followed signs back to the airport, from there we could see a main road that seemed to make sense given our instructions.
It was a while when we arrived and there was the mansion.
"Look whatever happens we are doing the right thing." Ralph said as we armed ourselves and slowly entered the building.
"Don't move an inch." Said a voice to the side of the door.
"Bloody hell Jack, you could have given me a heart attack." Ralph replied, greeting him with a hug.
Jack then let us all in, we didn't get a hug but then hey he had just cheated with my girl.
We were all sat in the kitchen, Jack gave us all drinks.

"I am assuming Ruben sent you?"
"Yes, how did you know?"
"Well to be honest Ralph it was a lucky guess. After killing his men I knew he would either send more and see if his luck would change or send you guys."
"How about the note?" I asked.
"Those goons of his wouldn't know even if you put it under their noses. But I knew one of you would look for ideas, clues."
I didn't really want to look at him, but when I did I could see that he had fought with those men. Bruises were all on the side of his face and his knuckles were cut.
"Did you find my other clue?"
We shook our heads.
"Sorry Jack, we had to run we heard sirens."
Jack looked annoyed, but he had obviously left us something there that maybe was important.
"Ruben probably just gave us enough time to see what you had done and get out of there, otherwise we would be probably be arrested."
"That's true." Thomas said.
"So did Ruben give you a message?"
"Yeah its more of a mission." I said
Ralph could tell I was getting angry, the more I thought about it the angrier I got.
So he decided to stop me from talking and did it for me.
"As James was about to say, Ruben has given us the week to a) find you, b)either kill you or bring you back for killing and c) return his ten million."
"Okay. What is your plan?" Jack asked.
"Where is Fiona?" I asked
"With her parents and Fred is there too. They are in the safe house."

"We had no plan." Thomas said, standing up and getting another drink.

"What we are all saying Jack is that we have no idea why we have a whole week. You see we have found you. Ruben knows us."

"That's true Ralph."

Then we heard knocking at the door. We hid in the kitchen, not knowing who could be out there.

"Expecting any visitors?" I whispered to Jack

"No."

We were armed and ready, Jack calmly went up to the door.

"Hello" was all I could hear at first. Then they were talking very fast. Jack then appeared in the kitchen.

"It was the cops asking if I had seen anyone suspicious in the area. They are looking for three armed men…"

"Seriously?"

"No you bloody idiots, they are looking for who killed those men. Apparently someone saw something and they were asking if I had seen anyone not from these parts."

"This is no time for joking Jack." Ralph bellowed, which gave us all a wakeup call.

"Sorry, I am not joking honest. I just don't know what it is you want me to do."

"We have to find you, take you or your body back and the ten million."

"How long do we have?"

"A week."

"Well technically that be less than a week."

"Fine, we best get to work then." And with that Jack set out a plan. We were still sat in the kitchen, as Jack started going through the options.

"Well I can just hand myself in."

I actually thought that was a good option right now, but then it occurred to me

"No, we have to think of an option that will keep Fiona and Fred safe."

He looked at me with respect and there it was the elephant in the room had been finally spoken about. Yet this was no time for arguments.

Ralph who was pacing around the kitchen, touched me on the shoulder. I got up and followed him in to the lounge.

"James, what are you planning to do about Jack?"

"I don't want to do anything."

"But Ruben wants you to act, he may even be watching us."

"I know, but if this as in this hell has taught me anything its patience. This isn't the right time Ralph. I am angry, very angry but seriously now is not the time."

"Okay, I trust you."

Thomas appeared at the door

"We need to go back to the hotel. The police have just issued an arrest warning for Jack."

We met Jack in the hall way.

"Go now. I will contact you tomorrow with directions."

"We can't keep running." Ralph said, looking like he wanted this all to end right now.

"I understand Ralph. I have an ace up my sleeve, but I need to play it at the right time."

Ralph looked at me. Yes two of a kind.

"I will contact you where you can find the money. Then you take it back, it will be a couple of days before you can do that. Then I return after you give Ruben the money."

"Then the rest of the plan just falls neatly in to place." I said with a heavy dose of sarcasm.

"That's my boy." Jack said smiling.

Maybe he was the calmest of us all, who knows what he had up his sleeve. But now it was time of leave.

We left via the front door and were just quick enough as three police cars drew up to the mansion. I wondered if Jack had gotten out. But all we could do is wait.

As we got back to the hotel, I felt relieved that Jack was alive. Ralph grabbed some rest whilst I had a nice hot long shower. Thomas decided that all could wait and that hunger was his first priority.

I wondered as I stood in the shower if Ralph was right. That Ruben was just watching us like some sick reality television game show.

After a short nap myself, I knew it was time to eat. So I woke Ralph and even though he said no I was determined.

"Jean would not be happy with you."

He smiled, that was all too true, and she wasn't going to be happy that we were here in Switzerland. But I knew deep down that if we all came back alive that maybe, just maybe one day we could put this all behind us.

That night was quiet, we didn't hear anything from Jack or Ruben. Time was still ticking away and I knew that if we couldn't find this ten million that would be the end of the game.

At three in the morning I needed to stretch my legs, Ralph was sound asleep and Thomas was snoring so I wasn't heard as I got out of the room and went down to the bar. The hotel was quiet, but relaxing.

"Anything I can get you sir?" asked a waiter

"Yes a whisky with ice."

I couldn't help but wonder if tomorrow we would hear on the news that Jack had been arrested. Maybe that was his plan and that his one phone call would be to get a message to us on how to find the ten million.

As I sipped my whisky, I was all too aware that any point Ruben could just bring this whole game to a stop. No-one was going to win.

I must have fell asleep on the bars couch, when a waiter woke me up

"Sir, I am sorry but your breakfast is waiting."

"Oh err thanks. Sorry"

"No problem sir. If you would just come right this way."

I straightened my shirt and followed him. We passed the main dining room and I was about to say something. But then we stopped.

"Sir, I have this for you."

He handed me a package.

I did wonder if I was going to get breakfast.

"I have sorted room service for you all."

"Thank you." I replied and went quickly back up to the room.

Thomas and Ralph were looking extremely fresh

"Good night on the couch?" Thomas asked.

"I needed space." I replied

Ralph looked at me with concern. He was tucking in to the breakfast and handed me one of the many pastries.

I was about to open the package, but Ralph stopped me.

"Let's enjoy breakfast."

It wasn't too long before we had finished all the food and were drinking the last of the coffee. When room service appeared at the door, it was the waiter from earlier.

"Please let me in, I can explain."

We did, it was right for us to be cautious. But then from his trolley, he gave us food supplies.

"I see you have yet to read your package Mr Folster."

"Look who do you work for?" I asked

"Jack sent me. I am his helper here in Switzerland. I am to tell you, follow those instructions. When you reach your destination you will have a new hotel where you will need to wait."

I ripped open the package and it was a map.

Thomas grabbed the map "This is miles away, the car we were given by Ruben will need to keep stopping."

The waiter who had now put the breakfast things back on his trolley, handed over us some keys. "I think you will find this a little more to your liking Thomas."

Thomas smiled and thanked the waiter.

We left him to clean up the room and began what would be a long journey.

I got hold of the map as we checked out of the hotel. I then realised we were not staying in Switzerland we were going to have to travel in to Germany.

On the back of the map, I noticed it was Jack's handwriting. "Do something touristy, you may need it."

I showed it to Ralph, who told Thomas to go get the car and that we would meet him out the front in half an hour.

"Where are we going?"

I followed Ralph out of the hotel, it was a bit of a route march and on a full stomach I realised how out of shape I was.

As we entered a new street I saw a man wave to Ralph. Did he have connections here too? I wondered.

We crossed over and he welcomed us in like we were family. I just had to go with the flow.

"How many of you are there?" the man asked Ralph.

Ralph put up three fingers, the man nodded. I didn't know why Ralph had not spoken but I followed his lead.

The man who was just over 4ft and I would say in his 60's rush out of the room we were in, which was a tailor shop. I noticed that Ralph had begun looking at some of the nice suits which were on the far side of the shop. I then noticed some rather nice ties and I began looking at them, then the man came back and gave Ralph three bags. They were plastic bags full of what turned out to be souvenirs.

He then hugged Ralph and wished me good luck and we then we raced back through the streets. As we were nearly back I noticed it hadn't been half an hour. I then noticed a rather nice coffee shop, which Ralph took me in to.

In the toilets we changed in to some jeans and t-shirt which had also been in the bag. I didn't dare ask questions, Ralph had maintained his silence. I just hoped that it wouldn't be too long before we could speak.

Even though we had our fill in the room, we decided to have another coffee, I then noticed Thomas appear. Ralph didn't acknowledge him, nor did I as we let him go and change in the toilets. By the time he had changed and grabbed a takeaway coffee, we were sat in the back of the car.

"I give up." I whispered.

"The waiter gave me another set of keys." Ralph said then laughing as he knew all too well that I didn't know how we had gotten in to the car.

"And the tailor?"

"It's not just Jack who has contacts. You'll learn."

Thomas got in to the front seat, and began setting off. We had a four hour journey to Germany and that was only part 1.

Of course we did as we had been instructed by Jack. We did tourist stuff, the bags contained enough souvenirs, so we only had to do photos. Which was hilarious, as Ralph had surprisingly never heard of a selfie.

"What do you mean you never heard of a selfie before?" asked Thomas who could hardly breathe after being in hysterics

"I don't know, I guess I haven't been out with the kids for a while." He said with a knowing smile.

"Hmm, me thinks you are playing with us?" I said, as we stood out on a vantage point

©TheExpirement

Ralph then admitted to us that of course he had heard of them, but he hadn't taken one. So that was first of many. He was too fussy, constantly deleting and trying them again.

A good few selfies, ice creams, yet more coffee, a few naps later we had finally made it in to Germany. Stuttgart airport came in to view where our hotel was. I didn't care how long we needed to wait a bed was calling me.

The next day, we went down for breakfast. I didn't know when we would receive any instructions, but no-one approached us like they did back in Switzerland.

The morning was slow, so we decided to do some more visiting, Thomas who we found to be a master in German took us to an old church that wasn't too far away. I noticed it wasn't meant to be open, but after some smooth talking, Thomas had gotten the key to let us in.

It was cold but fresh in the church. The stained glass windows were magnificent and yet the wooden pews could all do with replacing. The time in the church gave us some space, time to think, pray and just feel a little like normal.

As we wandered through the church, taking photos I wondered how long it would be before we were back on the road or in the air. In the far corner of the church I noticed some candles were burning. I found some change and lit one for Fred. I prayed that despite everything he would be kept safe and that he would have a great life. Even if it meant me not being in it.

I said some more prayers before Thomas's watch bleeped. Then his phone. "We have our instructions." He said.

We decided to take it outside, after we locked up the church Thomas left his phone with Ralph and I before going to find the old man who had lent us the key.

"I didn't realise you were religious."

"I am not particularly. I just felt a sense of peace in there and I thought it can't really hurt."

"That's very true son."

Ralph smiled and we then read the message.

"You will need to fly out of Stuttgart tonight to London. When in London go to the Darktronics no 6 safe house. There you will have half of the money."

As Rubens trail had gone cold, we would have to stomp up the cost of the tickets. But Ralph sorted it. I wondered if by the time I took over I would be able to just do that.

"We have tickets."

"Good. Now we rest until we fly."

At the hotel I noticed we had lost our handguns.

"When did that happen?" I asked out loud.

Thomas was about to ask, but he then noticed that Ralph was all ready to give an answer.

"Look, we can't board with them, as sadly our contacts do not work out of here."

"Okay, can you just next time tell me that. Or is this all a test."

Ralph just huffed and went back in to his book that he had brought from the hotel shop.

I wondered if this was all a test and how I longed to be back in my lab testing anything right now. Yes even the sewage.

©TheExpirement

Chapter Fifty Three

London was at its usual level of busy, everyone hurrying off to do what they had to do. Did anyone notice us jumping at anything that reminded us of Ruben? The fact that those two had showed up at the house had made me feel very vulnerable. Thomas looked a little bit how I was feeling, but Ralph was our air of calmness.
It wasn't long before we had reached the first of many tube stations, we travelled for what seemed like hours. Then after that, we had a route march along some good old streets of London when we reached the safe house.
Thomas was given the key by Ralph and only he went upstairs
"What if it's a trap?"
"Thomas knows the protocol. So we go if he doesn't come back." Ralph said looking at me slightly concerned.
"What?"
"You need to go back in the gym when all of this is over."
I know I thought to myself.
Thankfully Thomas came back out of the house with a duffle bag and another envelope of instructions.
"Please tell me it's not too far away."
Thomas smiled.
"Oh for…"
"Quiet." Ralph said suddenly. He pushed us in to an alley way.
We could hear two men.
"Look the duffle bag is still in there."
"Good. Let's do what Ruben has asked."
"Should we wait for them to arrive, I do love a good kill."
"No, Ruben said they were not to die. Just open the damn door and let's get this fire started."
"Sure thing boss."
I peeked round the corner and could see they were now taking

photos for Ruben.

Thomas had gone down the alley way, he then waved at us. We made a run for it.

We all breathed a sigh of relief as we realised the men hadn't followed us.

"How far ahead are we?" I whispered

"I don't know, this is a close game."

"How did they know the money would be there?" Thomas asked putting the bag on his other shoulder.

"You okay with that?"

"Sure." He was lying, I could tell that his shoulder was giving him grief. We decided to hire a car and then travel to our next destination.

It wasn't long before we were outside what I believed to be the hire car company, but no turns out that Ralph had brought us a car.

When we were inside, I asked Thomas to pull over. I needed answers and the question about the money definitely needed answering.

Ruben sighed and I knew from his face that he had to answer the questions.

"Where the hell are we going?"

"Back home."

"What to Darktronics?"

"No, my home of Cardiff."

I looked at Ralph, it was well known that his family originated from there, but I hadn't realised he would of called it home.

I could tell that there was more to this, so I was about to ask Thomas's question when he fessed up.

"Look, Jack knew all along that Ruben would somehow penetrate my inner circle. Even though I kept it close and even you two didn't know you were both in it. We knew he would find a way of breaking us down."

©TheExpirement

"So why Cardiff?" Thomas asked

Ralph raised his hand to pause us from asking too many questions, I could get the feeling that this was hard for him.

"When Jack and I had that conversation it was when we found out that Ruben was still around. So Jack and I created a plan. That if we needed safe houses to go to we would pick places like Cardiff, London and back at Darktronics. The two men we heard, are old employees of Jacks, when we were in the crime lab Jack sent me a coded text to tell me that this plan was put in place."

"You knew?" Thomas shouted.

"Yes, look I am sorry. There really was no time to explain. I honestly didn't know about Switzerland, it was obviously a last minute attempt to throw Ruben off the scent."

"Till he realised where you and Jack stored the money."

"Great, smashing, super."

Lots of questions were running through my mind.

"I'm guessing the two former employees of Jack had found his secret hiding places?"

"That I don't know. We didn't tell anyone or so I thought."

There was now silence in the car. But to be fair we had come this far, and people's lives were at risk.

"I am sorry for all of this, I should have opened up when we were at Darktronics."

"It doesn't matter now. Thomas do you still want to continue? I know that shoulder of yours is giving you grief."

"Yes, if we get to Cardiff and get the money then I am still in. Any sight of those or anyone suspicious then I am out."

"Are you still in this James?"

"I am, as there is nothing stopping Ruben from coming after me if I run. Ralph?"

"I owe it to Jack."

With that we all said "Let's go to Cardiff."

©TheExpirement

Most of the way we decided to listen to the radio, we weren't in the mood for talking. I don't think Thomas was ever going to forgive Ralph for knowing most of this plan.
However, it did give us a slight advantage. Ralph knew every place inside out and that was going to help.
We reached Cardiff in what seemed like no time at all. As for me I was undecided with Ralph, I was learning so much about him, and the company and that was enough for me.
We had parked up just outside this regular house in the middle of Cardiff.
Ralph decided due to Thomas's shoulder that he would go in to the safe house. Thankfully it seemed like we were still ahead of Ruben's men.
"Do you think we should have had a plan?" asked Thomas opening a new packet of mints.
"Probably." I said has he handed me a mint. It was a welcome taste, I hadn't realised my mouth was so dry.
"I know this isn't any of my business James, but do you think he knew about your son?"
I was about to turn to Thomas to answer it, when we heard an explosion.
Then before we could even jump out of the car to see, a bag came flying out of the top window from the house next door and landed on our car bonnet.
I jumped out and grabbed it, there was smoke and sirens filling the air.

"RALPH!" I shouted as loud as I could, not really being able to see much.
"Shush." Said a rather calm Ralph behind me.
"Sorry, I couldn't see you. Is this the money?"
"Yes. But it's short."

"What do you mean it's short?" I asked looking very perplexed
"I think someone has split it."
"Well surely that someone is Jack?"
"No James. I think it's time for the end game."
We jumped in the car, realising then that Thomas was hunched over the front of the wheel.
Ralph and I got back out, he said that he could handle it and I moved the bag to the boot and found that it was lighter than the other one.
I peered round.
"Is he okay?"
"Yeah, can you help move him to the back?"
"Sure."
After we moved Thomas to the back and strapped him in. We got back in to the front, Ralph decided to drive.
"Don't say a word till we are away from here." Ralph ordered me as we drove in silence.

©TheExpirement

Chapter Fifty Four

It was a while before we had found somewhere to park up. It was some old abandoned carpark, I think we were still somewhere in Wales but I couldn't be sure.

Ralph turned to me

"Look we knew Thomas wanted out if there was anything suspicious. So I have given him a little something."

I looked in the mirror Thomas was away with the fairies.

"Looks like you have given him what the doc gave me."

Ralph nodded.

"So why don't you want him gone?"

"Like you said there is nothing stopping Ruben getting any of us if we decided to run. He would just hunt and kill him."

"This way we keep him safe."

"Yeah, he may just hate us for doing it."

"Agreed."

Of course this seemed like an excellent opportunity to ask Ralph about Fred and find out how much he knew.

Ralph looked at me in a fatherly way, I thought he was reading my mind.

"I set up that explosion."

"You what?"

"The neighbour next door is an old friend. He had bad neighbours and a much worse landlord looking after the house."

"Oh so an insurance job?"

"No not quite James. I rigged it up to look like a gas cooker leak. "

"The money?"

"Was next door my friend got it and replaced it with another bag."

"He didn't steal the other money?"

"hahaha know, don't be fooled he is loaded. Just chooses to live humbly yet well is how he puts it."

"So who put the other half the money in Darktronics."
"I did."
"Say what?"
"I did. When we saw that those two men were on our trail, I had to give them another honey pot so to speak, to go after. Plus if we lost only 2 ½ million it was easier for me to raise another 2 ½ than it is 5."
"Okay, so where did you put it?"
"Well that is easy James. Your lab."
"My lab?"
"Yeah, why do I need my son's permission to his lab?"
"No, I'm…I'm just worried they may have damaged it."
I smiled, he smiled.
"Don't worry I'll get you a new one."
"Thanks Dad.."
"So ready?"
"Sure."
I tried to sleep but the conversation I did need with Ralph was whirring round my head.
It wasn't long when we were on the motorway that Ralph noticed I wasn't sleeping.
"You want to know if I knew about Fred?"
I simply nodded.
"Yes, I think I did."
We drove through the night, changing when we could. Not speaking much. As the elephant was firmly up and awake in the car.
"I didn't know for sure, until Jean was lying thankfully alive in your house."
Ralph suddenly said, making me stir.
"I know, its fine." I simply said. The elephant had gotten a little smaller in my mind, but then he asked me a question.
"You seem to be coping with this."

©TheExpirement

I couldn't answer not then, not yet. I wasn't ready to tell him.
So I lied.
"I'm not, trust me dad its bubbling inside, ready to pop just not yet."
He gave me a reassuring tap on the leg and we carried with our journey.
Darktronics came in to view, it was a welcome sight. When we arrived at the main carpark, it began to rain.
There was no time to wait for it all pass, I jumped out of the car and I could see three men running towards us.
I panicked, but the closer they came, I could see that they were paramedics.
Ralph calmly got out of the car and shouted to me
"There here to help Thomas. Get to your lab"
I nodded and began to run hoping not to slip in the rain.
It was time for the end game, the thing I had to do now was find the rest of the money in my lab.
I ran to the back entrance of my lab building.
Luckily the fire escape door was ajar and I was able to run up the stairs. I reached half way to catch my breath. When I heard voices from down in the stair well.
"Are you sure it's up here?"
"Yes that's what the map says. Now shut the hell up and let's go."
It was the men from London.
I couldn't believe they had caught up with us. But now I was spooked and that gave me another ounce of adrenalin which I needed. I reached my lab, not daring to look back and see where the two men were.
Luckily for me my lab door had several locks on it, if I locked them all it would buy me time.
Inside with the door locked, I could hear them outside
"Are you sure?"

"Nah I think it's the next one up. Let's go."
My heart was thumping hard, could I have literally dodged a bullet? Now I had to focus, I had to work out where someone had put the money. If it was me, I would put it in my wardrobe area as I have various bags in there. I rifled through there only to find my stuff and no money. I sighed. Now I had to think where else you would put 2 ½ million.
That's when my brain actually remembered what Ralph had said "..in your lab"
I was still in my office part of my lab. I opened the secure doors and went in. It was calm, quiet and refreshing.
Dennis the robot was still and silent.
"Of course" I said out loud.
There were only two ways of getting in to my lab. One was the way I had just come in, the other was of course being an object for testing.
Ralph had his friend break out the money, the guy would have been probably killed if anyone caught him coming in to my lab.
So the only safe way was sending the object in.
I looked in the usual places for packages but couldn't see anything.
Then I saw a strap peeking from a cupboard that I had put in.
"My secret hiding place."
Dennis was the only one that knew about it. He would have been the one to put the money inside if this secret too hadn't been found out.
I had to get on my hands and knees. Which was hard as I was physically and mentally tired.
I opened the door which was coded and found a rucksack.
I undid the zip and saw a load of cash. Now was not the time for checking it, but when I put it on my shoulder it felt about right.
Now it was time to face the music.
Just as we had approached Darktronics, Ralph said "When you get

the money, go out of your lab and show your face to the camera. Ruben will then know we are here."

I opened my main lab door which of course took longer due to my earlier issue. I then looked left and raised my face to the camera.

Chapter Fifty Five

It wasn't long before I was being escorted by the two goons that we saw in London. As we walked down a few of the corridors they started arguing about how much they should ask Ruben for as a reward.
"I say a million" one of them said as we entered a lift.
"Nah I think that's a little short man, we did have to burn that house down"
"Yeah but he was pissed that we didn't catch these idiots in Cardiff"
He kicked me in the leg and I laughed. I mean it did ruddy hurt but seriously I couldn't stop laughing at these goons.
"What you laughing at..."
"You two" I managed to say catching my breath from laughing
"Why?" the other one said as he was about to punch me.
"Ruben will kill you both, if he gives you anything take it. Otherwise you are both dead trust me."
With that the doors open and there was Ruben.
"Well I would listen to James." He grabbed me from the two idiots. And before I could realise where I was, the two goons were dead on the lift floor.
"They James are not worth anything to me."
He untied me and let me walk alongside him.
"Where we going?" I asked
"To see Ralph"
I was surprised how calm Ruben seemed.
I didn't say a word.
It wasn't long before we were in one of the more comfortable offices in the basement.
Ralph was sat on one of the soft chairs holding a gauze under his bleeding nose, he nodded to me to say that he was okay.
"Yet another one of my goons dead for that" Ruben came out with

©TheExpirement

suddenly.

"All I wanted you see James is my money and as you know my sister."

"Is that all you need?" I asked

He gave me a very angry stare

"Look I'm just saying for the past few years you have been really running us ragged. You could have easily got the money and well as for your sister, you have no idea?"

"NO" he shouted.

He started pacing round the room. He whispered to one of his suited goons who signalled to the others to get out.

Now it was just Ruben, Ralph and I.

There was silence which was suddenly broken by Ruben who started laughing.

"I am just pleased to see an angry James." He then said.

"I'm not angry."

"I think you are."

"No."

"Seriously."

"No."

"Boys" Ralph said

"I wondered how long it would take for daddy here to jump in."

"No, I just could do with ending this whole charade."

"Boring."

Ralph just looked at him.

It worked.

Ruben then begun talking seriously.

"You see James, Daniel and I received letters when we were at school." He put his hand inside his suit jacket and pulled out a very old small envelope.

I was now sat down on one of the couches.

"You may read it."

He handed it to me, this was the first time I saw some well emotion other than anger in him.

I read it to myself

"Dear Ruben and Daniel,

This letter I hope finds you both well, happy and studying hard. I sadly cannot tell you my name in case anyone else reads this, but I am your sister.

When you were both born I was already 10 and was taken abroad for what I thought I was going to be a holiday.

When we reached Cyprus I was told this was going to be where I was going to finish my schooling and live. Of course being a 10 year old I was scared but realised that there was no point in arguing.

I hope that we will meet one day soon and I will write when I can. If you have read this, then reply with fathers saying.

Love

your sister."

"I realise you have never met, but did you get any other letters?"

"Only Christmas cards, but I think other letters were written"

"But I'm guessing the school banned your post."

Ruben nodded.

I turned to Ralph in slight confusion.

"It was a favourite of the school to hide post so that you never got rewarded."

"What would they have done with the letters?

"Stored them in a safe."

"And the school now?"

"I like where this is going James, but I cant let you go."

"You have your money"

"I know but its not actually about the money."

He paced around.

"I don't know where he is"

"Sure you do James, you and Jack are best friends."

"Well not so much these days"
"I told you to take the test James."
"I didn't need a test."
I could tell they both were going to interrogate me as to what I meant. When a familiar voice made me jump.
"My pal" Jack shouted
He hugged me, as if we hadn't seen each other in years and as if nothing bad had ever happened.
However, the shock forced Ruben to pull his hand gun
"Seriously, Ruben" Jack said putting his hands up.
"What you doing here Jack" asked Ralph
"Hey Ralph, can you get this idiot to lower his gun and then maybe we can all get out of here alive."
"Ruben look I'll make you a deal" Ralph said
Jack looked confused at him.
I just sighed in despair. I moved to walk out.
"Don't you dare" Ruben shouted at me.
Ralph growled at me as if I was under his spell I decided to do as I was told and sat down.
I didn't want to be here anymore, but I knew I had to play this out.
"What deal do you have Ralph?" asked Ruben and Jack together, which caused them to grin at each other.
I was thinking that this was all part of some grand plan, but I had to pretend to be listening.
"Ralph, what can you do?" Jack repeated
"Look Jack is here and that's who you really want. Now let James and I go find your sister."
"Hmm tempting, but I just want to kill Jack and he won't get out of here alive…"
"That's true Ruben. You could kill us all. But I know what you really want apart from your sister."
"Intrigued."

©TheExpirement

"James."

My thoughts were now firmly back in the room. "Keep me out of this deal." I spurted out.

"Let me explain, I think what our good friend Ralph is trying to say is that I am very annoyed about how you have reacted to Jack here." Ralph nodded.

Jack had gone very quiet. It was true I felt like this had been some sort of test but then maybe just maybe it was time to bring out the truth.

"Oh so you think that if I tell you how I feel about Jack and Fiona you will make this deal happen?"

"Pretty much." Ruben said shrugging his shoulders.

"Then what."

"Sorry?"

"Well what says that when we find your sister, you don't just kill us and run this place in to the ground?"

"Good point Mr Folster"

Before he could go on, I decided to carry on. Not knowing what I was really getting myself or anyone else for that matter in to.

"Plus I don't see this being a deal for anyone. So here is my deal and my terms."

"Oh go on." He said in his most sarcastic voice.

"Jack stays here in your custody, but alive and well. Ralph and I will find your sister assuming she is alive we swap her for Jack. Then when all said and done you will find out how I feel about this whole sordid affair and you will either die or leave us alone forever."

"Hmmm I thinks that's very agreeable."

"We have a deal?" I put my hand out to shake his, but then I saw someone else come in to the room.

"Jean here will stay with me and if you find my sister dead she dies."

Ralph knew that this was the best deal that we could ever get.

301 –Expirement Series

©TheExpirement

"Do we have a deal now James?"
I shook his hand.
Ralph and I walked out of the room, knowing that we had one simple job to find his sister.

Chapter Fifty Six

There was actually a good chance that none of us were going to get out alive. Let alone be allowed to find his so called sister.
I stopped myself from fully going especially when I saw Jean being brought in
"Now, you see I have all the cards" Ruben announced
"So" I said which shocked everyone in the room
Ruben looked at me with a blank stare like he was looking in to my soul
"Well you may have all the cards, but you don't seem to have your sister."
"That's true. James"
"So let us go and find her." Ralph said
"Okay fine."
I didn't want to smile as the situation was just getting a whole lot worse and like most things in life I felt it was going to get a whole lot worse before it got better. But I was impressed how Ralph had authority over Ruben and that had made me smile as it gave me a sense of hope.
We were out in the Darktronics car park when two of his goons met us and gave us keys. One set was to brand new 4X4 which had caught my eye when we had reached the carpark. The other se of keys sent a shiver down my spine. I was going back to where I was held during my kidnapping, my Grandmother's house.
Ralph noticed that I wasn't right
"Where are they for?"
"My late Grandmothers house"
He gave me a reassuring look and we got in the new 4X4, it had its complete freshness even that new smell, you know the one. Yep in bucket fulls, he windows were soon opened as we drove away, not knowing if we would see anyone alive again.
Due to Ralphs illness I didn't want to chance it going away that he didn't have the right meds or equipment with him, so we stopped off at his house.
When we had stopped Ralph had gotten out of the car, when all of a sudden a noise was coming from one of the electronics in the car.

Of course this brand new 4X4 had more electronics than you could you get in an electronics store.

It had made me jump which isn't great when the person who could kill you in an instant is ringing you. I pressed what I hoped was the right button on the screen and said "Hello?"

"James its Ruben"

"Yes?"

"You don't sound very happy James"

"Well you did make me jump"

"Now, don't stick around at Ralphs for too long, you must get on. I have left you some money in the boot and if you need anything ring this number. I will be out of the country for a while so do be good."

"Sure."

"Manners James cost nothing, now I am going to put that down to tiredness and stress."

I managed to sum up the energy to say goodbye but I really didn't care if he was in the country or not. We were dead if we couldn't find her and possibly dead if we could. So I simply now was going down without a fight.

Next person to make me jump was Ralph, he tapped on the half opened window of the 4X4

I opened the door so I could speak to him properly

"Everything okay James?"

"Yeah that was Ruben, he has left us a present in the boot and he will be out of the country for a while."

"Great. Well you best lock up and come in, the doctor is getting what I need ready and may be a while. So let's rest before our adventure."

There was no time to argue or speak, I did quickly check the boot to find the money and that it wasn't a dead body or something.

It was some hours later before we set off, because Ralph had to have his next dosage which the doctor had said would help keep him going for a few weeks.

We had the next dosages all set up, I say we but I knew I had to give him the dosage and that was not going to be a pleasant experience.

It was in the middle of the night we had begun our journey and whilst my mind was focused on what we were doing. Like for many nights now I had been getting flashbacks of my childhood and visiting my Grandmother. I turned on the radio and hoped that my mind could stop going back.

The rain hammered down and as we got closer to our destination hailstones bounced of the windshield. I had luckily put on a hooded top, so I was first in to the house noticing an umbrella I grabbed it and got Ralph indoors. He was still tired and groggy.

It took a while for us to settle, but unlike before the place seemed more homely.

"Does it feel like your Grandmother's house?"

"Not really, there is no smell of cake or her anymore." I smiled, as Ralph came in to the lounge with freshly made cups of coffee.

"So why here?" He asked

"Well this is was where I was held during my kidnapping. Plus like every element of this so far has been personal."

"Agreed, do we know what's in the boxes?"

"Well I am hoping it's all the evidence I had before."

As I knelt on the floor opening each of the paper boxes I found various clippings and photos. One of the boxes contained just plain white paper and markers. I guess Ruben had not appreciated my work of art I had done before my new evidence wall was going to be more civilised and maybe understandable.

Ralph had made himself comfortable in a chair and was emptying one of the boxes in to piles, photographs, newspaper clippings and key documents. It was slowly beginning to make sense.

"Where shall we start?" he said

"Well let's make a wall of who we know to be involved. As if he has made this personal then it must be someone close?"

He nodded.

I emptied a few sheets of paper and markers and started writing names and then stuck them up on the wall

Ralph had gone to get more coffee and something to eat as the silence had enhanced my growls coming from my stomach.

By the time he had come back this was what I had on the wall

©TheExpirement

306 –Expirement Series

©TheExpirement

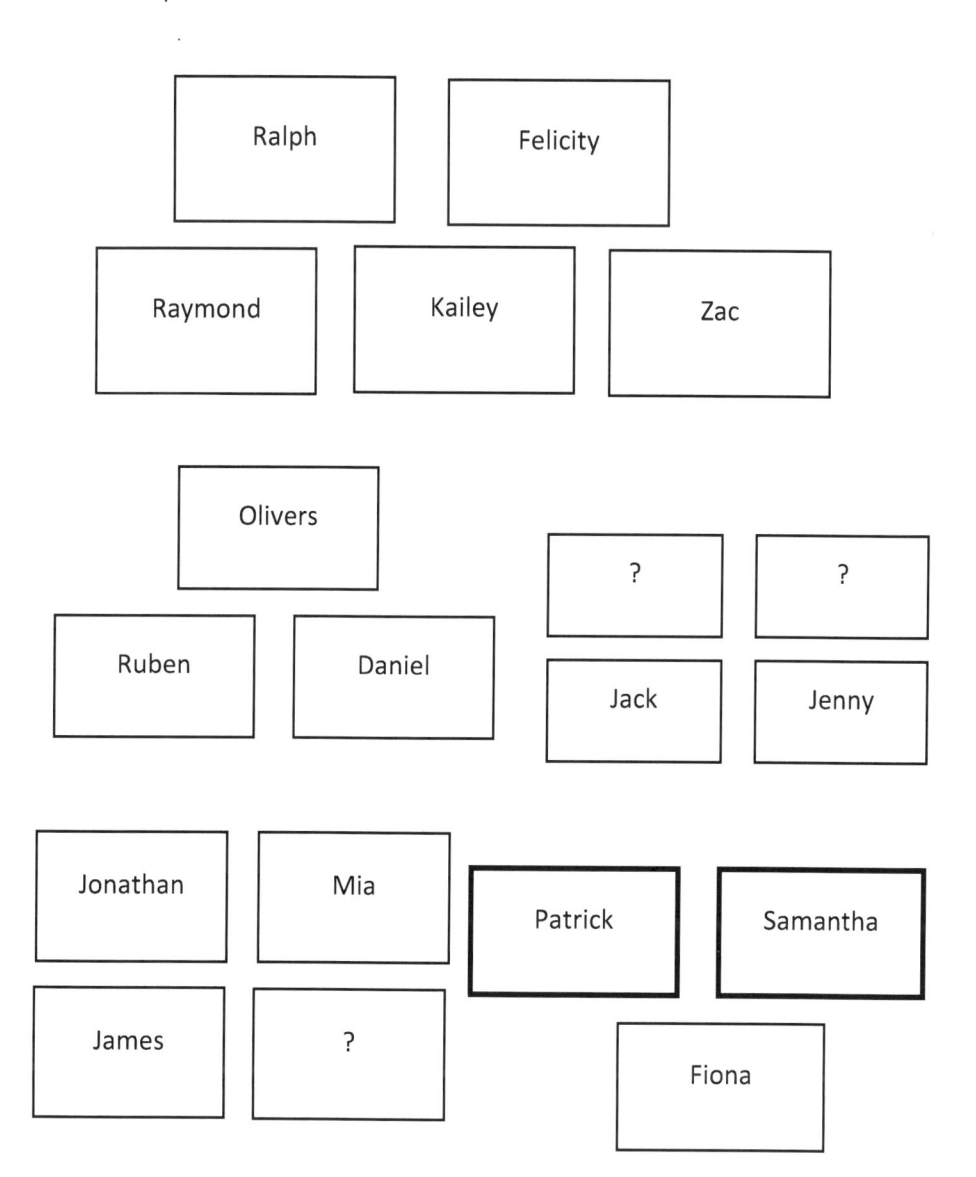

| Ralph | Felicity |

| Raymond | Kailey | Zac |

| Olivers |
| ? | ? |
| Ruben | Daniel | Jack | Jenny |

| Jonathan | Mia | **Patrick** | **Samantha** |
| James | ? | Fiona |

307 –Expirement Series

I didn't have all the answers and considering I was in my Grandmother's house I hadn't ruled out finding some unknown sibling, but when Ralph had put down the fresh cups and had told me that pizza was on its way. He took down one of the question marks above Jack and moved Jack under Felicity.
"He is my step son, he is the one that Ruben believes I don't know who the father is"
I stood there in silence shocked that Jack is the step son of Ralph.

Revenge is Bitter Sweet.

Like most things in life they have to get worse before getting better. However, stood in my Grandmother's house there didn't seem to be any light at the end of this dark tunnel.
It had made sense to me the way Ralph and Jack had been together that they were in many ways like father and son, but I hadn't realised how close to the semi-truth I had been.
Whilst I was stood there I had a sense of overwhelming anger which was about to explode and yet little did I know then I would be soon saving a certain person's life.

Printed in Great Britain
by Amazon